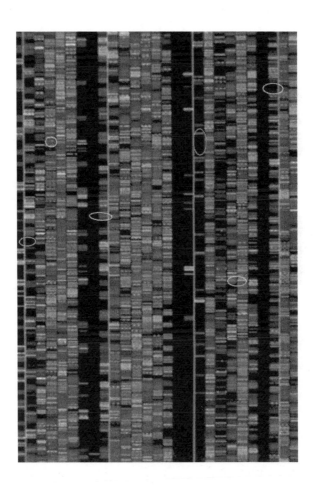

Project 01x

by

Alan Grieveson

As always my thanks to Andrea who helped so much with the editing.

Sometime soon.

It was getting late; James Mason Maurice locked his office door and descended the stairway to the atrium below. After nodding to the security guard, whom he didn't know by name, he stepped out into the colder air of the street where daytime activity was passing inexorably into the prelude for the nightlife. Turning right he felt the chill of the wind on his face and after stepping briskly a hundred paces he crossed the main road at the traffic lights. He turned right on the other side before taking a left hand turn and left the congested pedestrian highway for a less used side street. With each step the traffic hum decreased behind him, ahead he could see a steady line of traffic passing the end of the thoroughfare before him. Once he reached the end, as happened every day, his journey would take him right and after walking another two hundred paces he would arrive at the entrance of the building where he had an apartment. One he had owned before his divorce.

James was so wrapped up with his thoughts that he was aware of little that was going on around him that is until a hasty shuffling sound alerted his primitive hind brain, seconds before the blows fell, that something was wrong. The first blow struck him on the right shoulder muscle causing him to lean forward as his left hand moved towards the pain. The second impact struck him across the back of the head causing a cascade of white flashes to fill his vision as his head tilted back thrusting his chin forward. The assault concluded with a kick to the back of his legs causing him to fall forward, his knees crashing painfully onto the hard ground. He was totally disorientated as a heavy hand slammed onto his left shoulder; he felt his coat being pulled roughly aside. There was a pause; he thought he heard a voice far away then the pressure from the hand lessened as James felt the fingers slide away. A heavy thud to his left caused him to look round; his head broke out in a spasm of pain at the sudden movement. When his vision cleared he became aware of a pair of grey, lifeless and staring eyes directed upon him. His unconscious senses told him it was a male from the heaviness of what features he could make out, the face itself was cloaked in a scarf beneath the hood of the jacket.

Real death was a very rare event in the life of James Mason Maurice, the few occasions that he had come close were funerals where the body was safely boxed up. Sudden and violent death had never, until now, played a part in his sedate life. His first reaction was to recoil away from the corpse.

Unconscious responses flooded his system with chemicals; all he wanted to do was run as fast and as far away as he could. But he couldn't, another lighter hand held him in place, a soft accented but firm voice instructed him to be still.

"You are Jameth Mathon Maurithe?" The voiced asked softly.

Maurice took a moment to gather his fleeing wits, to try and understand through his clouded senses what had just been said to him. "What?" He finally asked when his comprehension skills gave up.

"You are Jameth Mathon Maurithe?" the voice repeated with patience.

Finally after his mind filtered the accent and the lisp he said, "Yes, yes I am James Mason Maurice."

"What ith your date of birth?" the voice asked further.

"Date of birth?" After a moment of confused recollection he told the seemingly female enquirer his date of birth.

He felt a hand lift from his shoulder before it gently but purposefully explored the injury to his head; he winced as he felt a cold sprayed jet of something with a not unfamiliar antiseptic smell strike the open wound.

"Is he dead?" he ventured to ask, with a voice that croaked.

"Yeth," the tone was matter of fact and the speaker seemingly considered the question of little importance. A bluish light lit the immediate area. "Hold thtill I need a blood thample."

Maurice didn't have a chance to consider the instruction before he felt a prick on his exposed neck. A moment passed, the light vanished. "Have you a mobile phone?"

Maurice fished inside his coat pocket before holding it up and behind him. "Here take it; I don't have much money on me." Maurice felt the latest model iPhone lifted from his grip, a few seconds later he felt it again resting upon his shoulder.

"I thuggetht you call for a medic to exthamine the injury you have acquired. If you are able to get up do tho, if not remain where you are."

James M. Maurice moved his weight forward in an attempt to stand but the world rotated alarmingly and only a steadying hand prevented him toppling forward, but it didn't prevent the upwelling of nausea. He wretched drily, it was some minutes before he felt able to focus on making a call to the emergency services but he didn't have to as members of the public had started to gather close by. One had made the call for him.

Eleanor Maurice gazed half awake at the flickering banal content of the television that illuminated the room. Her son Edward was upstairs in his own room applying himself voluntarily to his studies. Stretched out on the sofa she was enjoying that rare event in her life, a day off. Earlier in the day she and Edward had spent time together, after which he had prepared the evening meal. Edward was her only son and she was proud of him for many things but notably for his kitchen skills. Eleanor knew from other parents that a fifteen year old who can cook anything half edible is fairly rare. Yes, she was proud of him but that pride was masked by her concerns, the pains that had started to overwhelm Edward's life earlier had returned, but more severe than before. As yet they had had no sensible medical diagnosis that explained the symptoms. Of course the doctors had tried to fob her off with talk of arthritis, MS, ME and a dozen other tick box solutions, but none had stood up to serious investigation. As a last resort one of the younger, more enlightened doctors in the practice Edward attended had referred him to a contact at the Department of Genetics-University hospital.

The intrusive ring of the telephone shattered her reverie; unwillingly she brought her senses back under conscious control and looked at the clock hanging on the opposite wall. Eight minutes past eight, she noted out of habit as the second hand clicked inexorably onwards. The ringing continued.

Finally after the ringing refused to cease she snatched up the handset, "Yes?" she said curtly hating this disturbance in her own time.

"It's Tony," a voice said in the ear-piece. Slowly she recognised the voice of one of her team. "Sorry to call you so late boss, but there's been an attempted mugging that has resulted in a death, James is involved."

Her first thought had been to yell at him for disturbing her day off but when Tony had mentioned that her ex-husband was involved she stifled it. "Is he alright?" She said instinctively at the same time silently saying goodbye to her time off.

Tony Coltrain replied in his Lowland Scots accent, "As yet the details are sketchy but the emergency services were called nearly two hours ago. When the locals Bobbies arrived they found him covered in blood and a dead body nearby, Cordon is the investigating officer. James is currently in A&E at St Saviour's, when they release him he'll be brought in for a statement."

"Where did it happen?" she found herself asking although part of her didn't care.

"Near the junction of Sloane Street and Duke Street, he was probably on his way home as it's not far from his flat."

"Alright, thanks Tony," she heard a slight click then the dial tone before she put the phone down. "Edward," she called out to her son as she slipped her flat-heeled shoes on.

A door clicked open on the floor above, the sound of music drifted along the landing followed by a lanky young man with dishevelled curly brown hair. "What's up?" he asked.

"Your father's been involved in an incident and he's been taken to A&E. Will you be alright on your own for a while? I might be late getting back."

"Sure, no problem, I was going to bed early anyway, I feel pretty drained. Is it serious?"

"No I don't think so, that is I don't think he's hurt badly. How serious the incident is I have no idea except someone is dead."

"Pretty serious then I'd say. Say hi for me." Edward said as he turned back to his room, he really didn't feel well.

"I will," Eleanor called after him, "I'll look in on you when I get back." Then after gathering her things together she picked up the bag that contained her working life and left.

Two hours later after several cups of coffee and the purposeless passing of time, she had seen James Mason Maurice being escorted into the police station. After an intense period of questioning she now watched as he signed his statement. She'd heard most of the details from the observation room and instinctively knew that her ex-husband, knowingly or otherwise, had not given up all the information he had. The inspector handling the interview had not in her opinion been hard enough on the only witness to a death - perhaps because he was too aware of James's state of health and mind. She wouldn't have been so caring. Inspector Cordon entered the anteroom statement in hand and after closing the door he handed the handwritten pages to her.

"Technically Elle you should stay out of this," he said gruffly but not in an unfriendly tone. Alan Cordon worked one of the other teams in the same department and had known Eleanor since she was a newly promoted Sergeant.

"I know, but I also know he hasn't the capacity to kill mice let alone a human being." She replied as she scanned the statement pages in her hands.

"Well Tobbit could never be accused of being human, he was a drug dealer and user, about as low down on the evolutionary scale as you can get. Real pond life, he's got more form than a race horse. Nobody will miss him."

"Any family?"

"Nobody that'll own up to it, his father did a runner and never looked back or forward for that matter since a train hit him, probably not accidental. His mother died from sclerosis of the liver, if it hadn't been that it would have been the drugs or the cancer." Disinterestedly he took a sip of cool coffee from a cup on the desk, he didn't know who it belonged to and cared even less.

Eleanor finished absorbing the text of the statement, "Mind if I talk to him?"

"Be my guest; just don't go hitting him where it will show. The doctor said there were no skull fractures so let's keep it that way. He's on painkillers so he shouldn't feel much, oh, and has been told to rest up for a couple of days. If his eyes don't uncross in a day or two he has to go and see his doctor."

"Alan you are far too sensitive and empathetic for this job," she said with her hand on the door knob.

Cordon merely tilted his head sideways.

James Maurice didn't look up when the door opened, or even when it clicked shut, he didn't care. The numb feeling clung to him like a wet shirt; he wasn't sure whether it was better than the incessant thumping pain he'd had in his head and neck earlier.

"James?"

There was something familiar about the voice, he only got a second or two to ponder that thought before he was assailed by a loud noise.

"MASON, wake up!" The voice was loud, insistent and painful.

James Mason Maurice jumped, his eyes snapped upwards at the unsmiling face of his ex-wife looking down at him.

"Elle?" the sight of her only added to his confused state.

"Well that's good; your brains aren't totally addled." She dropped the statement onto the tabletop. "Do you want some more coffee?"

"Have you anything stronger?"

"Cold stewed tea or would you prefer that I bring in WPC Martindale from the tug of war team." She waited and when no response was forthcoming she continued. "Right then, this crappy statement of yours, let's go over it shall we?"

"I've already said all I know." He bleated, "Can't it wait until tomorrow?"

"No it can't, we need it now while it is still fresh in your mind and you haven't had time to churn it over and develop it into fantasy. So let's start at the point you entered Sloane Street, you are walking home approaching the half way point, when at some point you were struck from behind." If she cared about his suffering it didn't show in her face or body language.

"Yes. First on the right shoulder, then on the back of my head, the next thing I know I'm on my knees with my coat being pulled open."

"Not your usual position if memory serves me correctly or was prayer upper-most in your mind? I don't imagine you've changed the team you bat for."

"What?"

She ignored the question, she wanted him disorientated that way he might conceivably say something useful. "Now I want you to understand something James, something to help you focus your mind upon. You were found with a dead body and so far we only have you for a witness, the only person who was present. Now we don't know if it was a mugging gone wrong, a drug deal you were making that went wrong, perhaps even a lovers break up or perhaps just plain murder. For all I know your injuries are self-inflicted. So it's down to you to tell us the truth in very minute detail and skip this crap about you not remembering because you were in pain and seeing stars."

Maurice's eyes widened, "You can't think I killed him," his voice reflected the panic he suddenly felt.

"Oh but I can James." Eleanor moved her face close to that of her Ex, "I can think the unthinkable, the improbable even the impossible and without information to the contrary I can come to believe it."

"There was the girl."

"There always is a girl James. So tell me about the girl. Was she with you? Were you attacked because of her?"

"No, no, I was alone when he attacked me, I don't know where she came from."

"Alright tell me about her, everything you can remember and everything she said to you."

After a moment's recollection he looked up from the table, Eleanor watched his eyes as he finally spoke. "She asked me if I was James Mason Maurice and when I said yes she asked for my date of birth."

"Are you sure that is the first thing she said? Close your eyes and think back, on your knees, someone going through your pockets then the face staring at you."

"Stop, stop there, she said something but not to me. The guy who hit me had a hand on my shoulder, his left hand was inside my coat, and then she said, said....., yes she said, 'excuse me I need to speak with him first'. The next thing I know is that he's falling like a log next to me. Then she asked my name."

"So she knows you then?"

"What? No. I don't know her," James replied in confusion.

"She knew your name," Eleanor stated, staring him full in the face, her palms flat on the table.

"So do a lot of … people," he responded cautiously.

"But you say in your statement that she then went on to tend your wound, are you certain you don't know her? Because why else would she bother?" Her voice rose on the last question just to drive the point home.

"I'd remember if I knew her."

"How exactly, was it the perfume, body odour, touch? What makes you so certain you have never met her?"

"She's foreign for one thing, her voice was accented not easy to understand."

"Ah! The foreign femme fatale with an accent, so where would you say she was from?" Eleanor pressed on.

"No idea but she had a lisp as well, she couldn't say her 'esses' and she was quietly spoken. It wasn't easy to understand her, my head was banging away for Christ's sake."

"It gets better James, so the assailant is from foreign parts and speaks quietly with a lisp and cares enough about you to tend to your wounds before she disappears. Oh, and you don't know her."

"You don't believe me do you?" James Maurice's voice sounded almost resigned to his fate.

"What a thing to say, after all, whatever reason have you ever given me to totally believe every single word you say?"

James stayed quiet; this was not a topic he could win points on.

"Okay describe her, how big was she? And I don't mean breast size? How tall James? Was she slim, fat, or medium? I know you have plenty of experience to judge such matters."

"I never saw her, she was always behind me."

Eleanor was tempted to say 'really' but decided to stick to the topic, "She touched you on the head James; did she have big hands?"

James thought a moment, "No she had small hands, I think."

"Think? James if you could think you wouldn't have got caught out so often. So she could be smallish. What about her age?"

"She sounded young but she sounded as though she knew what she was doing, so she's probably older than she sounds."

"So to recap we have a soft, quietly spoken foreign dominatrix with a lisp, who is small and probably young. Are you sure you don't remember her from somewhere?" Her tone was intended to annoy and provoke, but when he failed to respond she moved on to the next question. "Now just before the victim became a victim did you hear a shot or the sound of anything that she could have used to kill a six foot thug like Tobbit?"

Frown lines crossed James's forehead as he rubbed his nose, "No, I'm sure I didn't hear anything; there was no sound at all. I don't even remember him making a sound; it was all so very quiet. But I couldn't think straight anyway I hurt too much."

"Then you say she asked for your mobile, yes? But she gave you it back after a few seconds?"

"Yes, she had it for maybe twenty seconds if that."

"And she took nothing else off you, wallet, papers, briefcase, address, telephone number?"

"No nothing. She just said I should call a medic for my head injury."

"Medic not doctor, you're sure?" Eleanor clarified.

"Definitely Medic," James Mason Maurice finally replied.

Without warning Inspector Maurice stood up and gathered up the statement papers. She had used the back of the originals to write her own notes. "I'll get these additional comments typed up and you can sign them in a day or so, if anything else comes to mind let us know." She said finally.

"Can I go now?" He asked more in hope than conviction.

"I'll call you a taxi. One last thing, injuries not-with-standing, do not forget you are taking Edward to the University Hospital on Thursday. Eleven o'clock on the dot."

"What? Yes, yes I know it's in my appointments. Check my phone if you don't believe me. When can I have it back my work diary is on it?"

"When we have checked it for prints, DNA, blood, semen, call register, contacts, we may even get around to your social media accounts. Who knows what we shall find, could be weeks before you see it again but I'm sure you will get by." His miserable demeanour on that news was to her a reward in itself.

On her way out Inspector Eleanor Maurice spoke briefly to the duty officer before returning to the observation room where Cordon had been listening in. He looked thoughtful as Eleanor re-entered the room.

"Can you keep me in the loop on this one?" Eleanor asked offering back the amended statement she had taken.

"I've got four weeks Elle; my transfer came through to Drugs Squad so I don't need complications like this. I'll see Doug in the morning and get it transferred to you, I see no conflict of interest; James is a witness and not a suspect in my opinion. This one is looking complicated; you have a mugging plain, a smack head looking to fund his next fix. The girl though is something else. You'll have to find her to make the connections."

"I totally agree. Who is she though? She obviously knows James even if he doesn't know her, so what is her interest in him? Anyway it'll keep until morning as I'm still officially off duty. Thanks Alan I owe you."

"My pleasure; you get off home I'll put what I can together and give you a running start tomorrow. I'll get the phone back to James as soon as forensics has checked it for prints but I doubt we'll find anything."

Eleanor nodded then left for home, she saw James Maurice leaving the building ahead of her.

Over breakfast Edward Clark Maurice was all ears when his mother outlined in the broadest terms the events of the previous evening. She had thought it best to give him some of the details, as the rumour mill on social media was certain to have started circulating the gory details. Witnesses to the scene were certain to have videoed the police presence, even the body before the forensics team put up their coverings, and she wanted her son to know the facts should any of his school friends ask. And there was of course the tittle-tattle that would surely appear on sites like Facebook and Twitter - truth, untruth, but mostly wild speculation.

When Eleanor had seen how Edward looked in the morning light she had considered keeping him in bed but he'd insisted he felt well enough to attend his classes. So with the proviso that he called her if things changed they both left and went their separate ways.

When she arrived at her office her team of four were already assembled, the renewed statement had been retyped over night and left on her desk along with some other notes. Witness statements would arrive in due course. Detective Chief Inspector Doug Fairclough was her line manager and he had called her in for a brief chat on the case. During this 'chat' he had expressed his main concern about finding the killer before any further killings took place. The last thing he wanted was the press advertising the presence of a psychopath on the streets. Eleanor had made it clear that she wasn't so sure the girl was psychopathic - it was too controlled. That the girl had no interest in the dead man may have been more to do with her main interest in being there - James Mason Maurice.

Eleanor looked at the dramatis persona marked on the flip chart paper and felt the drug dealer was a distraction, someone who was in the way of something that was more important to the girl. It was the link between the girl and her ex-husband that needed clarifying and quickly.

"Ceri, run copies of this statement off and these notes will you and distribute them. Read them everybody we need some ideas." The Inspector called out to the attentive team.

Once she had given them time to access the data in the statement she announced, "Before anyone asks or is too embarrassed to, yes the James Mason Maurice mentioned in the statement is the back stabbing, philandering piece of crap I was once married to."

"Does that mean we are to find this girl and charge her with failing to let him get mugged? Or for being useless as she took out the wrong man?" Commented Hazel Wilson who was the lowest ranked team member but only by time in service.

"Follow his money, but where will it lead Gov?" suggested Tony Coltrain, her Sergeant.

"Alright calm down, I don't want my biased feelings to get in the way of a fair and open investigation. I have spoken with Inspector Cordon and the D.C.I and for now we do not think James is responsible for the death of Jason Tobbit. As far as our investigation is concerned we are not interested in the attempted mugging, what we are interested in is the girl. As you will see in the statement James Maurice never got a look at her as she was behind him."

"Must be a new experience for him," commented Tony critically; he knew all the details of the messy break-up of his boss's marriage.

"For that Tony you're on door to door down Sloane Street, find out if anyone saw anything or knows of anyone fitting the limited description and who speaks with a lisp. Ceri see if you can find if there any cameras on the street, civil and private and any that have a view of the street ends. We need to find her fast; this girl has dispassionately killed someone and seemingly with little hesitation."

"But politely, I mean if what James said he heard is right, it's not as if every killer says 'excuse me' before delivering the final blow or whatever she did. Odd that don't you think?" Ceri interrupted her note taking seeking clarification.

"Good point Ceri and it's not the only oddity. She obviously knows James but he denies knowing anyone who is foreign and has a lisp. So we need a connection, and why take the blood sample, what is that all about?"

"Trophy maybe boss," suggested Hazel.

"Unlikely as it was only a pin prick worth and she took it from James and not Jason Tobbit but if that was the reason she was there it has to be important. Yes Tony?"

"Well there was that TV serial killer that kept blood sample slides of his victims, who knows what goes through the minds of such people? Anyway at the risk of walking about with a sandwich board asking for witnesses could she be an unknown daughter that needs blood for a paternity test?" the sergeant suggested.

"Hmm an interesting speculation, although it's an odd way of going about it, however if she's young, say twenty-five maximum James would have been fifteen at the time of her conception. Which means …." Eleanor left the question hanging.

"He'd have some interesting questions to answer," said Tony.

"Indeed so, however I hope it isn't true as there are many things

I might wish on this girl but having James Maurice for a father isn't one of them. Now, as yet we don't know how Tobbit died and it'll be early tomorrow before we get the autopsy report. So for now let's start on the basics."

"Boss, I notice she used the word 'medic' when suggesting James gets some help, not the usual word, most of us would say doctor or medical help. Could she be military or ex-military?" pondered Coltrain as he highlighted the word on the statement.

Eleanor pursed her lips; the idea of an unhinged ex-special op's agent running loose was not something she wished to contemplate. "Let's hope not, for now we are looking for female, possibly early twenties but could be younger, possibly of small stature, she has a foreign accent and speaks with a lisp. We have no fingerprints as yet and we are awaiting the examination of James Maurice's phone and clothes to see if there are any prints or DNA evidence. I think we can rule out special op's she is probably too young."

"We have bugger all then," voiced Tony.

"Quite so, so find that camera footage Ceri so we can put a face to her, or find someone who has seen her and can describe her. Hazel organise somebody to put up some signs appealing for witnesses at each end of the street, I'll arrange for the local Bobbies to ask around the area, shops and the like. Okay let's get to it."

Thursday 10.45a.m.

The Department of Genetics - University Hospital.

Edward Maurice sat in the waiting area scanning his tablet screen onto which he had loaded earlier his study project notes. His mother had dropped him off ten minutes before and all he had to do now was await the arrival of his father. Unlike most hospitals he had familiarity with, this place lacked the same odours, and the staff had different uniforms. In the short time he'd been there several people had passed him by who he assumed were post-graduates or doctrinal students specializing in human genetics. It amused him to think that one day soon one of them may write a thesis on his condition, hopefully with a positive conclusion.

"Hello." The voice was soft and accented with a slightly husky overtone.

Edward jumped out of his reverie and looked up. On seeing the girl he straightened up trying not to look as young as he was. God she must walk quietly he thought, everybody else around here seemed to squeak as they walked on the polished plasticised floor coating. She stood about four feet six inches tall he guessed and she was of a slight build, two dark brown pigtails hung down across her ears the ends resting just below her collar bones. The oval face he noted was accentuated by well applied but not over done make-up. He couldn't see her eyes as they were hidden by large round glasses, the lenses of which shimmered like oil on water. Her mouth was straight but curved slightly down at the centre; it looked as if she was half smiling. Dressed in a white blouse and dark trousers he took her for one of the students and she held across her chest a pink leather satchel.

"Are you Edward Clark Maurithe? She asked quietly.

"Edward Clark Maurice," he corrected, "yes, yes I am," he replied clearing his throat.

"And your date of birth ith?" she asked in an unthreatening tone.

He told her and her smile didn't alter.

"I am Rethearcher Oo-neh Maurithe, do you mind if I take a thmall blood thample?" she said as she sat down in the vacant seat beside him.

"No go right ahead," he offered his thumb automatically, not taking his eyes off her. To him she was something else, so different from the other girls he knew, far more exotic but focused. She didn't seem as interested in him as much as he was in her.

Removing an object, barely eight inches square by a half inch thick, from her bag she switched it on, a pale blue light shone out. Her tongue protruded slightly, moving slowly up and down as she placed a pen like device on his index finger, Edward winced as he felt a sharp pain. The pen was then pushed into a slot in the device. Oo-neh Maurice hummed slightly while rubbing what seemed like a crayon over the prick site. After a few minutes the screen colour changed, a flickering readout cascaded sideways across the face of the square. She examined it, slid the data sideways then up, zoomed in, and then looked up at Edward so intently he felt uneasy. Edward felt rather than observed her smile widen. Her tongue curled slightly upwards and stayed there for a fraction of a second before she finally said, "I mutht go now, your father will be here directly."

"Will I see you again?" he asked, more in hope than expectation.

"Yeth of courthe, you are the reathon I am here." She bowed slightly before disappearing down the corridor clutching what Edward thought of as a school satchel.

When his father came into view James was slightly shocked by his appearance, he looked rough with dark rings around his eyes. However Edward seemed strangely elated, now he had something positive to look forward to on his future visits. He turned his head to look again down the now empty corridor. Then he started berating himself for not asking if he could take her picture. "Hi Dad how's the head?" He said turning his attention back to his father.

It was late in the day when Eleanor scanned Jason Tobbit's autopsy report to remind her of the recent conversation she had had with Doctor Edgar Gains earlier. He was a man in his late fifties, prematurely white haired and not very tall with a tanned leathery complexion, more from ancestry than standing in the sun a lot. The doctor had swiftly gone over the state of the internal organs; both liver and kidneys were damaged beyond hope of repair from a lifestyle that was anything but healthy. Stomach ulceration and indications of pre-cancerous tissue in addition gave a life expectancy, had he still been breathing, of only a few months at best. He expected the blood analysis to show the presence of any number of drugs taken orally, by injection and/or snorted.

On hearing this, her first reaction was that the victim, or perpetrator depending on your stance, had died of self-inflicted injuries. This as the pathologist was to point out, was not so. He produced a photograph of Tobbit's right ear and awaited comment. When one wasn't forthcoming he began to explain his findings.

"As you can see there are no apparent or obvious marks or even blood to suggest he had in anyway been struck with anything. We can discount old bruising and the head abrasion, which probably resulted from contact with the ground when he fell. However when I came to examine the brain I found this, he held up an x-ray plate. I am seeking confirmation but that will have to wait until I get the MRI scan done but quite frankly I have never seen anything quite like it."

Eleanor looked closely at the backlit grey image, "What am I looking for?"

"Look just here." He traced a line with his finger, starting on the centre right hand side of the brain and moving towards the front of the left hemisphere. A faint line lay beneath his extended digit.

"What is it?" She queried peering close up at the image.

"It appears to be a fine tube about two millimetres in diameter, whatever caused it was placed inside the ear. There is no blood seepage and it is difficult to spot externally. What caused it however I have no idea, as I have never in all my days seen anything similar. Had it been a sharp pointed object like a fine needle there would have been an entry wound and the blood from severed veins and capillaries. On the other hand if someone had developed an ultra small bullet, there would most certainly be some evidence of a cavity from the pressure wave. After the scan the image may tell us more but I do not feel confident, this is unusual to say the least."

"Would death have been instantaneous?" Eleanor asked.

"From its apparent path more than likely, he might have

twitched a bit but probably didn't make a sound. What happened to him? It's not some spy stuff is it?"

"All I know for certain is that he is dead, it's the how and why I'm trying to find out. All we know is that he was a known addict and dealer that had tried to mug my ex-husband. There is a girl involved about whom we know nothing, but foreign agents with secret weapons - I doubt that very much!"

"Ah! Might be able to help you with the girl, we found a long hair on the decease's sleeve which was not his, however it could have come from the ground he fell on, so it may not be important."

"Well it's something to work on. Thanks." She took the proffered plastic bag that Gains had removed from a box on the side counter.

"These items are a few odds and sods we found in his clothing and on his body, a most insanitary person in my opinion. In this little plastic bag, containing what appears to be cocaine, there is a partial print but it's probably his; however that it is not for me to say. I'll call you when the image file from the scan comes back." The full stop was tangible; he waited for Eleanor to leave, her education being over.

She took the hint.

After working on the available street camera footage, both public and private, nothing had turned up. There were no images of a female fitting the description, vague as it was, entering either end of Sloane Street, before, during or after the incident. Door knocking at the shops and residential property nearby had produced nothing. Nobody knew of anyone with the described speech impediment and nobody had seen anyone even close to the vague description of the girl.

Eleanor brought the team together to update them on the cause of death, acknowledging that the more they discovered the more unusual the case seemed to become. After the meeting she reported what little she knew for definite to her senior officer D.C.I. Doug Fairclough. The meeting didn't last long but just as she was leaving for the day the report on the hair fibre came through. It indicated that although the hair fibre was natural and dark brown in colour, due to the presence of chemical residues it had probably come from a high-end wig or hair accessory.

The smell of cooking met her as Eleanor entered the kitchen by way of the rear door. Edward looked up from the pan he stirred in front of him, "Hi Mum," he said with a smile.

"Something new?" she asked.

"Something Italian," replied her son cryptically.

"How did it go?" She asked referring to the appointment he'd had at the hospital, removing her coat as she did so.

"Just asked a load of questions, same oh, same oh. Anyway they'd like me to go in for exploratory tests for two or three days so they can check out my DNA." Edward answered without much interest.

"Did your father turn up on time?"

"No, he was a bit late," he reluctantly replied in between making some culinary adjustments. "But I didn't mind, I met one of the people handling my case, seems I am interesting to the females of our species at last. You'd love her she's an absolute stunner, reminds me of an elf."

"What, with pointy ears and all?" She laughed.

"I couldn't see her ears they were hidden behind plaits and she had these big glasses on, they had lenses that seemed to ripple when she moved." He paused as the phone rang. "Don't be long it's ready now."

From his position in the kitchen Edward could overhear one part of the telephone conversation and it didn't seem to be going well for his father who he assumed was the caller. Well he only had himself to blame he thought. James Maurice was calling to tell Eleanor about the hospital meeting, the details of which were more in depth than those her son had mentioned. What displeased her was the discovery that her son was scheduled to go in the following day. He had a list of the things he would need to take with him. When the call was over she slammed the handset down into its cradle.

"You forgot to mention you're to go in tomorrow," her irritability was obvious. The meal gave Eleanor time to cool down and on reflection her displeasure wasn't with her son. "Your father is coming round about ten-thirty to take you," Eleanor finally said when the meal was over.

The rest of the night was more tranquil; the meal had at least made up for her son's laid back attitude. Sitting with a frothy coffee, as she called a Cappuccino, she reviewed the case again in her mind and there were many strange factors standing out when you apply the Who, What, Where, When, Why and How technique. It never crossed her mind that things would get to be even stranger.

Brightly's Café the following day.

"Good morning Proprietor Alexthandria Brightly."

Alexandria Brightly didn't have to look up to notice who the speaker was, but she did so out of politeness, "Good morning Miss Oo-neh Maurice." She smiled widely because she genuinely liked the girl in front of her; there weren't many of her customers she could say that about. Alex had to look down at the young woman as she was less than five feet tall, or as she corrected herself, one point five metres, and of slim build. Blonde haired today she noticed, what her eye colour was she had no idea as they were always covered by a pair of fashionable sunglasses, and she was smartly dressed in a white blouse and black trousers. A light grey coat and a coloured satchel completed her appearance. "What would you like today?"

"A pot of tea and...." the customer perused the selection of delicacies, ".....one of the thothe pleathe."

"Very good, now you go and sit yourself down and I'll be right with you." Missus Brightly watched the figure go to her usual seat in the corner by the window. She sighed slightly; a bonny enough girl she thought but she seemed sad, as though she was trying hard to appear as if everything was all right. Missus Brightly speculated that it was because she was foreign and possibly missing home, wherever home was, however she was pleased to note she had been taught to be very polite.

Across the road Inspector Eleanor Maurice was walking to work as she often did. She stopped at the 'Future Treasures' art gallery and looked in the window for the picture she had looked at many times. It had gone. Peering through the glass she tried to see if it had been moved inside, but she couldn't see it. Moving to the door Eleanor tried the handle but it was locked and according to the sign wouldn't open again until later in the morning. He who hesitates, she reminded herself, mentally committing herself to ring up later to see if the picture had been sold or just moved. Glancing at her watch she noted there was time enough to get a coffee to take in with her to the office. Crossing the busy road she entered Brightly's Café.

The owner was at the far end, by the window serving a blonde girl.

Oo-neh looked up as the woman entered and froze, "Maw her," she said almost silently.

Alexandria Brightly heard the words and the tone they were said in and she looked at the young woman's face, it looked in a state of shock. "Whatever is the matter?" she reached out taking hold of a small hand, it was icy cold. Looking around she tried to see the cause of this sudden state of alarm but only saw a regular. "Be right with you Elle," she called out. "Now my love whatever is the matter?" she said turning back to her young customer.

"That woman, do you know her?" Oo-neh asked gathering her composure.

"Yes she often comes in, her name is Elle, Eleanor Maurice she's a police inspector, been a customer for a few years now. No need to be frightened of her, she's a very kind woman doing a difficult job."

Oo-neh withdrew a square electronic unit from her bag and manipulated the controls until a coloured image showed upon the screen, "My mother," she said turning the screen around.

Alex looked down at the almost three-dimensional picture; it showed a woman possibly in her late thirties. The face was smiling as she held a young girl close to her; the dark haired girl was dressed in a yellow jumpsuit and wore glasses similar to the pair worn by the girl next to her. But it was the woman's face that drew her full attention; she was identical to Eleanor Maurice. "Where is your mother now?" She asked wondering if the girl's mother had just up and left the family.

"My mother died a month after the picture wath recorded on my eighth birthday, I loved her very much and my mother loved me." The girl said distractedly as though her thoughts were far away.

"I am truly sorry to hear that Oo-neh, no wonder it was a shock seeing Elle. Now you drink your tea, put some sugar in it, it's good for shock and it'll warm you up while I see to Elle."

After administering her maternal duties Alexandria moved briskly to the main counter, "Sorry to keep you but the young lady has had a bit of a shock."

Eleanor glanced briefly at the figure seated by the window, "What happened?"

"You walked in, gave her quite a start." Alex said, stating the facts as they were.

"Must have a guilty conscience," Eleanor said as she glanced back to the now empty table. "She seems to have run off."

"Probably outback throwing up I expect. You don't happen to have a secret daughter do you?" Missus Brightly asked as she straightened up a few items on display.

"No, just a very rather obvious teenage son, why do you ask?"

"She has a picture of her mother on one of those tablet things, taken when she was eight years old and her mother is the image of you, not similar. Even accounting for a change of hair style she's the absolute image of you."

"Really, who is she?" Eleanor said reaching into her coat pocket for the chiming phone, "Excuse me." After listening a moment she said, "I'll be there in five minutes," then closed the cover over the display.

"Her name is Oo-neh Maurice another coincidence, I think from her accent she's foreign but speaks very good English, she tries really hard to be clear. She's a researcher of some sort but I have no idea into what. Personally I think she is lonely being away from home; she's friendly enough but reserved if you know what I mean. I suppose living in a strange country is hard, away from everything you know." Alex handed the usual order of coffee over in a sealed plastic cup. "How is Edward doing?"

"He's going in today for more tests, let's hope they find something conclusive this time." Handing over the correct coins for the drink Eleanor picked up the cup in a gloved hand and turned before turning back as though a sudden thought had struck her. "You say she's foreign and accented, does she happen to speak with a lisp, you know, can't pronounce her 'esses?'"

"How did you know that? Yes it takes a while to attune your hearing to get a full grasp of what she is saying sometimes but she does very well."

Eleanor didn't hesitate on hearing the news, putting her cup down she went through the café to the facilities beyond, they were empty. Her eyes scanned the surrounds before concluding it was near impossible to get out that way but gone she was. On returning back to the counter to a bemused proprietor she held the cup and plate the girl had used. "Look Alex it may or may not be important but I'll be back later to get a full description of her if you don't mind. Can I take these, I'll let you have them back as soon as I can, I need to rule her out of a crime scene." Eleanor said.

"No I don't mind but what can she have done, she's such a sweet well mannered girl."

"Maybe nothing, anyway I have to go; I'll be back as soon as I can."

Entering the police building through the main entrance she glanced at the desk sergeant who in turn nodded towards two figures seated across the atrium. Both stood about five feet nine or maybe ten inches tall, wore matching dark suits with pale blue shirts and black shoes. To the inspector they had a predatory stillness about them, not the meditative stillness of someone just waiting but someone watching and awaiting the moment to act. She didn't like them on face value.

"Give me two minutes," she said to Sergeant Hoyle, "Does the D.C.I. know?"

"Yes, he's waiting for you, he'll have notified the Super' by now, Hoyle replied inferring much.

After swiping her ID card across the pad by the door she went directly to her office on the second floor, dropped her things onto her desk with the coffee and went to see her superior officer. It was nearly fifteen minutes later when Inspector Eleanor Maurice and her Sergeant, Tony Coltrain entered interview room one where the two dark suited men were already sitting. They stood up as she stepped through the doorway.

"Good morning Inspector of Police Eleanor Maurice, a pleasure to meet you. I am Agent O. F. V Tyler-Wolfe and my companion is Agent O. F. R. Tyler-Wolfe."

Slightly taken aback by the unusual address Eleanor recovered quickly, "For the record this is Detective Sergeant Tony Coltrain, please take a seat." To both police officers there seemed to be an unnatural pause before the two agents reacted to the invitation, it seemed as if they only sat when they themselves started to sit down. "Now I understand you are representatives of one of the Security Services. Is that so?"

Agent O. F. V Tyler-Wolfe slid a holographic, credit card sized object across the table, Eleanor picked it up; turning it slightly she observed the facial image of the man opposite in three-dimensional detail. She was impressed at the quality and the detail. Underneath was the agent's name above the legend 'Agent of Investigation and Enforcement – Scientific and Technological Development and Engagement - Military Division'. In the right hand corner was a reference, 005TW. In her hand the card felt heavier than the usual plastic I.D. card; the reason occurred to her when she tilted it. The light illuminated one edge and she could make out what may have been fine circuitry embedded within it. She passed it to her sergeant.

"I don't imagine you can copy those very easily," she observed.

"In thirty years it has never been achieved," the seeming spokesperson of the pair replied without pride, just stating the facts.

"Interesting that a technology that has existed for thirty years has yet to be talked about let alone filtered down to us mortals. Most unusual," Eleanor observed. "As you can imagine until we verify the details of who you may or may not be, I cannot discuss any ongoing investigations with you. So I fail to see the purpose of your visit and request to see me personally." Eleanor was curt; she did not like interference from either politicians or members of the security forces when it came to her investigations. Unless of course they were to provide accurate information, that was both pertinent and helpful in bringing culprits to justice. "Would you mind saying exactly what the organisation you belong to actually is?"

"It is one of the many developments arms of government; its main purpose is to discover solutions to problems."

"Military solutions?" Eleanor asked bluntly.

"Every government has such facilities; it is what keeps us all safe from foreign aggression. As you would expect I can elaborate no further, but I ask your discretion, that you do not discuss our part in any assistance we may give you. The work we do is by its very nature sensitive or more accurately extremely sensitive and because of that, ultra secret."

"I have heard similar arguments before; to me they appear designed to make me feel good about abhorrent activity. Activity that I am forced to accept but it is often both morally and ethically beyond the pale."

"Perhaps, but if an enemy of the State realises that we will do the unthinkable to preserve our way of life they hopefully will take several steps back from incurring that response," O.F.V Tyler-Wolfe did not have the look of a man who was joking.

"I hadn't realised that Hitler had won the war? Eleanor replied without smiling. His tone, his air of superiority and patronising style made Eleanor like him less than before.

"I keep my country safe." He reached over and took the card back from D.S Coltrain's hand, "And we protect our secrets as well as we may. Without this," he held the rectangular plate up, "I would not even get through the first gate into the transit area. In all the facilities I have access to the security level is set very high. Believe me when I tell you the security systems at those facilities do not just look at the surface of this card." The agent paused as he slipped the I.D device out of sight.

"However we have not come to fight about jurisdiction, you protect the civil population by the means available to you, and we do the same."

Tyler-Wolfe's tone hadn't changed; if it had been intended to be conciliatory it failed to impress the police officers. From Eleanor's position that fact - that lack of social empathy, was interesting, the agent was starting to sound like a psychopath or sociopath. The inspector listened more intently to what else these two had to say.

"We will do nothing to impede your investigation Detective Inspector Eleanor Maurice," Agent O.F.V Tyler-Wolfe continued, "nor ask for any information but to assist you with information. How you may assist us in return will become clear as we go along. Your current investigation I understand, involves the death of a young man witnessed by Finance Transactor James Mason Maurice."

Eleanor noted the use of her ex-husband's full name, just as the girl had done and also the mispronunciation of her surname, Maur-ice instead of Maur-eece. What she found strange was the description of her ex-husband's profession prefixed to his name. "That is public knowledge to be found in the press coverage," she replied wishing to give nothing away.

"The executed person, Jason Tobbit died from unusual damage to the brain caused by a means you have yet to discover." He waited for a response.

Eleanor tried not to show anything on her face for that information was not public knowledge. "Executed?" she found herself asking.

"Executed, yes he was of no importance or benefit to society; I believe I am correct in saying so. Regardless, you and I are looking for the same person."

Slowly Agent Tyler-Wolfe removed a hard photo image from an inside pocket and slid it purposefully across the table in the same way he had done with the I.D card.

As Eleanor examined the picture she made an easy assessment. It was an image from a surveillance camera judging by the angle but the colour quality and definition was remarkable, high resolution photo quality. Clearly seen was the face of a girl with brown hair that cascaded around her head, dropping below the shoulders. An angular but not unpleasing face looked around and up at the camera. The mouth had a slight smile on it and the eyes were hidden behind what appeared to be sunglasses. An image flickered to life in her mind, an image so recently formed, that when compared with the photo' they were identical. "Do you mind if I take a copy of this?" She found herself asking, trying to hide the excitement in her voice. She motioned her sergeant to follow.

Outside the room Eleanor checked the photograph again, "Tony I saw her this morning at Brightly's Café, from Alex's brief description she sounded like our girl. It's a long shot but take a couple of the others with you and see if she has gone back there. Send Hazel down to me here once this has been scanned. Ask Ceri to take the cup and plate on my desk and have it analysed for prints and DNA, its urgent tell her. When you speak with Alex ask her for a DNA sample to exclude her from anything we get off the plate, better include that girl of hers if she's been in today."

"Right boss," The sergeant said turning.

"Tony do not go in mob handed, she's a regular there, if she's not there now she will be sometime. So we don't want to put her off," Eleanor cautioned.

Tony Coltrain disappeared up the stairs at a pace whilst she returned to the room.

She hadn't seen the smile that had appeared on the faces of the agents still sitting at the table behind the closed interview room door.

When she entered the room the inspector asked her informants a casual, pass the time question, "Would you like a coffee or maybe tea whilst we wait?" Elle smiled as the request was turned down.

Hazel joined them in interview room one eight minutes later with the original hard copy and a couple of her own copies. In between time Sergeant Coltrain and another plain clothes officer had entered the café and commenced visually checking all the customers. They then searched the toilet facilities and the rear of the building but it was to no avail, the girl was no longer there. Alexandria Brightly was slightly bemused by this turn up of events but none the less it would be something to talk about when she got home but that would be after supplying the police with a more detailed description of her elusive client..

Back in interview room one Inspector Maurice slid the photograph back across the table, "Who is she?" She said in a hardened voice, a reaction she knew deep down was due to these weird, yes she reinforced, weird and seemingly fascist duo. Her observations led her to think of them as statues that occasionally found a reason to move, and without a reason they remained motionless. Their eyes blinked slowly and infrequently giving them a fixed, glazed look which made her feel decidedly uncomfortable. This wasn't the feeling of being mentally undressed by a man - more of having your very soul analysed.

Why did she feel so scrutinised she wondered until Hazel distracted her by leaning across and whispering in her ear, "They don't blink much do they?" No, she had replied as if another question had been asked. She took some small comfort in knowing it wasn't her imagination but these observations reinforced her initial assessment that these two were predators.

"She goes by the name of Oonex," the agent pronounced the name Oo-necks, "and she has for many years passed as the daughter of Principal Engineer Ioan Maurice, a name not unlike your own. However a recent security check on all personnel revealed that there is no record of her birth, in fact no records exist of her at all. Officially she doesn't exist and since the area she lives in, is, as I said earlier, one with an ultra high level of security, unregistered or unmonitored individuals have no place being there. Investigations revealed she has in her possession a file of an unrecorded, detailed experiment into creating a genetically manipulated human being for the purposes of warfare. The file is designated Project 01x."

"Forgive me but experimentation into creating a genetically modified human is illegal in this and many other countries." Eleanor elaborated, "Would you care to be more specific? Who did this work and why? Or is it also ultra secret? I am guessing it's not an officially sanctioned government experiment otherwise I'm sure you'd know more, if not everything about it." Eleanor sensed a slight hint of discomfort in the two sat before her and the reason they had come to her was now starting to become clear. They had a problem and they weren't sure how to handle it.

"I cannot for security reasons give you that information suffice to say she must be apprehended before any knowledge of this matter becomes public. There is a further problem, we understand she is unstable, which is why she has probably had no medical examinations on record. It appears she has only been kept in check by continual observation and a specific range of drugs; drugs not currently available to her. Until our investigations showed us that she is a non-person, nobody on the facility beyond her father seems to have been aware of her status, even the girl herself. Regrettably that revelation and the fact her father had lied to her all her life has tipped her mental balance. She left a note saying she was going to make Principal Engineer Ioan Maurice pay. He has an undisclosed, rare and damaging gene mutation. We believe she is tracking anyone with that gene, all of his line, anyone with it we believe she is intent on killing. She is dangerous." To highlight that point he continued, "When we started out six months ago my team had five members we are the only two left."

"She doesn't look very old, she must be extraordinarily clever to get around all your ultra-high security measures and escape," Eleanor couldn't help rubbing salt in an obviously open wound. "However from the death of the drug addict it appears she has a weapon. What is it? It appears to be anything but conventional." Eleanor pressed hard with the question, restraining the tension that was steadily building up within her. Any hint of friendliness she might have had, had long evaporated.

"We believe it is one of the pulse weapons under current development, she took it from her father's laboratory. That is something else we are also keen to recover." Tyler-Wolfe, the spokesman did not look anymore discomforted by the way the interview was developing.

The detective ignored the latter comment for a moment, "What kind of ammunition does it use and how much of it has she got?"

"It is a pulse generated personal protection weapon, the mark one version, it doesn't use the hard rounds that you are familiar with but a compressed energy bolt. How many discharges she gets will depend upon the setting." He gave the appearance of being helpful but both officers felt he was holding back what could be vital evidence.

"How about a setting that drills a fine two millimetre hole through somebody's head," Eleanor said acidly.

"Close contact, medium to low setting, about six hundred discharges," was the disturbingly blunt response from the lead agent.

"Jesus Christ," Hazel swore.

"What kind of security do you have at this ultra secure facility? The Inspector's question was rhetorical, "It may well be that nobody can get in without a card like yours but it seems anyone can get out with whatever they can stick in their pockets. I am not surprised that this little girl has for years been allowed to wander about a secure facility and leave unhindered. Notwithstanding she had access to a weapon that has the potential to kill hundreds of people?" Eleanor paused to gather her thoughts and to repress the anger she was feeling. "What kind of range does it have?"

"High setting, about half a kilometre but do not be over concerned she may even know how to initiate another charging."

"Why doesn't that comfort me? How did she kill the other members of your team?" Eleanor shook her head and looked at Hazel to gauge her thoughts.

"We don't know - their bodies are unaccounted for."

There was something about the answers she'd got which caused a light to flash in her mind; they lacked a natural emotional flow. "Then it's possible they might still be alive."

"A remote but unlikely possibility, as they have not reported in and their tracking signals have disappeared so we assume the worst."

Eleanor shook her head in total disbelief, "What else has she taken?"

"Nothing so far as we know, what may have been discovered post deployment is not currently available to us. The data file she has is now the only copy in existence, as the main database file sequence where it was stored has been deleted then corrupted with an encryption that may take years to break."

Voicing her thoughts Eleanor wondered at the miracles or in this case the curses of science, "She looks barely a child, and so what kind of genus is she that allows her to by-pass your security? What exactly are we dealing with here, Hmm? We might be grateful she has the only file because it has a positive side; you will not be able to perform the experiments and create God alone knows what monstrosities. It might be a good thing if the file remains lost. And your intentions or shall I say orders are precisely what?"

The agents looked at each other momentarily before the spokesman replied, "We do not know her specification and therefore have no ideas as to her capabilities. Her father has not been helpful. Our orders are to recover both file and subject and return them back to the facility."

"Alive or dead?" she asked bluntly.

"Preferably alive but if the means justify the ends we are allowed to use force."

"Well let me spell this out, so you can fully understand my position, you are not in some high security unit here. You are out in the real world where there are laws to protect the public. Unless I see any authorisation to the contrary, you are not permitted to carry weapons or use lethal force against any person including the girl. She is wanted for questioning relating to a murder not a mile from here. When she is captured she will be questioned and charged with that offence should we have the evidence and then she will stand trial. That is unless some orders from on high, tell me to hand her over to other officials of the State. Any weapons or files found upon her will all be held as evidence. So do not impede my investigation, otherwise I shall be forced to incarcerate you two for obstruction of justice. Do I make myself clear?"

"Perfectly Detective Inspector Eleanor Maurice, I have my orders, you have yours and should I find the Institute's property first we shall return it to its lawful owners. We are not enemies Inspector of Police we have a common problem so I would also like you to know that Principal Engineer Ioan Maurice created a modified influenza virus that is lethal beyond any virus you know about. According to my briefing, once infected with the NAF01 the individual will show no symptoms in the first twenty-four hours as the virus colonises the host.

The person is highly contagious during this time. During the second day the sufferer will experience high fever, on the third day ninety-nine percent of people die. I tell you this because this little girl, as you call her, was part of a project to trial this agent in the North African States. Estimated losses of thirty million people within the first week were beyond the projected result.

She has already killed one person here and none of us knows what the consequences of that action will be in the long term. If she attacks and kills the target she is aiming at, the results I do assure you will be catastrophic for the world as we know it." Both men stood up, practically as one, "You may find this data useful, it gives some metrics of the girl and her tracker frequency," he pushed a single white folded sheet across the table. "Thank you for your time and good morning to you Inspector of Police Eleanor Maurice and to you too Detective Constable of Police Hazel Wilson."

"Wait a moment, tracker, what tracker?" Eleanor spat out as though she had just realised what had been said to her.

"She has an embedded passive pulse unit in her leg. Regrettably it appears faulty as its signal is intermittent but provided she is within thirty miles you may be able to triangulate her position when it is operable."

Eleanor was a little bemused by this new revelation, "I assume you didn't put it there. So who did and why?" she found herself asking.

"We do not know, we can assume it was her parents but why, we have no idea." Both agents straightened up as if conjoined, and then they left much to the relief of both women.

Both police officers stayed seated and watched them leave, each shuddering.

"What a pair of freaks, they give me the creeps," commented Hazel.

"But interesting nonetheless," replied Eleanor

"Not an interest I'd wish to cultivate," replied her sub-ordinate.

"Well to begin with they have an interesting way of addressing people, using their full name and title. James Maurice said the girl called him by all his names as well. I thought that may have been just to confirm his identity but if it is a usual form of addressing people common to all three of them, then they come from the same place."

"Foreign parts do you think, their English is accented after all."

"Possibly Hazel," the inspector said thoughtfully, "but nowhere I'm familiar with, however if true then we might end up in a political shit storm as to who gets this girl and file. In that direction lies another ten years in the courts, because if she has any sense she'll claim asylum. The relevant country will want her back for stealing state secrets but also the file she took. I can imagine a lot of people will want such a file if it exists, even our Government. If people are willing to go to court to get primates human rights there is no telling where this will end. Tell you what, get off to the University and ask around some of the academics and see if such a human genetic manipulation is even possible. Ask them about that virus as well; especially if there have been large-scale deaths in Africa.

For all we know she simply nicked some secret research papers that they want back at any cost because they are about internationally banned experiments. Of course it could be nonsense. There's something about their story that sounds contrived and their delivery is anything but fluid. It could be that this "Scientific and Technological Development and Engagement - Military Division place," she read from her notes, "has been developing the super virulent virus themselves, in contravention of International law. But I can't get this nagging doubt out of my mind; the girl I saw earlier looked normal enough, in fact she looked like any other teenager, a bit smarter and smaller than average perhaps but she didn't look like the picture of a homicidal maniac those two are painting, That they are, I could believe without much effort. So is she just a dupe, sideshow for some other event? Or are we?"

With that rhetorical question left hanging in the ether they parted; Eleanor went to the upper floor just as Sergeant Coltrain returned. "Anything?" she asked.

"No boss, I've got a good description of her and I've asked Missus Brightly to call us if she comes back which she might since she's been a regular for a few months. We tried not to look too obvious. Oh! And I got the samples you asked for."

"Good, we'll see then, it all depends if she knows we're onto her. Anyway you missed a treat with those two weirdoes. When everyone is back gather them together for an update, see you in about ten minutes I want a quick word with the D.C.I."

Edward Clark Maurice sat in his assigned room at the hospital reading up on his examination notes. His father hadn't stayed, he'd quickly signed the mandatory paperwork, without checking to see if he was signing over his son's body parts for harvesting before departing, his filial duties complete.

Engrossed as he was in his work he never noticed the door open and close or the figure that quietly approached his bedside.

"Good morning Edward Clark Maurithe." The voice had a singular cadence to it.

Edward jumped visibly.

"I am thorry to have thartled you. Would you like a moment to compothe yourthelf?" the figure before him said calmly.

"No, no I'm fine, just swotting up for my exams, I didn't hear you that's all." Edward put his notes down onto the bed. "You've changed your hair, the red suits you."

"Doth it, you are very kind to notithe, I shall not keep you for long." She laid a brown, card wrapped package on the side table and started to rummage in her satchel before laying it down at the foot of the bed, "Do you remember the blood tetht I did when we latht met?" She asked almost chattily.

"Yes," Edward said warily as the oblong device he had seen before was placed in front of him.

"Thith ith the rethult." Pointing to the screen, the girl he knew as Oo-neh continued, "You thee thith group I indicate here, it ith a mutated gene and that ith what ith cauthing your problemth. My father hath it, as did hith father and grandfather going back to hith great, four timeth grandfather. They all died before their fiftieth birthday, having lotht motht of their mental and phythical facultieth. That ith what you and all your male heirth have to look forward to."

"Well that **is** something to look forward to," Edward said not without irony. "Is there a cure?" He asked out of politeness because even he knew that gene therapy was in its infancy and as yet unreliable.

"Of courthe, would I mention it at all if there wath no tholution? That would be too cruel! Pleathe lithen Edward Clark Maurithe, I am going to give you an injection, well two ath it happenth, one in the arm, the other in the thigh muthle."

"And that will do what exactly?" Edward warily watched her withdraw a box from a side pocket in her coat.

"Today nothing at all, thmile and be happy becauthe tomorrow you will have a high fever, you may not remember much of the day, your body will ache, you will thweat a lot. You will cry out, perhaps a good time to athk for ithe-cream, tootie fruitie might be a good choithe."

"Why?"

"It it'th what I would choothe, it'th my favouritc. On the third day you will feel tired, every muthle will ache but it will be all over; you will never have to worry about thith problem ever again." She smiled; at least that is what Edward thought it was.

"Will they hurt, the injections I mean?"

"You will hardly feel them. Jutht clothe your eyeth and be brave"

"You're sure…" Edward asked warily, "it'll work?"

"Athk me again in three dayth time? Clothe your eyeth."

Edward felt his sleeve being pushed up, he felt his breathing turn slightly erratic, he'd hated injections for as long as he could remember. He felt pressure on his thigh for a moment then nothing. "Changed your mind?"

"No, it ith all done," she said replacing her equipment back in the box.

"But I didn't feel anything?" Edward said in surprise.

"Did you want to?"

"No."

"Then why are you complaining? You will feel bad enough tomorrow if you enjoy thuffering, tho enjoy today." Oo-neh packed all her equipment back into the satchel that still lay on the end of the bed. Then picking it up putting the strap over her shoulder she turned, moving towards the door.

Edward noticed the seemingly ever present half smile was still present all the time, he wasn't sure if she was half sad or half happy. "Will I see you again? He asked not without hope, even with the knowledge that to have her job she must be older than he was. "Can I have a picture of you?" He finally blurted out.

"To the firtht part of your quethtion, I do not know. Tomorrow ith a day that will change many thingth, you may not even remember I exithted."

"No fear of that. The picture will remind me," he insisted.

"You are very kind, but I am really nobody, not worth your conthideration." Her tongue passed over her upper lip momentarily. "I mutht go now, don't forget the tootie-fruitie you may never get another chanthe."

Then she was gone as silently as she came. A moment later a nurse popped her head around the door to see if he was okay and to tell him he'd be taken down for an MRI scan and a blood test in about half an hour. He wondered why, but considered it was probably to see what was going on, before the treatment kicked in. He looked at his tablet and smiled, "Well at least I have her picture even if she hadn't posed for one." He said to himself.

The team sitting around the conference table went silent when Inspector Maurice returned.

"If you don't already know we have just received our first solid lead into this case." She held up a copy of the photograph. "Now this is where it all gets a bit surreal. According to our informants this girl has stolen some highly classified data called Project 01x, which is about, if I interpret things correctly, creating a genetically modified human weapon. That is not to be discussed outside this room." Eleanor paused; looking at each face in turn to make sure that message had gone home. "If that is true then it is either a private company acting outside of the law, or a foreign country that believes itself beyond the law or even the possibility a covert unit belonging to our own Government. I have just spoken with the D.C.I. to see if he can find out anything through higher channels. If this company, Scientific and Technological Engagement and Development exists here or anywhere else then the whole case may pass out of our hands. The source of our information is allegedly part of the security structure of this alleged military operation, and frankly they are creepy. I put no trust in them as they seem to be repeating a script." She paused once more as the door opened; eyes flickered away from her to see who it was.

"Yoséf, I thought you weren't back for at least a couple of days." Eleanor smiled at the welcome return of an absent team member.

"That was the plan Ma'am but there is only so much a man can take from his family. It was fortunate you recalled me for some undisclosed case that only I can solve."

"I did?"

"Yes Ma'am by telephone not an hour ago."

"Then it's obvious your psychic skills are much in need. Grab a coffee and take a seat." Eleanor liked Yoséf as did the whole team; he was bright and applied himself to the job, rarely getting distracted. "Now the picture you have in front of you is that of the girl we are looking for. It looks to be very high quality surveillance video. Strange as it may seem I saw her this morning in Brightly's café although she was blonde whereas in this image she is a brunette. From the proprietor's comments she is very polite and may be foreign. From what I saw of her she is small in stature, about four foot-six, which makes it hard for me to believe she has killed three out of the five members of the security team that were sent after her. Especially since the ones we met earlier were a well-set pair. For those of you who didn't see them this is an image taken from the reception camera. I read them as being dangerous so on no account are you to try restraining them for any reason without armed backup. Personally I'd be surprised if you find either of them on their own as they appear oddly paired. Our priority is to find the girl before they do, even if it is only to save her. Ceri look into these three names see when they entered the country, it'll be about six months ago. If that fails see if they are registered on any database in this country. Tony take the photo to James Maurice see if the photo jogs his memory, ask at his office, if she's been stalking him someone may have seen her hanging about. If James knows her, bring him in for further questions. Yoséf you're with me, I'm going back to speak with the café owner and I'll update you on the case as we go."

After filling in more of the details she and Hazel had heard earlier she ended the briefing, "One last thing, she has a weapon that may have been used to kill Tobbit. From what these security agents said it is a secret model in development, which has, if she knows how to use it, the capacity for six hundred lethal shots. They are hoping she doesn't know how to reload it, however if she's as clever as she seems I don't think it should take her too long to work it out. Tony, get this picture circulated amongst the mobile teams and beat Bobbies, with this instruction. If anyone sees her they are not to approach just observe and report back to me a.s.a.p. If any of you see her, approach with caution; do not be threatening as all we need for now is to talk to her. If she is foreign she may not be legally here and with those two goons after here she may well be frightened, be careful frightened people can be unpredictable as some of you well know."

It was an eight-minute walk later that the door chime tinkled as Eleanor and Yoséf entered Brightly's Café. Eleanor looked around hopeful but not expectant. About half the tables were occupied. A young woman stepped out from the kitchen.

"Can I help you?" she asked in a voice that suggested she did not really care whether she could or not.

"Is Alex about, I need to speak with her?"

The woman disappeared back into the back room; Alex appeared a few seconds later.

"Hi Elle, what can I do for you this time?"

"Can we talk in private?"

Alex looked a little perplexed then said, "Sure, come through. Wendy the tables need clearing – now." They passed through the kitchen space which, thanks to the efficiency of the extractor, held few odours and into a small staff room at the rear.

"Take a seat," Alex said as she seated herself in a well used armchair.

"Alex this is Detective Constable Yoséf Aziz just in case you see him again. Now do you remember the foreign girl that was here this morning when I came in?"

"Oo-neh, do you mean? Of course, some of your lot came looking for her earlier."

"Yes I know, I didn't know it for certain at the time but she has come up in an investigation. What do you know about her?"

"Not much really, as I said earlier from the way she talks she's foreign - couldn't say where from though. She first came here a bit over six months ago, generally has a cup of tea and a cake of some sort. Apart from an excess of politeness, always using my full name and always appearing smartly turned out she doesn't stand out. Never causes any trouble, she just sits there for about an hour then off she goes. It took me a while to convince her she didn't have to return the cup and plate on her way."

"Does she ever meet anyone?" Eleanor asked.

"Never seen her with anybody, she just comes in, puts in her order then sits in the same seat you saw her in earlier and puts her satchel on the seat next to her. Did I say she was a researcher? No idea what in mind you but she spends some time looking at one of those electronic things all the kids have these days. What's she done?"

"To be honest I don't really know for certain, this is one of the strangest cases I've been involved in but I need to speak with her as soon as possible. I think she might be in danger so the sooner I find her the better."

"Danger, whatever from, she such a quiet harmless little soul," Alex sounded and looked surprised.

"There are two men looking for her," Eleanor showed Alex the image of the agents, "you'll know them when you meet them because they will make you feel creepy. They are about five-ten and may have forgotten how to smile. If they show up give me a call as soon as possible but do be careful as they never gave me the impression they would care much if they hurt you."

"Oh! Right," Alex said taking the business card offered to her.

"If anything else comes to mind let me know, I really need to find her before they do."

"Yes, right I will, don't you worry."

Eleanor's phone chimed, "Excuse me," she said pressing the answer icon, "Maurice."

The conversation didn't take long but Eleanor's complexion was noticeably paler by the time she pressed the red phone icon. Quickly she called her sergeant Tony Coltrain to pick her up as soon as he could at the café, cursing that this was one of those days she had not brought her car. It was ten minutes later that she heard the double blast of Tony's car horn.

"What's up?" he said as she and Yoséf got in the car.

"University Hospital as fast as you can, someone's given Edward an unscheduled injection." Eleanor said not without a hint of panic in her voice.

On hearing the news Tony switched on his police issue siren and lights in the hope it would move the traffic out of the way. The journey took less time than both had expected for the time of day, arriving at the drop off point some twenty minutes later.

"Do you want me to wait?" Coltrain called out as she alone exited the car.

"I doubt it will do any good but both of you have a look around the area, Doctor Forbes said it was a girl so it just might be the one we're after. Show the picture to some of the staff, they might have seen her. Yoséf you do the same in the immediate area."

"But why would she, what possible motive would she have for going after your family?" The sergeant queried.

"I have no idea for certain, it was something those agents said she was intent on doing but it didn't make a lot of sense." With that final word she crossed the block work pedestrian access and went into the hospital through the large glass doors. Doctor Forbes, the superintending physician awaited her.

"Before you see him," he began hurriedly, "he appears perfectly normal, there are no apparent adverse affects. This way, I'll show you to his room. I haven't questioned him much about this yet; I thought it better if you do that. However I have ascertained that a young woman he'd met previously at the interview session gave him two injections, although I must admit I cannot see the needle marks. There have been no injections scheduled only taking a blood and skin sample for the DNA testing. We have no idea who she is or what he was injected with, if he was injected with anything. Tell me has he ever had any hallucinations or delusions of any description?"

The question caught Eleanor off guard and she stopped moving. "No never, if he said it happened, it happened."

"Very well, we have taken a blood sample to see if we can isolate what Edward has been given, that has already been sent to the lab as a matter of priority. Here we are." He knocked once on the door then entered.

Apart from her son there was only a male nurse in the room who left on a silent instruction from Doctor Forbes.

"Do you wish me to stay?" Forbes asked.

"If you will, there may be details that make sense to you."

"Ili mum, what's the panic about," Edward asked more out of curiosity than concern.

"Are you feeling okay?" His mother asked trying not to show concern.

"Yes, shouldn't I be?"

"You were given an injection earlier the doctor tells me."

"Yes," he replied guardedly. "One here and one here," he said indicating the sites.

"Are you sure? The doctor says there are no needle marks."

"Well I wasn't looking, you know me and needles don't get along. Whatever she did, it didn't hurt, didn't even know she'd done anything. Why, is there a problem?"

"Perhaps, because there were no scheduled injections planned. Do you know who did it, have you seen them before?"

"Yes, she's the girl I told you about, the one that looks like an elf. Remember I met her when I went for the initial meeting with Dad."

"Did your father see her there?" the question was more in hope than expectancy.

"No idea, she came up just after you'd left, all she did was ask me my name and checked my date of birth before she asked for a blood sample. She even did that without hurting too much, just a finger prick mind you." He looked over at the doctor wondering if he could do as much.

"Think carefully Edward, did she call you by your full name?"

"Yes, she always has done, it's never Edward or Mister Maurice always Edward Clark Maurice, or Maur-ice the way she says it. She's really cute."

Eleanor felt her worst fears rise up as she held up the copy of the photograph she'd received earlier. "Is that her?"

"Yeh, that's her except when I first met her she had pigtails and brown hair, today it was red and a shorter cut, suited her. Can I have a copy of that? I took this one just as she was leaving." Edward turned his tablet around to show the picture he'd taken earlier.

"Doctor if you will, alert your security to be on the lookout for this girl, you can keep the picture." She handed over the printed copy she had. Her name is Oonecks Maurice, she stands about one point five metres tall maybe a bit less and of slight build. Do not try to detain her, she may have already killed one person, possibly three more, we don't know for certain."

"Mum you can't be serious, she's real nice. Anyway her name is pronounced Oo-neh not Oonecks."

"She told you her name?" His mother said slightly puzzled.

"Yes why wouldn't she? She said she was a researcher or as she said it, 'I am Rethearcher Oo-neh Maurithe' and that I am the reason she is here. I did mention that I am at last attractive to girls even if it is because of my health issues."

"What else did she say, the details Edward and do not skimp on anything, it's important."

"Well she said she had the results of the blood sample and that it showed I had a gene mutation, she showed me the read-out on this tablet thing she's got. Her father has the same issue and it means you have a crap end by the time your fifty with your mind and body disintegrating on the way."

The doctor coughed slightly, "You say this is the Genetic data from the blood sample she took a couple of days ago?"

"Yes, from the finger prick." Edward glanced at the doctor.

"That's too soon to have it processed and analysed with any precision." The medic was emphatic.

"Well she says so and when I asked if there was a cure, she said yes, otherwise she wouldn't have said anything. Then she told me about the injections and what would happen."

"Details Edward," his mother said in frustration.

"She said I'd be okay today but tomorrow I'd have a high temperature so it would be a good time to ask for some ice-cream. Tootie Fruitee is her favourite so if I can order some now. Day two would be spent in a fever rambling or some such and then by day three I wouldn't have the pains anymore. I'd feel wrung out but I assumed the worst would be over by then."

Eleanor was pale hearing that news, "I'll be back in a minute, Edward. Doctor if you please." She motioned to the door. In the corridor outside she turned, "My son may have been infected with an engineered flu virus called NAF01, have you heard of it?"

"No, it is not one of the usual references I know of. Where is it from do you know?"

"No idea doctor but it may have a mortality rate of ninety-nine percent if my information is accurate. If it is then the first twenty-four hours represent the contagion period, so for safety's sake you may have to quarantine this area."

"Are you certain about this, if true it could have devastating consequences if it got out?"

"In truth I am not, but if she wanted to decimate the whole population I doubt she'd start in a hospital. My information suggested a more targeted approach so let's assume the worst for now, please check on the possibility. I'll ask my son what else he knows."

"Then you might need this," he held a face mask out, "avoid touching him until we know how it's spread. You might consider staying here for the next day or two, if he is contagious at this early stage you may already be infected." The doctor looked grim.

"Good point. STOP," the warning was to her sergeant who was returning having checked if there had been any sightings. "Tony stay where you are, Edward may have been infected with the flu virus I mentioned at the briefing. I may already be infected so I won't be in the office for a couple of days. Keep everybody away until we know for certain."

"Are you sure?" Coltrain asked concerned.

"No I'm not, but the symptoms described to Edward sound the same as the agent described, better to be safe, tell D.C.I. Fairclough that finding the girl has become more urgent. Her name is pronounced Oo-neh not Oonecks."

"Will do, anything you want bringing in?"

"No not for now. I'll see you later, hopefully. Tony?"

"Yes."

"Don't apply for my job just yet," Eleanor said trying to lighten the atmosphere.

"No, I'll give it a couple of days," her sergeant winked then turned and walked away, the doctor followed at a distance stopping at the nurse's office to inform them of the situation. Slowly, thoughtfully Eleanor returned to her son's room.

"You still haven't said what's wrong," said Edward grumpily.

She breathed out, "This morning we received information that Oo-neh Maurice was involved in a plot to infect North Africa with a flu virus that has exactly the same symptoms as you described."

"But I've had flu before."

"Not like this one, you haven't."

"But why, she seems real nice? What possible reason would she have? We don't know her."

"Did your father tell you about the mugging?"

"Yes and then somebody killed the mugger."

"We think it was her." Eleanor said flatly.

"You're kidding, right? How? She's tiny?"

"I can't go into details but she's more than she appears it seems. What's this?" She held up a brown card wrapped package.

"Oo-neh left it."

Eleanor turned the rectangular package over, "Well it has your name on it, 'Edward Clark Maurice, to be opened after the third day'. She has nice handwriting." The latter comment she made absently as she broke the sealing tape, she gasped when she saw the contents."

"What is it mum?"

"It doesn't make sense," she said turning the framed painting around. "I have been looking at this picture for nearly a month, I had just convinced myself to buy it when it was no longer on sale."

The oil on canvas picture was of a three arch stone-built bridge; the legend affixed to the backing board identified the work as 'Crossing Over' the bridge itself being located near Banbridge, Northern Ireland. She turned it back, looked at it again then gave it to Edward as she opened an envelope glued to the outer wrapping. It read:

'Greetings Edward Clark Maurice,

As you read this letter you can look forward to a long life, with many happinesses, please do not waste a moment of it. The painting is of a bridge that stood near my home in Engleire; perhaps it will remind you of the day your life changed.

Keep it as an heirloom, hand it down to your eldest son with instructions to hand it down to his eldest boy until one day in the future there will be no sons. On that day your descendant may sell it for a substantial fortune so that he may fulfil his dreams.

0|X.'

As Eleanor refolded the single sheet of paper she felt tears well up in her eyes without really knowing why.

"What does it say mum?"

She quietly handed the letter to her son then wiped her eyes as he read it.

"None of this makes any sense, no sense at all. If she was intent on killing you or making you ill as a warning to stay away, why on earth would she buy a painting worth five hundred pounds for an heirloom?"

"Could it be," Edward said sounding as only a teenager can when stating the obvious, "she is making me well just as she said. Have a bit of faith, why would she harm us."

Picking up her mobile phone she called her sergeant, on the sixth ring he answered. "Tony, things may not be as I first thought but the priority now is to find those agents, I think they are spinning us a yarn. If you find the girl take her into protective custody until we get to the truth."

"Okay boss, Hazel has reported back that the academics know of no way to genetically engineer a human successfully or of any attempts to achieve the specific end the agents outlined. China and the U.S seem to have developed Gene Editing equipment for who knows what purpose. The medical field is the main area for consideration, for getting rid of various medical conditions that have a genetic base. However there is no specific gene linked to a specific condition. It may be combinations of genes, and trying to manipulate them has led to a few disastrous outcomes. So either the plan is a secret military one, Dreamland, Area 51 and all that, or it's claptrap."

"I'll go with the latter for now. So let us assume she has taken something important and the opposition is willing and probably capable of killing to get it. Any news on the organisation they belong to?"

"No not yet, we tried a search on the Internet for 'Secret Spy organisations' but nothing came up, no listings for 'Covert or Clandestine genetic experimentation' either," Coltrain mocked. "The D.C.I. hasn't said anything, at least not to me when I spoke to him about your position."

"Disappointing but not unexpected," she smiled, "but it gives me an idea. Get in touch with cybercrime and see if they have a technical hacker we can talk to about this. Oh, one other point, it occurs to me this girl isn't hiding, she's just not obvious, and she seems to change her hairstyle fairly frequently so it may be a wig she wears, which would tally with a strand of hair found on Tobbit. Edward says she's a researcher but for whom? So check out the National Insurance database and see if they have a record of her, failing that the Internet providers, if she's researching she must be online."

"If she's keeping a low profile she might use Internet cafes I'll get someone onto those. Any idea what her field might be?"

"No idea, but send Yoséf to look into the Internet cafes, however do remind him to be careful, I'm not so sure she's as dangerous as we've been led to believe but let's err on the side of caution until we know for certain. She left a gift for Edward and she even put a circle slash cross on a letter to Edward."

"Meaning?"

"When I was younger it was hugs and kisses, so she can't be all bad."

"But she's younger than you."

"You have such a way with women, but it, like all fashion is probably making a comeback. Speak to you later."

The day dragged on but it meant Eleanor got more time with her son. They talked about this mysterious girl that had for some reason come into their lives but it led nowhere. If Edward was the target, what had his father got to do with any of it they both wondered?

It was nearly an hour later in one of the quiet moments that Eleanor had a thought, after cogitating on what the security agents had said, but the thought itself raised a question. What if what they said was half true? What if Oo-neh, strangely she found herself now thinking of the girl as a person with a name, really was looking for a genetic marker. A marker that she associated with her family, what if the blood test on James was negative, the next logical step would be his son, who it seems had the genetic mutation.

The question then arose as to how she had determined that so quickly, if the analysis and interpretation took days and not minutes? What was the purpose of the flu virus if that is what her son had been injected with? Lost in her thoughts she didn't hear her son's first call to her.

"What?" she said startled out of her reverie.

"I've found the bridge on the Internet," Edward flicked around his tablet showing the stone bridge in the painting but from a slightly different angle.

"Put in 'Engleire', the place she names in the letter, see what comes up."

Nothing did.

Flicking her phone on Eleanor called her sergeant once again. "Tony her home is at a place called Engleire, it may be a home name as nothing comes up on the Internet, but it's near a place called Banbridge in Northern Ireland."

"I'll give our opposite number over there a call and see what they can tell us. The Border Agency has no record of anyone using the names the agents used or Oonecks/Oo-neh Maurice entering the country at anytime in the last twelve months. You don't happen to know how her Christian name is spelt, do you?"

Eleanor thought for a moment, "The girl pronounces her name as Oo-neh, probably a 'y'; maybe an 'h' if Edward's interpretation is correct or you might try an 'x' if the pronunciation used by the agents reflects the last letter. It has occurred to me the agents whoever they are, may be telling half truths - the problem is we don't know which half." She looked at the clock, "Better call it a day as none of the agencies will be open now. Make a fresh start in the morning."

"Okay boss. How are things there?"

"Alright at the moment I'll be here all night so we shall know more in the morning. You might drop my phone battery charger off in the morning."

"Will do, bye for now."

Barely had she said her farewells when Doctor Forbes put his head around the door and nodded for her to come into the hallway.

"What is it?"

"Initial blood analysis shows that it appears to be a flu virus and it has some differences to types we know about. The main difference is that it appears to replicate extremely fast, practically exploding when it enters the bloodstream. I'm having its DNA tested to see if there are any major changes compared to the avian or swine flu samples we have. They'll be working through the night to get a result because if this thing is as deadly as you say we need to know sooner rather than later. Its behaviour is frightening. We should have some idea in the morning." He handed Eleanor a card. "This will give you access to the food and drinks facilities in the recreation area along the hall, there are sandwiches and drinks, the usual fare. Since it wouldn't be wise for me to go home I shall be spending the night in the lab where I can keep abreast of events as they occur. If you need me or Edward's condition changes rapidly, call me on this number, the nurse that was in here earlier will be in the first room on the right, just beyond the recreation area if you need him. If you want a comfortable sleep there is a free bed in the first room beyond the recreation area on the left, we've had to cancel a few patients due to possible contagion so nobody will bother you."

"Thank you, I must say though that there are some things that are odd about all this and my initial worst fears may prove to be groundless." Eleanor told the doctor about the painting and the letter.

"Let us hope it is so." He bowed slightly and left taking with him the busy active atmosphere of the daytime working, leaving behind a quieter more tranquil state than Eleanor usually found working late in the day.

The evening moved inexorably into night, inevitably sleep overcame both Edward and his mother. While he slept deeply, Eleanor's sleep was fitful, waking occasionally to find a nurse by Edward's bedside silently observing her patient and deftly taking his pulse without awakening him. Six o'clock registered on the wall clock as Eleanor finally awoke, stiff from sleeping in the chair. She stretched and shrugged several times to loosen her muscles, looking over towards her son, she could see the droplets of sweat gathering upon his forehead causing her to move closer to his side. Passing a hand over his head she could feel the heat generated by the increase in his temperature. Checking the chart clipped to the foot of the bed she noted that his temperature had shown a steady hourly increase since just after midnight.

Stepping out of the room the detective instinctively noted the differences, the trolley with its cargo, a square counter top freezer. She opened it and smiled, her theory strengthened. She called the male nurse from the office. Immediately on entering the room he took Edward's temperature, muttering something Eleanor couldn't hear but it sounded like surprise. Taking up the record chart he paused seemingly puzzled for a moment before entering the thermometer reading, and then rushed out. Returning moments later with some cold compresses the nurse fussed about his charge as though trying to rectify some earlier omission.

Eleanor dialled her second in command, "Tony? Sorry if I woke you but can you pick me up from the hospital on your way in."

"Sure if that's what you want. Is everything alright?" Concern sounded in his voice lest the news be bad.

"Yes, yes everything is fine, it's just that I doubt a mass murderer would go to the trouble of visiting the victim through the night to check his temperature and leave a freezer with two tubs of ice-cream in it. She's not out to kill him, if she had been he'd be dead already, nor does it seem like a warning. I don't think she's the enemy."

"Who is then?" Coltrain sounded surprised, "Are you saying she didn't kill Tobbit?"

"No I'm not saying that but everything we have found out so far doesn't suggest she's in any way a danger to the public. We still have to find her to help us clear this mess up, but now we have a lead. She bought Edward a painting."

It was an hour later when Coltrain drew up outside the reception centre in his car, and by the time Eleanor had been home to freshen up it was a quarter past eight. That gave Eleanor and her sergeant time for breakfast at Brightly's Café.

"You don't expect her to show up do you?" Tony asked.

"No not really but it's as good a place as any to eat especially since the gallery we are to visit is just across the road."

"Sorry boss but this is all starting to look as though your family really is the focus of all this, whatever all this is. So where are we now? Is this still a murder enquiry or are we involved in something else?"

"If we look at the initial conditions," Eleanor began, "we started looking for the person who killed a drug dealer whilst he was mugging my ex-husband. Right from the start if we re-examine the statement of James Maurice, the girl we now know as Oonecks or Oo-neh Maurice, seemed to have no interest in the deceased. He was peripheral to the reason she was there."

"Have you ever thought there may be a family association?" Tony asked.

"It had crossed my mind but I have never heard the name Oonecks or Oo-neh, anywhere let alone in terms of my family or even James's. Probably coincidence, but what I find interesting is that she is searching for a gene mutation. Now the 'Chuckle Brothers'...."

"Who?"

"Those two security agents, they told us that she was seeking anyone that held this gene with the intent to kill them in some sort of revenge against her father. Now that seems patently untrue, so why are they lying?"

"So far that appears to be true but forgive me saying this; Edward is not yet out of the woods so to speak."

"I know, but I feel positive about it, after all she told Edward what was about to happen. If you are going to kill someone, at least in my experience, you do it and not spend the night popping in and out to see how the victim is. Do you know of any murderer who has left two tubs of ice cream behind for the deceased to eat? Edward said she was going to rectify the gene mutation but there are questions there. Firstly how did she analyse Edward's genome so fast? Secondly gene therapy is still largely unproven in a practical sense, so how is she doing it by infecting him with a virulent flu virus that has been genetically engineered?"

"So you don't think then, that this is a terrorist event where she is trying to cause an epidemic?"

"No, I don't Tony. What would be the point if she is only targeting people with a specific mutation? After we've seen the owner of the gallery will you check up and see if there's been any joy finding out who they all are and if the organisation they represent actually exists. The girl is the centre of this for them and for us; we need to speak with her." The emotion in her voice was not lost on Coltrain.

Alexandria Brightly walked up with a tray before setting down the fried breakfasts, two drinks and two cream cakes on little plates.

"I'm sorry Alex but we didn't order the cakes," Eleanor said pleasantly.

"No I know, Oo-neh did yesterday, she told me you were to have two cakes when you came in. She has paid for them so you don't need to worry on that score."

The two police officers looked at each other, "You're kidding?" said Eleanor.

"No, as God is my judge she was most specific. Enjoy your breakfast." She smiled and walked away to attend to another customer.

"Are we dealing with a psychic now or are we just so predictable?" enquired Coltrain.

"I have -" her handset chimed, "no idea. "

"Maurice. Oh! Hi Ceri, any news?"

The conversation took a few minutes before Eleanor finally ended the call. "Well it seems we can find no evidence for the organisation or any of the people involved, it's as though they don't exist."

"Spooky stuff maybe, or is it an elaborate charade?" wondered Tony.

"The agents are lying, that is all I can be certain about. Fairclough wants to see me when I get in so maybe his contacts up the ladder know something. Northern Ireland came back to you; they've sent a package special delivery with something that may be linked to our interest."

"Such as?"

"They didn't say except let them know what we make of it because to them it makes no sense. Looks like we're not the only ones groping in the dark it seems."

"That sounds about right in this case." Tony smiled faintly. "Better eat your breakfast before it gets cold."

Eleanor's phone chimed again, the call was shorter than the first. "Good news at last, Edward's temperature is high but he has asked for ice-cream, and Doctor Forbes thinks I may have left too early since he hasn't seen the results yet to confirm if the virus really is contagious. So take comfort in your last meal."

The meal ended just as Eleanor saw the gallery shutters being raised, time for them to pursue their enquiries. The door chime tinkled as she entered 'Future Treasures' the name of the Art Gallery. Once the jingling ceased, only silence remained. Eleanor looked around at the paintings briefly before someone entered through a rear door.

"Good morning," the proprietor said in a slightly excitable camp tone. "How can I help you?"

He was a corpulent man of medium height suitably dressed in tweeds; however his yellow pattern cravat looked slightly out of place.

Eleanor held up her warrant card, "Detective Inspector Eleanor Maurice and this is Detective Sergeant Tony Coltrain."

"Oo Police! I do hope you've brought your handcuffs! Just slip them on and I tell you anything you want to know." The man said pleasantly.

"I don't think that will be necessary sir, at least not yet anyway but who knows what the future may bring." Eleanor said returning the banter.

"You tease, you."

"And you are?" asked Tony.

"Yes I am, always have been, always will be I imagine. You should try it; put some colour in your cheeks." The owner of the establishment replied good humouredly.

"Your name sir, just for the record if you wouldn't mind," Coltrain replied, refusing to engage in the older man's machinations.

"Anthony Sinclaire with an 'e', sole proprietor of this august establishment for over twenty years, I'll get you my card. Did you know I got a mention in Who's Who?" His latter comment was made whilst leaning provocatively over the counter.

"Thank you Mister Sinclaire," the sergeant said taking the card.

"Please call me Anthony....Tony." Sinclaire's voice had a heavy whispering quality about it that suggested all and nothing.

"Have you seen this girl? Eleanor pushed in to regain control and explained the reason they were there by holding the photograph copy in front of him."

"Absolutely, one would never forget such a child, absolutely adorable. So well mannered even when she was chastising me." He saw the vague look on Tony's face, "Telling me off, you naughty boy."

"What can you tell us about her?" Eleanor pursued.

"Is she wanted for something, I do hope not, she's totally

charming in every way? Well let me think, she came in two days ago as soon as I opened the door and asked to see a painting I had in the window. It was of an old stone bridge over a stream, painted by an up and coming young woman of whom I expect great things. I brought the painting to this table here so she could examine it in the light and do you know the first thing she did was to turn it over and examine the back - most unusual. Then she looked at this small device she had, a bit like the things all young people seem to have these days. Then she asked me if the catalogue number was correct. I ask you what an odd question! Of course I said it was fine, but she was so insistent, in such an utterly adorable way that I went to check."

"And when you came back she'd run off with the painting?" suggested Coltrain.

"What an absurd idea! Lovely girl like that, positively enchanting, can't imagine it crossed her mind." Sinclaire gave Sergeant Coltrain a withering look. "Anyway I looked up the number and would you believe it, she was perfectly right. I had transposed two of the numbers on the label. She was positively prescient; I mean how could she have known? Absolutely astounding, I had thought to ask if I would win the lottery in the near future, but decided it would be too base a question for such an angel."

"What happened then?" Eleanor urged.

"I replaced the sticker of course with the correct number, after all if some issue were ever to arise, well; one has to have accurate records. Provenance is everything. Anyway she consulted her electronic thingy again and she seemed satisfied and said she would take it. A wise choice I said, it will be a good investment for her future and do you know what she said? I shall remember this till my dying day; she said that she had no such expectations, for her life may only be measured in days before she ceased to exist."

The two police officers looked at each other.

"Did she say why?" enquired Eleanor.

"Alas no and I did not wish to pry, such a lovely girl, so tragic. Then she said the painting was a gift for someone who did have a future, and if he kept it in the family, she was sure that in time to come it would indeed be worth a small fortune. My heart broke," he fanned himself rapidly, "how noble of her to consider someone else, knowing her own life was to be all too brief. I just wanted to wrap my arms around her."

"Then what happened?" Tony said trying to keep the witness on point.

"She asked me if I would be so kind as to wrap it for her. As if she had to ask! How could such a paltry act compare with her kindness? Then she pointed to another picture, a small piece by another local artist who shows great promise. I told her as such and she said she believed me and that he too would become very collectable in a decade or so. She asked me to wrap it also, and then she wrote a message on the card covering. What it said you will not believe if you guess for a hundred years, so I will show it to you." Mister Sinclaire scuttled off into the back office returning moments later with a brown card wrapped package, he thrust it forward towards the detectives.

Eleanor read it aloud, "To Proprietor Anthony Sinclaire who was so very kind to a stranger. Do not open until 1st of November 2036; any ideas why she should write that?"

"Absolutely none," replied the art dealer. "I protested of course and said she shouldn't waste her money on an old fool like me." He stifled a sniffle, "My heart breaks because she said she had nobody else and repeated that I had been so very kind. Absolutely tragic, when I have a sister who is the most loathsome of beings whose mere existence pollutes the very air I breathe." Sinclaire drew a breath before asking, "You wouldn't do me a great kindness would you? Arrest my sister for something, she's bound to be guilty of some infraction of the law, maybe soliciting, that should get her kicked out of a few lunch clubs. Make it up if you have to."

"Does she? Solicit I mean?" asked Tony.

"Alas officer if she ever went to court on such a charge the judge would take one look at her and realise that anyone who was unfortunate enough to pull over and have her look in the car would drive away as fast as possible. They would probably take Holy Orders and spend the rest of their life in a stone cell in a desert in some God forsaken hole, begging for forgiveness. Alas a forlorn hope. God she really is awful."

"Did the girl pay by card or cheque?" Eleanor asked returning to the purpose of their visit.

"No, she paid cash, mostly twenties; took it out of a pink satchel she carried with her, she even insisted I check every note which I did to please her but it wasn't necessary. I imagine you'll want her address." Sinclaire added the last comment in the hope they would say no and go away.

"Have you got it?" Coltrain asked disbelievingly.

"Of course I've got it, wouldn't mention it otherwise, would I? You see we issue a certificate of authenticity on behalf of the artist and I like to match my records and certificates with the purchaser's details just in case there is a future issue as to ownership. Provenance is everything, as I said, in the collectibles world, believe me. Come this way." In the rear office the proprietor removed a large ledger from a shelf and opened it at a silver place marker, then flicking back a page he drew a finger down the page. "There you are," he said laying a ruler under the entry.

"You've spelt her Christian name as Oonex," Eleanor said by way of comment.

"Yes, but it is apparently pronounced Oo-neh, her mother's choice I believe."

DI Maurice noted down the address. "My son met her at the hospital a week ago he was quite captivated by her, as you seem to be. He thought she looked like an elf."

"Oh yes, I can quite see how he would think that, there was something ethereal about her, different and pleasingly so. An old head on young shoulders as my grandmother would say, not about me of course. Totally unlike those two Orcs, if you'll forgive the Tolkien comparison, who came looking for her not long after she'd left."

"Orcs?" queried D.S. Coltrain.

"Yes, a couple of big unpleasant types, waving some security card about enough to make one dizzy. I don't mind admitting they gave me the willies and not the sort of willies I would wish to look forward to. Even Carl, he does jobs for me you understand, six foot three and spends his days punching some leathery old bag about, not my sister sadly, even he was a little unnerved by them. I mean what sort of person goes around sniffing at picture frames."

"Sniffing?"

"Yes the sort of sniffing that a dog does trying to identify the smells on a lamp-post. Wanted to know if she bought anything, well I said no of course, didn't care for them one bit. I said she had been interested in that portrait but felt it was far too expensive, which it is of course, but these up and coming artists have such ambition or as my grandmother would say, they are full of themselves. Anyway Carl came in fortuitously at which point they went, hopefully never to return."

"Did they sound foreign?"

"Oh yes their English was good but not that good, well I only heard one of them speak, bit like the Marx brothers but only two of them. He was very accented, not like her of course much more refined, even the impediment she has was in itself endearing."

"You think she's foreign then?" pursued Eleanor.

"I would have said she had an Irish lilt to her accent but if so then she probably speaks English as a second language."

"Leprechaun then, not elf," suggested Coltrain smiling.

Anthony Sinclaire merely sniffed in his direction. "Well if there is anything else I can help you with please do call again. I hope your intentions are good ones, I think the poor lamb has enough tragedy in her life already."

The senior officer thanked him for his assistance turned and left, Sergeant Coltrain followed behind. Not a word passed between them until they were sitting in the car. "Tony, I hope you can come up with something really positive at your next appraisal because you are going to have to work on your people skills. For all we know this girl's life is in danger and just because she has an appearance that others find endearing, it is not for you to ridicule them. Let's hope when we catch up with her you can be more civil. Right let's visit the address she gave."

"Probably fake," said Coltrain grumpily.

"Possibly, we shall soon find out but I get the feeling she isn't hiding, she's in plain sight all we have to do is look."

"Well I'd be hiding if those two were after me. What I can't understand is how she has survived against five of them if she is as small as people seem to think." Coltrain queried out loud.

"Well don't forget she has that weapon and doesn't seem afraid to use it. I doubt she would take them on in a scrap, perhaps a good example of brain against brawn."

"Or perhaps she just sneaks up on them from behind and bang they're dead." Coltrain finally offered.

The journey took nearly half an hour to reach their destination. The area had once been a middle class gentile area but had over the years declined. Fashions change and it was now on the up with a great deal of evidence of improvement work going on. The house they sought was like those surrounding it, late Victorian to Edwardian. The front façade still retained its original mock timber frame painted dark green, which complemented the front garden area. After ringing the bell they waited until eventually a tall spare woman opened the heavy front door. On seeing their identification she stepped to one side allowing them entry into the hallway before escorting them through to her rear sitting room.

After brief introductions the landlady said, "Sit yourselves down, no need to stand on ceremony," in a mild Black Country accent.

"Do you know this girl?" Eleanor held up the photographic copy.

"Yes, it's Oo-neh Maurice she's been living here a few months now. Has anything happened to her?”

“No nothing like that, as far as we know she’s fine but we do need to find her. What’s she like?”

“Oo-neh, bless her she’s no trouble at all, pays her rent well up front and as polite as can be. She’s a lovely girl.”

Eleanor led the questioning, “Does she have any friends that you know of?”

“She’s never mentioned any, never brought anyone back as far as I know but she does go out in the evening, generally back before I lock up.”

“Do you know where she goes?”

“Somehow I don’t think it’s clubbing, she doesn’t seem the type. Maybe she’s at the library for some of it; she does research of some kind. I know that she goes to the health club early when the swimming pools are practically empty.”

“Any idea which health club she goes to?” Eleanor probed.

“Probably the one up the road about ten minutes walk away. In truth I don’t think she’s a socialiser which must be hard when you’re away from your home, especially the first time.”

“Home sick you mean?”

“Yes, I’ve had students over the years and for some it was their first time away from home but most got over it when they started making new friends.”

“And Oo-neh?”

“I think she’s lonely, and I also think she tries to put it to one side by engrossing herself in her work. Not that she complains, always pleasant.” Missus Wainscroft wrung her hands slightly.

“How does she pay her rent?”

“Always cash; never needs reminding like some I’ve had. I gave her a special deal because she’s staying a long time. I wish I had more like her; she never gives me a moment’s concern unlike one of the young men that comes fairly regular. I think he was trying it on with her but came to regret it.”

“Any idea how long she plans on staying?” Eleanor probed.

“Not really, but she did say that she’ll always pay in advance so if one day she unexpectedly has to leave I will not lose out. May I ask what this is all about?” The landlady finally asked what was on her mind.

“All I can say is that her name has come up in an investigation and we need to speak to her as soon as possible. When she comes back can you ask her to call me, the number is on this card?” She held a business card out. “Or will you call me when she’s in. Now is it possible to see her room?"

"Well you being the police I imagine it will be okay so long as you don't go touching anything, she might not like it. Come this way, her room is on the first floor at the back."

The stairwell and first floor were as well kept as the lower floor, Missus Wainscroft stopped at the end of a short corridor. Inserting a key in the lock she stood to one side allowing the officers to walk in.

It was a bright room painted in light shades of pink; the furniture was tastefully painted to match. A single bed projected from the wall opposite the window and on it lay a medium sized suitcase its handle pushed in. A cloth protecting the bed cover from any dirt on the small rollers was spread out underneath it. On the case lay a white C5 envelope.

"Looks like she's leaving boss," suggested Coltrain.

"Perhaps," Eleanor said absentmindedly as she opened the drawers, noting the neat piles of clothes, and in the lower one stationery. "She's very neat." Then she opened the wardrobe noted the assortment of clothing neatly hanging and some shoes, again neatly arranged beneath them. A second case lay on the top of the wardrobe. Coltrain reached up to take hold of it.

"Leave it Tony, we don't have a warrant. What I'm curious about is why; with all her clothes still in their place does she have the suitcase on the bed."

"Possibly an escape pack, maybe she keeps all her important stuff in it, just in case she has to make a quick escape."

Eleanor moved to the bed and took up the envelope and read the neat handwriting. She paused not quite believing what she read.

"What's wrong?" Tony asked.

"It's addressed to me, Detective Inspector of Police Eleanor Maurice." She turned the envelope around to show him and then to Missus Wainscroft, the landlady. Slitting the seal open with her finger Eleanor removed a folded sheet, it read;

'Detective Inspector of Police Eleanor Maurice, I do not know how much time I have left so I leave the results of my research for you to examine. It is not totally complete but it is as far as I have got. Please forgive my manners for there is much I do not understand about your society. I would like to have spoken more to you to see if you really are like my mother who you so much resemble, but alas I cannot now plan too far ahead. Give my wishes of happiness to Edward, he is very nice.

0|X'

"Missus Wainscroft, Oo-neh has left the case for me as you will see in the letter."

After a brief examination the landlady nodded in agreement and led the way downstairs, Eleanor carried the case leaving Tony to close the door and follow them down, then expressing their thanks the officers left. Once seated back in the car having placed the case in the car boot they contemplated events.

"She knew we would find her then," pointed out Coltrain.

"So it seems, but then she's a researcher, she collates information so I imagine she thought it was only a matter of time. So it should come as no surprise really."

"What's in the case, do you think?"

"At the moment no idea but it must be relevant somehow for her to have gone to the trouble. After all you don't research something without good reason and then pass it on to us, there's no point to it. We'll open it back at the office."

With Coltrain driving, the first part of the return trip was quiet, Tony had tried to make comment but Eleanor was too wrapped up in the predicament of this girl. She even tried imagining what it must feel like to be Oo-neh, only to fail at getting close to a complete understanding. Then without warning her sub-conscious mind kicked in, "Pull over, pull over now," she yelled.

Tony braked hard as he pulled into the kerb, causing him to jolt forward as the brakes gripped. "What's up?" he said looking across at his senior officer.

"Over there by the newsagent, the girl in the black three-quarter coat, white hair, it's her. I'm getting out, you drive ahead and get in front of her and we might stand a chance of talking to her." So saying Eleanor opened the door and stepped out onto the kerb.

"Boss, what's she doing?" She heard Coltrain say. Eleanor looked across the road.

The girl, Oo-neh had stopped moving, she was moving her head slowly from side to side moving through nearly one hundred and eighty degrees. Rolling her sleeve back a little she examined her wrist before turning around to scan the pathway behind her. Then clutching her satchel she started to run. Eleanor looked right along the row of shops opposite, examining the people to see what had startled her, and then she saw them, the two agents a hundred yards behind. The security agents were running as well now, disregarding the people they pushed out of the way in their pursuit. Looking back left she saw the diminutive figure turn down a side access road that lead behind a series of shops lining the road at the next junction.

"Request backup with an armed response unit then get around the other side and pick her up if you can, be careful she's spooked and may not come willingly."

"Right boss," Tony said ramming the gear stick forward, then checked the traffic before moving out. At the same time he pressed the speed dial on his hands free unit and called the police control centre.

When safety permitted Eleanor crossed the road as quickly as she could, bringing her closely behind the pursuing agents as they too turned into the alleyway. Then they stopped suddenly, one of them checked his wrist as Eleanor had seen the girl do, before looking along the empty space in front of them. Slowly they moved forward. The sound of approaching sirens caused both men to pause momentarily, before they moved forward again their heads moving slowly from side to side. One intermittently checked his wrist as though it gave him some sort of guidance.

"Halt, police," called out Eleanor as she saw Tony's car with its blue grill lights flashing draw into the other end of the access road and stop. A siren went quiet behind her, car doors slammed shut as two uniformed officers armed with pistols approached, a third had opened the vehicle boot to withdraw a standard issue Heckler & Koch MP5. Eleanor held up her warrant card as the two agents in front of her turned. "Police; lost something?" She said walking towards them, the other officers moving in support as they fanned out behind her to gain clear lines of sight.

"Good day Detective Inspector of Police Eleanor Maurice, fortunately you have arrived as we are close to engaging the quarry that both we seek."

"We both seek," Eleanor corrected, "Yes I saw her run as soon as she set eyes on you. So where is she?"

The assumed leader, O.F.V Tyler-Wolfe looked at his wrist, "In that direction, within thirty feet." He pointed north-easterly.

"And how would you know that?" The inspector asked almost scornfully.

A wrist was held up, as far she could tell from where she stood, there was what appeared to be a piece of plastic stuck to the skin. Three pulsing lights lay close together whilst a third blue light on the side of the screen flickered up and then down again.

"What is that, a tracking device?"

"Do you recall me mentioning she had a location beacon inserted in her leg? The specification of which is on the data sheet I gave you on our first meeting. We have lost the signal, the flickering light in the centre is her last position so she cannot be far away." He tilted his head to scan the roof tops.

"Fortunate for her, otherwise you might have caught up with her long ago. What are the other lights?"

"Us," the humourless agent didn't elaborate further.

Eleanor scanned the near empty roadway with the occasional rubbish skip, nothing moved. Where was she, she wondered as the girl cannot have passed her sergeant without being seen. "Well it seems you have lost her again, so I'd like you to accompany me to the police station. It is starting to become clear in my investigations that some of what you've told me previously is anything but the truth."

"I think you'll find the truth is above your comprehension." O.F.V Tyler-Wolfe commented with an air of superiority.

"I'll be the judge of that and in case you misinterpret my words it isn't a choice, and I would advise you to keep your hands in sight at all times. I suspect you are armed and I am sure you would not wish me to misinterpret your actions and this end in a shooting match." She noticed them briefly glance at each other and exchange a few brief unintelligible words. "Tony did you see her?" She called out to her approaching sergeant.

"No, but I can't see how she can have run that distance in so short a time she'd have to be an Olympic sprinter. She must be somewhere here about."

Eleanor surveyed the rear of the properties, the closed doors, and the lack of side passages. She may have entered an open door leading into the shops and closed it behind her, thought the detective to herself but she had a feeling it was not that simple. Nothing about this case was. "Okay, you," she pointed to the main spokesman for the duo, "come with me, you go with them." Turning she said, "We're going to Central, if he gives you any trouble, any trouble at all, Taser him." The latter comment she made to the police constables who nodded in complicit understanding.

The police officers moved forward just as Eleanor heard her phone ring, she checked the display, 'unknown number'. "Hello," she said anonymously.

"Good day Detective Inthpector of Polithe Eleanor Maurithe," the voice said rapidly, "I am Rethearcher Oo-neh Maurithe. Pleathe do not end thith communication."

Eleanor was taken aback slightly, although previous interviewees had stated Oo-neh was quietly spoken and had a speech impediment she was quite unprepared when she actually heard the voice of the girl she was looking for. The voice had a much more whispery quality that nobody had previously mentioned and she spoke her surname as Maur-ice instead of the usual Maur-eece as Edward had said.

Oo-neh continued without pause, "If you are conthidering taking the Drothophila twinth into cuthtody I urge you to reconthider. Watch their reaction ath I thpeak with you, they were dethigned to have more acute thentheth, they can hear what I am thaying to you. If you thtep back about ten patheth you'll thee what I mean."

Eleanor started walking back to the main road, she got nearly eleven paces.

"That'th far enough," the voice said.

As Eleanor stopped moving she realised that Oo-neh must be watching her. She also noted that within half a second both of the agents started scanning the upper stories around them. She shivered, wondering how it was possible for her to be on the roof in the time available.

Oo-neh's voice continued in her ear. "They were created with one purpothe, they are a kill thquad and are only deployed in that role, you can try to shoot them but they have better reflexeth than you. If you try to take them on it it'th not a quethtion of how many men you will lothe but how many thurvive. Oh-Five he'th the one that talkth a lot, he'th the only one with anything clothe to a thenthe of humour."

"Oonecks, Oonecks," the one identified as Oh-Five yelled upwards in a language unfamiliar to the police officers present, *"Give us the zero-one-ex Genome file and we'll leave you to rot in this backward hole. You have my word."* If it was intended to be encouraging then he failed as even to Eleanor, who didn't understand the message, it sounded threatening.

"Thee he can't even thay my name correctly. He hath juth given me hith word that if I give him what he wantth he'll go away. They follow orderth to the letter and he knowth I am not going to give him what he wantth, he doeth not know that I can't, becauthe there ith no file." Oo-neh paused briefly, perhaps to appraise the situation. "I think you might conthider leaving ath they have little patienthe. You can't negotiate with them. Pleathe go now."

Eleanor paused, weighing up the limited options; but her mind was made up for her when a series of explosions occurred on the concrete surface that advanced on the agents before her. Immediately they raised their arms, pieces of brickwork and tiles high up on the walls started to fill the air. "Run," she cried to her officers, the agents followed close behind.

When the explosions ceased the police officers paused to look back, the roadway was clear of life, Eleanor could see Tony turn around as he slowed down at the other end of the alley, the agents were gone.

Back at her base of operations, Central Police headquarters, Eleanor reported to her superior D.C.I. Fairclough.

"Sit down Elle, how's the investigation going?" He asked.

"Well sir we have a girl that could pass for a twelve year old, who is currently on the run from two seriously weird guys. They carry some kind of high powered weapon up their sleeves, probably similar to the weapon she used to kill Tobbit. They want a file from her called Project 01x, which they say she stole from the facility I spoke to you about. They appear willing and able do anything to get it back. All the players are foreign by their accents but from where, I have no ideas. The only clue is in a letter she left Edward at the hospital, she's from a place called Engleire but that may only be a house name.

I was intent on bringing the two agents in for more questioning but as I was about to do so she called me on my mobile, how she got my number I don't know. Her purpose was to warn me off as these so called agents are in fact a kill squad. I can't get a grasp on this at all. Everyone that I have spoken to that has met the girl says she is very polite, pleasant and absolutely no trouble. From my limited contact she seems exactly that. She has a speech impediment and can't say the 'ess' sounds. However the Drosophila twins as she calls them, if I understand her properly, say she's become unstable and without medication could be dangerous. In the brief contact I had with her she says they are a creation, designed to kill, hard as that may be to accept I certainly find her more believable. I mean what normal person can hear a phone call from twenty feet away; but it seems they can by the way they responded, just as she said they could.

Other people who have met them also get this creepy feeling when in close contact. However scientific evidence says that genetic manipulation to create a 'super-human' at this level, apart from being illegal, has never been done or is ever likely to be. None of the players we know about seem to exist in the databases we have access to, and there is no evidence they entered the country legally. Finally the girl, she's called Oo-neh Maurice by the way, the Christian name is spelt 'O-o-n-e-x', knows we are looking for her, somehow she's predicting our movements. That was clear when we went to her residence, a B&B, the address of which she either intentionally or unintentionally gave to the art gallery. Everything was very ordered, very neat bordering on obsessive but she could be military trained. At the address she had left me a brief note saying that a medium sized suitcase with some research in it was for me. I haven't examined it yet."

"What's an art gallery got to do with it?" Fairclough intervened whilst she drew breath, referring to a line of enquiry he hadn't heard about.

"As you know Edward, my son is in hospital for tests. Well she's been there. According to the agents she is supposed to be intent on killing anyone with a specific gene mutation, her father has it apparently and she has taken against him."

"She's killing people because her father has a mutant gene, bit odd isn't it?"

"It's all odd, but that's what they say, but according to Edward she'd told him that he has this gene and she has given him an injection of what we first thought may have been a highly infectious form of flu virus. However her actions do not remotely suggest she's trying to kill him, quite the opposite. We simply can't rely on what these so called agents are telling us. Anyway she purchased an oil painting from the gallery opposite Brightly's Café. It is apparently intended as a gift for Edward to hand down to his descendants. Oddly enough it is a picture I had taken a liking to and was thinking of buying. The subject matter is a bridge near her home in Northern Ireland, somewhere called Engleire, a place we have as yet to locate."

"Well as regards those characters who are flashing security cards and this went as high as the Commissioner, nobody has heard of them or their organisation either domestic or foreign which begs many a new question. Could be far East of course there's been claims of bio engineering going on for years, they'll even clone your dog if you want, provided you can afford it." Fairclough fiddled with his pen, "And you say they may be a kill squad?"

"That's what the girl said. None of them look in the least oriental and where does Ireland fit in? Oh, and one other thing, she told Mister Sinclaire at the gallery that she has no expectations of a long life, weeks not years, in fact the note she left me suggested she could die any time soon."

Fairclough stood up and looked out of the window, "Do you mean she's ill or that she doesn't expect to outrun them for much longer?"

"I don't know but I expect the former, she seems quite adept at outpacing them provided she knows they are there. How she detected them in the street earlier I don't know. They have a locator unit, very high tech if I'm any judge that can home in on a passive unit implanted on her which gives them an advantage. Fortunately or otherwise her passive transponder is faulty so it gives an unreliable signal."

"A tracker chip you mean I assume, but why?" Fairclough was surprised and showed it.

"No idea, I assume she had it before she ran as it's not likely they caught her, fitted it and she escaped. They claim her parents put it in. If she's been here for six months she must have been out of range for sometime before they caught up with her." Eleanor leafed through the file she'd brought into the interview. "On the data sheet the weird ones left with us there is a unit frequency relating to what may be the tracker, some of the terms used aren't in English."

"Okay, leave it with me and I'll see if the techs can rig up our own detector that might help us find her. However what is the involvement with Jason Tobbit, and why kill him?"

"I am beginning to think he was in the wrong place, doing the wrong thing, to the wrong person at the wrong time. Somehow James Mason Maurice, my ex-husband is linked to all this but how or why I have no certain idea."

"The report says she took a blood sample from him, maybe she thought he had this gene problem. Is it hereditary? Maybe she's following a family tree. That would make more sense than knocking off anyone with the gene. Any ideas how common it is?"

"None, and if she is following a family tree then it will take an age to find all the links. Having said that of course, with her skill set who knows. She may be in her early twenties, looks at lot younger mind you, so her father must be of a similar age to James, maybe we are looking at a cousin or aunt-uncle link. Another puzzling thing is also the speed with which she can analyze the genetic code of the blood sample; normally it takes days."

"We aren't talking the X-files here are we?"

"That depends on what this file is that they want so badly and what they can do with it."

"Okay continue to focus on the girl, at least she's not killing any more people - yet anyway."

"Sir," gathering her papers together Eleanor left the room.

On the way to her desk she eyed the case stood on the floor, that could wait she thought and dialled the number on the card Doctor Forbes had given her, it rang a few times then a male voiced answered, "Forbes," it said bluntly.

"Doctor Forbes, this is Eleanor Maurice, Edward's mother."

"Good afternoon, Missus Maurice, well we have some good news. Edward's temperature has been falling for the last couple of hours and he has regained some lucidity. I received the report from the laboratory and the virus used was indeed a version of bird flu but it has characteristics that we are unfamiliar with. On the amount of information I have received so far, and I only got that because I asked the question and pressed for an answer, it may have been altered in a non-natural way."

"You mean it has been bio-engineered?"

"Quite possibly and it is causing some concern, because if someone can manipulate a virus in this way, and nobody is even guessing how it was done, they could easily create a pathogen worse than Spanish flu or the Plague."

"From what I understand so far they might have done that already."

"Then fortunately they have never used it, probably fearing the consequences of letting that particular genie out of the bottle. The version we have isolated from Edward's blood appears to be sterile, the last results I received show a marked decline in numbers. It's as though it had a shelf life limited to mere days before it naturally decays and that is worrying. Regrettably, and I have to consider all possibilities, I have to ask if you think Edward was being used as a test subject."

"No I don't, I think she knew precisely what it would do, and he was injected for a single purpose. Tell me, have you got the genome report on Edward?"

"Not yet I expect it later today or early tomorrow, why?"

"Well doctor I would like you to test a theory. What I want you to do is analyze his genome again with a sample taken today or tomorrow and compare the two profiles."

"Why?"

"Because I think that will answer a lot of our questions, if I'm right the samples will differ in some way. Should that be true then the case I'm working on will be a lot more complicated. I'll call in when I leave the office, bye for now." She pressed the red phone icon and ended the call.

"Boss, you are going to want to see this," Tony called over from his desk.

"What is it?" she asked moving closer, other members of the team gathered around.

"This DVD arrived from the Northern Ireland Police, it shows an event that took place in a leisure centre swimming baths which they have no explanation for." He pressed play on the media player. "This is the foyer, now watch this guy, he flashes an I.D. and walks though to the swimming area. The cameras in there are set on the balcony looking along the length of the pool, right there he is. He stands near the edge of the pool and seems to be talking to someone, possibly the lifeguard."

A collective gasp rose from the viewers as they saw, as if from nowhere a figure shot out of the water before wrapping their arms around the neck of the man standing on the pool edge, over-balancing him. As they watched both figures fell forward hitting the water and disappearing beneath the surface. Thirty seconds later the smaller of the two swam to the side and disappeared into the changing area.

"Now here we see the lifeguard jump in and bring the guy, the one that came in flashing his badge, to the surface and with the help of this other attendant." He pointed out another man with his finger. "He's lifted onto the side where they start pumping his lungs. See he's moving, so he's still alive. Now watch."

From the side of the screen an indistinct figure could be seen emerging from the changing rooms dressed in a white blouse, black trousers and a jacket, a pink satchel slung over one shoulder.

"Oo-neh," exclaimed Eleanor.

"Looks like, now watch. The victim is starting to sit up, she doesn't stop, walks right up to him bends forward, there he's slumped forward. Now watch this bit."

They watched as the pool attendant grabbed hold of the figure identified as Oo-neh Maurice, as she straightened up. With a speed that was almost unreal her left leg came up in an arc, her toecap catching the male attendant between the eyes as he leant forward, causing him to fall backwards into the pool. As the lifeguard jumped into the pool Oo-neh leant forward, did something with the prostrate figure's sleeve before stamping on his chest and then walked calmly away, unmolested, out through the foyer never to be seen again.

"Well...." Eleanor started to say.

"Wait just watch the body, this is what is causing the N.I. Police sleepless nights."

Eleanor and the others strained closer, she spoke first, "Where is it? Run it back."

Tony took the image back to the point where the attendant fell backwards into the pool and replayed it. Nobody was any clearer after the second viewing - the body simply disappeared from view.

"Has the video been cut up?"

"No, that's what they thought at first. They had a forensics team look at it and they can see no abnormalities, the time and date markers follow smoothly. What you see is what happened. Nobody at the pool would have any reason to alter it. To all intents and purpose it looks like a killing or attempted killing for reasons unknown, but without a body who will ever know?"

"When we questioned the agents they said three of their team were dead and the bodies hadn't been found. That could be why, but how on earth did she do it?"

Tony turned in his seat, "I looked at the earlier bit in slow motion, she was in the water yet she wasn't clearly visible, he obviously wasn't aware of her. When she came out of the water it looks like she punched him in the nuts and solar plexus on the way up knocking the wind out of him. He bent forward and with her weight around his neck she unbalanced him. Why he doesn't seem to have struggled in the water isn't clear, maybe she kept punching him causing him to suck in water. She certainly doesn't hold back."

"No she doesn't. When we were going to apprehend those two agents she called me as you saw and she said then that if we took them on it wasn't a case of how many they'd kill but how many of us managed to survive. She obviously believes that and believes in the pre-emptive strike So we have her and them in Ireland, what....," Eleanor looked at the time and date code, "Six and a half months ago, shortly after that she appears here and has remained here ever since. They must have lost track of her so she was relatively safe to get on with whatever she was engaged in, then they show up again."

"Does she seem ex-military with fighting skills like that? She must be very fit," pondered Ceri a little envious.

"I don't know, she calls herself a researcher, not a role you'd think required martial skills, but then is that a cover? The two we've seen are military no doubt in my mind, she calls them a kill squad, which is probably what they'll do to her if they catch up. This all started out as her being the villain but it is beginning to look like she's the victim. What is worse she seems alone with no known associates, unless any of you have discovered anything.

Hazel volunteered, "The only thing for certain Ma'am is that much of this is simply not possible. The science people say gene manipulation on the human scale is simply science fiction, we know a lot, but not enough to know how most of the genes work or how genes work and interact together."

"And yet she said the agents were created. I don't think she was talking in the terms of 'Jason Bourne' I think she was being literal. Not to mention the weapons they carry, powerful, small, easily hidden. Best not say too much to the D.C.I. he's already worried we're being invaded by aliens. Alright our main target is still the girl; we need to speak with her a.s.a.p."

Moving back to her desk Eleanor wrote out a list of names and addresses that she passed to Hazel. "Take Ceri with you and visit all these people, they are all family members related to James Mason. Show all of them the girl's photo and see if anyone recognises her." When they'd left, using her own private email account she sent email's to all her family with an attachment of the photograph. If the girl was related somehow to Edward, somebody must know her.

After checking with Yoséf by phone she discovered that so far nobody he had spoken to, in or around James's place of work or residence knew the girl. She recalled him back to the office where she wanted him to check if any of the known suspects had a recorded entry into Northern Ireland. With the E.U. open border policy that might be wasted effort but she had to try. She asked Tony to request the N.I police search their databases for any of the names, just in case they had been listed as resident in the blank six months.

Having run out of immediate ideas to pursue other lines of enquiry she picked up the case and laid it flat on the surface of her desk. Unzipping the lid she re-read the letter that had previously lain on the top of it. Lifting the canvas lid carefully she scanned for any potential threats; there were none she could see. She felt a bit melodramatic because from her own experience she felt if any of this odd trio wanted her dead she already would be. The inside space was filled with coloured ring binders each containing several A4 clear pouches, each as far as she could see had a self adhesive label attached. She lifted the first clear pouch that sat at the front outside of a binder; the label read 'Brightly's café'. Eleanor's eyes widened on reading the name then she read to herself;

'If you sit in Brightly's Café at nine-thirty in the morning on a Wednesday and wait for ten minutes or less, you will see a man in a green three-quarter length coat pass the window. He will stop outside as he looks at the menu affixed to the window. If you watch his eyes you will see he is actually looking at the reflection of the road behind him or himself. He never orders anything from that menu, ever. He always orders the same things, a pot of tea and a sandwich usually meat.

He enters and scans the room before sitting at the second table by the window facing the door. Without exception he always carries the same shopping bag which he places on the floor on his left. By its shape the bag contains a box the contents of which I know to be paper money. Once seated the man, it's always the same man, takes the menu off the table and places it on the window ledge.

Five minutes later another man dressed in a casual fashion and wearing a red woollen hat will walk across the road and enter the café.

On seeing the first man he smiles, greeting him as a casual friend. Something regulars to a single place often do I have found. He then sits down opposite the first man placing an identical bag to the first man's, on his left under the window. He orders a coffee only, nothing to eat. This bag too contains a box but contains at least five different drugs and sometimes others in smaller amounts, possible samples of a new type.

They talk about nothing important, weather, government, politicians or stock market trends for fifteen minutes then the second man finishes his coffee, picks up the bag on his right, which the other man has brought in and leaves. The first man waits usually ten minutes more and then he too leaves, walking across the road to the brokerage business. Folder three contains what I have discovered about the buyer and his contacts as well as the contacts of the second man.'

Eleanor re-read the text not quite believing her eyes. "Hazel, find D.C.I Fairclough will you and ask him to come here as soon as." Then she took from the case a roll of what looked like lining paper. On unwinding part of it she exclaimed "Jesus Christ," under her breath as her eyes scanned the family tree like structure. Putting it back she then took out the first folder, it was heavy; the reason was obvious as she opened the rigid card cover. The first clear pouch contained a revolver, possibly a thirty-eight she thought. In other plastic sleeves were three mobile phones, two wallets, half a dozen credit cards and some loose change in a separate bag. The white label read, 'Jason Tobbit'.

"Tony," she called over to her sergeant.

"What the hell is all that?" Coltrain said when he saw the contents of the case.

"You couldn't guess if you lived to be a hundred. Our little girl has been very busy in the time she's been here, look at this." She held up the plastic pouch with the revolver and other contents in it.

"Bloody hell, if Tobbit was carrying that she could claim she was acting in self-defence."

"Quite so, and from what we've already seen she doesn't react kindly to people who try to assault her. Get it all logged and down to forensics, fingerprints, the lot. We've had this case all wrong from the beginning so let's get it put right." As Tony turned away D.C.I. Fairclough approached.

He eyed the case and its contents, "This what the girl left for you?" He asked rhetorically.

"Yes sir. I've just given D.S. Coltrain a folder with sleeves containing various items marked as previously belonging to Jason Tobbit, although I suspect the wallet and credit cards were not his."

"She robbed him you mean?" Fairclough said bluntly.

"Yes and no, the main item was a revolver which analysis may show it to be the object that struck James Mason Maurice, if so and it has Tobbit's prints all over it then she may have been responding in self-defence. Be difficult to get a conviction, she being at least in part a member of the pubic preventing a mugging."

"Don't forget an armed member of the public." He cautioned.

"Might have trouble there if the weapon she has is classified, nobody is going to want that aired in the press. Anyway put it into context, just read this." She offered up the neatly hand written note she had just read twice.

"Is this right?" Fairclough grunted as he reached the end of the script.

"Only one way to find out, now look at this," she opened up the roll of paper with its schematics. She watched her superior's eyes widen as he scanned the lines of text, following the links.

"Can we verify any of this?"

"I expect the contents of this case will provide the evidence, look here, photographs, and we know who he is, him as well but I don't think we ever connected them together. There's a file on both players this one has a list of addresses."

"I wonder how up to date it all is."

"Six month or less, she was in Northern Ireland before that."

Fairclough grunted again, then picked up the phone and punched in a number. "Drug Squad will want this. Colin, Doug here can you drag yourself away and come downstairs we have an item or two you may want to grovel for, sorry, see. Charming, does your wife know you use such language? I must ask her when we next meet. See you in ten." He replaced the handset. "What worries me is that she just gave it to you, a set up maybe? Doesn't she know what negotiating power is?"

"I'd be surprised if it wasn't genuine, if you read this letter that effectively signed it over to me you'll see she suggests she isn't going to be with us long and she may not get another chance." Eleanor handed her superior the envelope containing the hand written page.

"But why, she's young, right? Why would she spend her final days and nights gathering all this stuff, can't see my daughter doing anything like with a full life ahead of her."

"Like everything else about this girl we know nothing except what others have said about her. I think she might be responding to her training, how she was brought up, and the last preserve when all options run out. All I can say for certain is she has an odd way of opening a conversation; she has on the few occasions written and verbally given my rank and then my name. When saying who she is, she precedes it with 'Researcher' Oo-neh Maurice, and she pronounces her surname as Maur-ice not Maur-eece as I said before. The 'Oo' is long and the 'neh' brief like an adolescent saying no."

"Definitely foreign then, not the English way of address, but I can't think who else may speak that way."

"More than likely she's an illegal, the other two likewise. If it hadn't been for the mugging they would have remained under the radar. Frankly I have no idea what she's up to, how it all fits together but I doubt she is just killing time. There's a plan somewhere."

"Maybe we'll find out one day, anyway for now better not reveal the source of this stuff. We're not going to hand her over to 'Drugs' so they can play her."

"Somehow I don't think that will ever be an option. Sir, just to keep you in the frame with all this, the flu virus that my son was injected with was non-contagious. So far all the doctors can tell us is that it was definitely genetically altered in some way as it corresponds with no virus in their database." Eleanor went on to explain what had been discovered from the academics before commenting further. "So even though the experts say these things are not within the real world, I am beginning to see it might have been done. Someone somewhere may have found a way to bio-engineer the human genome. If Oo-neh's information about the agents is to be relied upon they might be the result of that technology. The scary thing is that to them this technology is over thirty years old. One can only speculate what advances there have been since then."

"That's maybe what the girl has then, a file containing the latest technology." Fairclough speculated further.

"She said on the phone she couldn't give them the file as she doesn't have it. Whatever we say or think, it is mere supposition sir, we need to speak with Oo-neh and get some solid facts, because the agents won't tell us the truth."

"Do you think she will?" Fairclough looked at her squarely.

"As a matter of fact I do, whoever her parents were they have given her manners and I expect they have taught her to be truthful."

"A rare bird in our job. Ah! Colin, out of breath are we? It's all those big dinners and no exercise you mark my words."

Colin Wright was a large man it was true but not as a result of over eating, in his younger days he had been a keen rugby player but with marriage, his work and injuries his muscle tone had declined. "Sod off Doug, hello Elle, long time no see. I hope you're not waiting for him to die before you become a D.C.I, you know what they say about creaking gates. He'll linger longer than you or I well after his sell by date expires."

"No sir, I'm just waiting for the right time." She liked D.C.I Wright, unlike most upwardly mobile people she'd met he had no side to him, a copper from the ground up, who would not tolerate poor standards or inefficiency.

"Well don't leave it too long there are too many aspiring geniuses climbing the ladder. Right then what have you dragged me here for, not a cup a weak tea and a stale bun I hope."

"No my friend I think you will find the journey worth the while, read that." Fairclough handed the sheet containing the description of events at Brightly's café.

D.C.I Wright read it without comment then read it again, "Is this a good source?" he finally said.

"Judge for yourself, if this hasn't some basis in fact someone has gone to a lot of work fabricating evidence," Fairclough's arm swept across the contents of the case.

Eleanor was aware of the other team members making glances in their direction, intrigued with events as they unfolded. She opened up the roll of paper to show the Drug Squad's D.C.I. the summary of what the case contained. His eyes scanned the names; mobile telephone numbers, links to other people all of which finally coalesced at the end with six named individuals, their addresses, all known phone numbers, web addresses and passwords. Annotations linked the data to file numbers.

Colin Wright lifted one of the files out of the case, on opening it he saw the clear plastic inserts, the mobiles phones, sometimes several to a sleeve, photographs, notes relating to meetings observed and the occasional handgun. He checked out another three before he finally stopped looking.

"Where did this all come from?" he asked replacing the blue folder he had last held.

"It came up in the course of an investigation," said Fairclough without committal or elaboration.

"We have removed one file as it's pertinent to someone involved in one of our investigations," said Eleanor.

Wright fingered a name on the chart, "we've been after this sod for months, he's damn careful and we can't get close enough to gather any real intel'." He rewound the roll stopping when he noticed a clear plastic pencil box containing three keys. Releasing the clips he opened the cover, the key fobs stated the name of storage facility, an internal legend denoted file references. D.C.I Wright drummed his fingers on the desk, "Okay Doug what do I have to do to walk out of here with this lot?"

Fairclough didn't answer fast enough, Elle got in first, "Nothing sir, I believe the source felt it was important enough to gather and important enough to give it to us. Make it count sir."

Wright looked at Fairclough, who nodded, "I'll let you know how it all checks out, and if it does can you arrange a meeting with the source?"

"No sir," said Eleanor emphatically. "There are already too many people after this source I will not risk a leak that could further endanger them."

Wright nodded, accepting the point of the argument, "Then give them my thanks at least."

"I will sir." She said.

"I'll probably owe somebody a great deal when I've sifted through this lot and realised its true worth." Wright said to no one in particular.

"You will Colin, Oh! You will," said Fairclough smiling brightly. He watched his colleague as he dragged the case out of the door, "You should think about it Elle, you know."

"Think about what sir?" she asked absently.

"Promotion Elle, promotion, and don't give me that nonsense about waiting until Edward is settled. It's just an excuse and if it weren't him then it would be something else, you know it, and I know it. Besides you're likely to be home nights more than you are now."

"Do you mind if I think about it? At least until we get this case sorted out."

"As long as it's this case and not the next, now get off and see how that boy of yours is doing."

As Eleanor gathered her things together, and tidied her desk her mind wandered over the basic outline of the case trying to fit the facts into some coherent scenario but try as she might she could see no feasible way the dots connected. As far as she knew her ex-husband had no drug related connections and even if he had, what or more to the point who was Oo-neh. She gave up with a sigh; it wouldn't take long before she became aware of the fallout from the contents of that ordinary suitcase on wheels. Even as she walked down the staircase three cars from the Drug Squad left to find out just what was in the storage lockers, storage to which they now held the keys.

The taxi pulled into the bay outside the hospital; Eleanor paid the Latvian driver and walked into the reception. She sensed rather than observed that there seemed to be more chaotic activity than usual. Without obstruction she made her way to the corridor where her son was located. Dodging to one side of the corridor as she allowed two members of the nursing staff to pass through the swing doors, before she herself passed through them, but going the other way. The corridor was painted the usual vile colour such places were painted - at least in her opinion. The vertical walls were protected by the well scuffed wooden boards that projected from the plasterwork to stop the trolleys damaging the smooth surface. One such empty trolley lay at rest at the furthest end, parked against the wall. She knocked on the door to Edward's room, opened it and saw it was empty. Assuming he was off having some test or other, she went to the waiting area further along, acquired a coffee from the machine and sat down to wait.

Five minutes elapsed before Doctor Forbes put his head around the corner, "Ah, Missus Maurice one of the staff said you'd arrived. Now I don't wish you to be alarmed but Edward has gone walkabout."

"Meaning?" Eleanor asked slowly putting the paper cup down.

"Well when we went to check on him he simply wasn't there and as yet we have no idea where he is. I've just come back from security and as far as we can tell he never went out through any of the camera monitored doors since the last time we checked on him."

"How long has he been missing?" She asked with little hint of the concern she felt.

"About an hour, he was fine then, practically back to normal but we can't rule out some aberrant behaviour from his recent fever, he could have just wandered off. No need to worry as we have people looking for him, he can't be far away."

"Has he got his clothes, do you know?" the rising concern started to grip the usually calm woman.

"No, just his hospital attire, you don't know if his father may have come for him do you?"

"Highly unlikely it would mean thinking about somebody else but himself. Have you seen the girl Oo-neh, the one in the picture I showed you? Small, about four feet seven, maybe less, slim build usually carries a satchel"

"No, we have been especially vigilant for her, nobody has reported seeing her."

The figure that appeared around the corner at that point did so silently. On seeing him Eleanor felt a jolt pass through her, not just from the shock of the sudden appearance but also because of who the figure was. The doctor turned on seeing Eleanor's attention shift, "Can I help you," he said in a mildly imperious tone.

The darkly clad figure looked him up and down, then dismissing him with a curt, "No", before saying "Detective Inspector of Police Eleanor Maurice we have business to transact."

Without taking her eyes off Agent O.F.V Tyler-Wolfe Inspector Maurice told Forbes, "Doctor, I think you'd better go."

"But," he said in protest.

"There's nothing you can do here, if I'm right you can call off the search for my son."

Tyler-Wolfe nodded as the doctor, whose primitive brain stem responded to signals he hadn't consciously registered, scuttled away, feeling relief the further away he got.

"Where's my son?" Eleanor said a hard edge to her tone.

"Somewhere safe and he will remain that way for I have no orders to cause him any direct harm. All I want is the girl or the file then we shall be gone in no time at all." His tone was measured, whether the menace was intended or just normal for him she did not know for certain but felt the latter.

"I have no idea where she is." Eleanor said moving into the corridor to check that nobody was likely to become involved in something she had no control over.

He followed her out, positioning himself directly in front of the police officer.

"Oonecks Maurice will contact you or come here to see your son that much I can safely assume, and when she does you can help me detain her."

"Don't you mean kill?"

"Detective Inspector of Police you do not seem to understand that we are both officers trying to enforce the law. My orders specify I must try to take her alive if possible; failing that slightly damaged is an option. Killing her is not beneficial but as she has shown herself to use deadly force against us then to defend myself I will use the same. If, and only if it becomes necessary to do so."

"I saw what happened to your colleague in Northern Ireland in the moments leading up to his literal disappearance. Now I don't know who you are or where you're from, or indeed who she is, all I know for certain is that you have lied to my colleagues and me. But one thing I am beginning to wonder is if you're actually up to the task of taking her down before she takes you down."

"She's a researcher nothing more nothing less."

"Perhaps, but a researcher that has skills enabling her to avoid you and your team." Eleanor paused not quite certain whether she saw a head look around the corner at the far end of the corridor or not before it disappeared from view. "She nearly drowned your Northern Ireland colleague in a swimming pool; she would have done had he not been pulled out of the water by some bystanders."

"She must have caught him unawares due to the noise and smells of the area."

He almost sounded like he was looking for an excuse, Eleanor thought; maybe he was human after all. Or was he unwittingly revealing a weakness they had.

"Oh, she did that most impressively." She stopped talking as a figure moved into view, it was the girl and all she wanted to do was scream for her to run. Eleanor looked at the agent before her, looking for signs he was aware of his target, he appeared not to be. Surely, if his hearing was as acute as it seemed to be, he'd already heard her. Thirty feet away the small figure moved soundlessly, holding the satchel, which seemed to be a constant part of her attire in her right hand. Her attention seemed to be fixed on the back of agent O.F.V Tyler-Wolfe as she lifted the leather satchel up and placed it on the trolley parked against the wall. The agent tilted his head and started to turn his head clockwise and sniffed the air.

"Shist," was all he said as he brought his arm up.

Oo-neh started to run towards him, she was fast. Eleanor expected, on seeing the bigger foe, that she would run away and not towards him. In three strides the girl seemed almost to walk up the wall before taking another three strides along the wooden wall protector before dropping once more low onto the floor. As she repeated the same movement on the opposite wall the agent moved and fired at the wall she had just left.

"Run," Eleanor screamed loudly at the fast approaching girl unaware of the effect it would have on the agent.

The agent cursed loudly as he thrust an arm out to push Eleanor away, shook his head and tried to relocate his approaching target. Eventually registering her new position he fired again but she was no longer at the spot his visual processes said she would be. Oo-neh then changed direction again running straight at him before performing a cartwheel that brought her skimming along the wall inside his blind spot on his right side. But before he could complete a turning motion Oo-neh made two jabbing motions at his back. To Eleanor such a move was impractical as the girl was too small to have the physical strength to do any real damage. Nonetheless the agent crumpled at the knees and fell forward like a puppet that had just had its strings cut.

Ignoring the now prostrate and immobile male, Oo-neh quickly straightened her clothes and stood before the older woman, "Good afternoon Detective Inthpector of Polithe Eleanor Maurithe, I am Rethearcher Oo-neh Maurithe. She waited for a response but Eleanor was still trying to understand what she had just witnessed and wasn't prepared for this seemingly out of place introduction. She wasn't even sure she fully understood what had been said. The girl was certainly athletic, but then from the Irish CCTV footage Eleanor already knew that. She looked at the girl; whose face was set in what her son had described as a half smile, as if she was unsure whether to be happy or not.

"I'm sorry," she started to say, still in slight shock at the turn out of events, before she held out her hand, "Pleased to meet you at last." Then wished she hadn't, for the girl's half smile faded slipping rapidly into one of sadness as her mouth crumpled slightly. Then as if the cause had quickly passed by the half smile returned.

Oo-neh looked directly at her then asked quietly, "Would you mind keeping the corridor clear I need a word with Oh-Five."

It took Eleanor a moment to realise she must be referring to the agent. "He's not dead?" Eleanor asked in surprise. From the way he'd gone down she'd expected his next visitor would be the pathologist.

"No, he ith unable to move hith legth or armth but he can thtill breathe." There was no emotion in her tone.

"I'll get a doctor."

"No need he will be recovered shortly. Pleathe keep them away, it'th important." she indicated the advancing medical staff.

"Alright," even as she walked down the corridor Eleanor couldn't understand her own behaviour but for the moment thought it better to keep the potential crime scene clear. Looking back she saw the diminutive figure, for Oo-neh seemed smaller close up than she had imagined, kneel down by the agent's head her back towards her.

After a brief argument the medical staff retreated beyond the fire doors allowing the detective to return to the Oo-neh, who was just returning from collecting her satchel. On the short walk back Eleanor had considered the brief hint of emotion Oo-neh had shown. "Are you alright?" she found herself asking.

"Yeth thank you, I am quite well. Have you recovered? If you want to thit down I shall get you a thweet drink."

"No I am fine honestly. How did you do what you just did?"

"With thith," Oo-neh held up a flat skin coloured object the length of a hand from finger tip to wrist, "It'th a Mark One, thtandard military issue perthonel protection Thkite. It'th quite old technology now, he hath the Mark four, on full power it will make a wall dithappear. Do you want to thee?"

"Er, no not at present thank you." Eleanor was slightly amazed at the enthusiasm in the girl's voice, she somehow seemed younger than she imagined. "Can he talk?"

"Oh, yeth he has been very helpful. Out of them all he ith the likable one, I have exthchanged a confidenthe with him and he told me where Edward ith, but he didn't have to." Oo-neh rolled up her sleeve to show what looked like a clear plastic patch on her wrist, on its surface two lights pulsed steadily whilst a blue one flickered up the side. "I took it off him, it mapth the local tracking-ware, Oh-Four ith the blue one, with thith they know where the retht of the team are." She rolled her sleeve back down.

"Confidence, you mean you've told him where the file is?"

"Yeth and I altho agreed not to kill him, when he ith recovered he will be treated and be back on hith feet in a month. I told him to athk my father to remove the Drothophila gene and rectify the vithual updating problem."

"You shouldn't have told him," Eleanor argued before moving on to a subject she did understand. "We'd have got Edward back, maybe it would have taken us a bit longer but we would have got him back." She knew she was trying to convince herself because these people were uncharted territory for her and outcomes were not guaranteed.

"It doethn't matter it ith too late now for them to interfere they cannot change the outcome." Oo-neh moved to the middle of the corridor then placed a circular disc onto the taupe coloured wall and then returned. "I'm going to record thomething for my father; he will be interethted in how I am doing and if all ith well. Will you be in the record?"

"I? I don't imagine your father would want to see me, he doesn't know me."

"But he will be happy to thee I have a friend and that I am happy. He loveth me and I love him and ath we will never meet again, he will know all ith ath well ath it can be. This will be my latht opportunity, pleathe. pleathe be in it, it will thurprithe him."

Was it the earnest plea that swayed her, Eleanor didn't know, but she sensed a sadness in Oo-neh, possibly because she'd left her father. Perhaps there was something more, something she hadn't yet told her concerning her imminent demise. Perhaps, Eleanor considered, if she involves herself with this young woman she will open up and tell her what is actually going on around here. "Alright what do you want me to do?"

"Would you put your arm around me? Look at the thentre of the dithc, try to look ath though you love me a little and when I raithe my hand, thmile?"

"I think I can manage that." Crouching down Eleanor moved closer to Oo-neh and placed an arm around her slim waist and then she smiled. As she did so a bright light seemed to emanate from the disc on the wall, eventually forming an extended circle in the space around it with her and Oo-neh at the focus. Then with a flourish Oo-neh slid her glasses onto her head and smiled her best smile and raised her hand, index finger pointing up. A second later she dropped her hand and replaced her glasses.

"Something wrong?" Eleanor asked having expected a flash or something.

Oo-neh picked up the square tablet that Eleanor had heard about from others, and with a rapid movement of her fingers Oo-neh eventually seemed satisfied. "No everything ith good," she said removing a crystalline disk from the side of the unit. "I exthpect my father will be very happy, tho will Project leader Antoniuth Dioth when he lookth at the record of my journey. However he will not be really happy ath it ith all he will get." Bending down she placed the disc onto agent Oh-Five's forehead, "He'll find it there." Into the limp hand Oo-neh placed the Personal Protection device, Mark one version.

Detaching the disc off the wall Oo-neh relocated it into a side recess on the tablet before finally taking a rectangular crystal block from one of her pockets. She showed it to the prone figure, his eyes widened. *"I'm not going back becauthe what I left will no longer be there,"* she said in her own language. Then Oo-neh looked at Eleanor. "Ith there anything you want to athk him before he is recovered."

"What? No, not unless he can tell me what is going on."

"He can't, but I may." Then she stamped on agent Oh-Five's chest and took one step back, then with no discernible movement or sound the floor area became empty.

When Eleanor had seen it on the CCTV recording she had found it hard to believe, having been next to the actual event she found it impossible to accept. "Where's he gone?" she asked probing the floor space with her hand where seconds previously had been a mass weighing about seventy-eight kilos or more.

"Home, he will be recovered about…." the elfin girl watched the analogue display on her left wrist, the second hand evenly sweeping around the dial, "…now. They will have a medical team on thtandby. Within one hour they will be performing a neural graft on both the injury thiteth to rebuild the nerve bundleth that feed his legth and armth. Oh-Five will be debriefed early tomorrow by which time my father will have recovered the crythtal memory from Oh-Five'th forehead and returned to the Inthtitute at the TholarThea Thecurity Zone. He doethn't want to be at Donderry when the next one ith recovered."

"How did it happen?" Eleanor found herself asking.

"How did what happen?"

"How did he just disappear?"

"Did you notithe the crythtal block I took from my pocket? He had one like it attached to hith chetht. It wath my Rethonant Plotting and Location Thequenther and without it I cannot be recovered. When I thtamped on him it broke the plotting thignal cauthing an automatic recovery, utheful if you are in danger or need immediate help."

"I wish I hadn't asked! Sorry but it doesn't mean anything to me. Is there a simpler explanation?" Eleanor doubted there was.

Oo-neh smiled a little more brightly, "I will try later, but now I have to re-acquire Edward Clark Maurithe."

"You know where he is?"

"Not exthactly but the locator will lead me, he'th not tho very far away."

"Wait, before you go I'll get a team from the armed response unit." Eleanor flicked on her phone app but before she could tap in a number a small gloved hand covered the screen.

"Not a good idea, when you conthider who ith holding him."

"But the agent, Oh-Five said they don't have orders to kill Edward."

"They probably don't, they rithk their own exithtenthe by harming him but that ith no guarantee. Oh-Four ith neither very bright or nithe, by now he will have developed an audio map of the area around him. It ith probably where they have located themthelveth thince they arrived, he will have ethtablished an olfactory map ath well. Not to mention hith eyethight ith a factor of five better than anyone you know. There ith no way you will be able to creep up on him. He will hear your vehicleth five to eight hundred metreth away; he will hear the movement of your men'th feet well before they get into pothition."

"You are not serious?" Eleanor could not believe what she was hearing.

"Oh yeth, he ith the end rethult of a project by Tyler-Wolfe, a clever man but an idiot ath well becauthe the Drothophila Team, actually Team Prometheuth, are flawed. They shouldn't be allowed out on their own. Not that they ever are, they are alwayth deployed together. Without the otherth Oh-Four ith itholated and he may take it into hith head to thtart killing anything and everybody within range until you give me to him. I know him, you do not, and he won't thtop until he hath fulfilled hith orderth. Perhapth you should go home. I do not think it will be of benefit for you to wait here." Oo-neh drew her satchel close to her chest, "Perhapth we will meet again, I would like that. I never really thought I would get to meet you." Quickly she reached out and touched Eleanor's hand, her face crumpled slightly, "I'm glad I did even if it ith for jutht a little while."

Eleanor could easily imagine tears welling up in the girl's eyes, hidden as they were by the oily film lenses, but she had no idea why. Then the moment passed, she watched the girl turn and run back along the corridor retracing the route she had followed when she entered the building and was soon gone from sight.

Edward Maurice sat sullenly against the lined wall of the office he was locked in. The air was filled with the damp mustiness of dilapidation. Outside and below the office was the fabrication floor of some defunct engineering company and he could smell the old oil that permeated everything. On his journey through the silently decaying equipment he'd recognised some of the machinery from his own limited experience in the engineering classes he'd had. The lack of rust suggested to him that the works hadn't been closed all that long. Oily grime coated the floor giving it a blackened appearance, evidence that lubricants had been trodden into the concrete over the years, perhaps decades. The light levels were decreasing outside he noticed, as he glanced up at the filthy transparent panels set in the metal roof, giving him a rough idea of the time.

A half hour or so passed and all that happened was a steady darkening of the room until he heard a brief commotion somewhere in the interior of the factory. Then silence. His ears ached listening for some sound to suggest armed police had raided the place but all he could hear was the far away hum of traffic. Finally he drew breath and sighed, "No rescue yet," he said to nobody.

Without warning he heard three soft thuds before the door fell forward into the room, devoid of lock or hinges. He sat shocked for a moment then he saw a small figure standing in the doorway.

"Good evening Edward Clark Maurithe, rethcue may not alwayth happen in the way you imagine and not alwayth by the people you exthpect," said Oo-neh as she stepped onto the door.

"Oo-neh? What are you doing here? How did you find me?" Edward said after recovering his senses.

In reply she pointed to a single small pulsing yellow light on her forehead.

"What is it?" Edward found himself asking, wondering if it was her third eye but was prepared to be disappointed.

"A tracking unit, it belonged to Oh-Four, I have one that belonged to Oh-Five. It showed me where Oh-Four wath located and thince he wath unlikely to leave you alone, that ith where I would find you altho."

"Where is he, the tall creepy guy?"

"He had to go home; he won't be back for some time if ever. You can have thith if you want." She said peeling off the locator. Then grabbing Edward's wrist she applied it to the smooth skin on the under surface. "Now you'll alwayth know where I am, at leatht you will if I'm within thirty mileth, if not there will be no light. The blue light on the edge will show the direction of the passive unit."

Edward experimentally peeled back the thin layer of a clear something or other, plastic he thought, no thicker than the protective plastic used to cover electronic equipment surfaces and yet it must be filled with electronics. He held it up trying to see anything but the subdued light made it impossible. "Ow," he yelled startled at the prick he felt in his neck.

"I brought thome ithe-cream, in the bag by the door, it probably ith melting by now." Oo-neh sat down on the blanket Edward had recently vacated on the floor. "I imagine you are feeling well," she said absently, her attention focused on the square screen of her tablet.

"Yes fine, the muzziness has gone, no headaches and the muscle twitching has gone completely. Have you come with the bill?"

"Bill?" she queried.

"Yes, the cost for the treatment, even though I gather you're not a doctor."

"No I'm a rethearcher and the bill hath been paid already, come thit here I will show you what hath changed."

Intrigued he sat close by her side and looked at the screen.

"You thtink," she said catching him off guard.

"So would you cooped up in here. What am I looking at?"

"Wherever your eyeth are pointing. Now thith wath the firtht blood thample. You thee the group outlined here that wath the gene pair that created your problem, it ith one of many such pairth hidden within the tho called redundant part of the genome. Now here ith the thample I've jutht taken, the thame thite ith here and you notice it ith different. It will be replicated like that from now on and keep thpreading through each thell and you will not die before you are fifty, provided you take reathonable care and avoid too much ithe-cream. Promithe me you will not wathte your life, I gave up everything tho you would not die."

"Why, why would you do that? I don't even know you," Edward was surprised and showed it.

"Becauthe my father thaid I mutht to be thafe. Now eat your ithe-cream I don't want that wathted either, if you don't want it I'll eat it." After which comment Oo-neh fell silent as she pondered upon the things she had had to do to become safe, the least of which was attaching the explosive device to Oh-Four on his recovery. Sending her Resonant Plotting and Location Sequencer back with Oh-Five didn't guarantee they would cease looking for her, but destroying the Rotating Torus at Project RoTos that was something different. A smoking hole in the ground a mile wide would not encourage further development of the project. There would, she knew, be an enquiry but holes and smoke gave nothing away, besides there had been voices raised against the idea from the beginning about the inherent instability of the Torus itself. What would happen now she didn't know for certain, all she had was a bunch of untested theories but whether they had any basis in reality she did not know. She'd be the first to test them.

Suddenly the twilight of the room was filled with a soft radiant light. When Edward looked at it he saw what he interpreted as a hologram, a three dimensional image floating in the air but of a quality he'd not heard about.

"That ith my mother and me when I wath little." Oo-neh said. Edward barely heard her as she spoke so quietly.

He was distracted as he walked over to the shining image, squinting and frowning as he tried to grasp what he saw. "She looks just like my mother," he finally said. "Do you think we're related?"

"Dithtantly, I don't think you'd want to be any clother."

"Oh, I don't know, we might be cousins."

"We're not," Oo-neh said emphatically shutting down the spectral image. "We'd better go; your mother will be worried about you." As she stood up the glow vanished as quickly as it had appeared. "She'll want to give you lotth of hugth and kiththeth when you get home."

"I hope not, is that what you have to look forward to?"

"No, my mother died when I wath eight and I cannot go home again, ever. I have no one to give me hugth and kitheth anymore."

Edward felt his stomach tighten. "Look, I'm sorry Oo-neh I didn't know," he finally said reproaching himself.

"How could you, as you thay, you do not know me?" Looping the satchel strap around her neck she left the gloomy office.

Edward followed listening for any possible threats in the dark spaces; all he heard was the scuffing of his own feet on the steel stairs. He had barely walked fifteen steps when he stopped, in the partial light from the skylight he looked at one of the machines, a large section was missing, it wasn't just smashed or melted but the damage was more akin to an extremely sharp blade slicing through it. Two of the floor retaining bolts had been sheered. "I wonder what happened to that."

"He miththed me, that ith all," Oo-neh replied.

"What; missed you, who missed you?"

"Oh-Four, he wath aiming at where I wathn't. On their own the Drothophila Quinth can only hit thomething bolted down, they are truly awful when it cometh to a moving target."

"Useful to know I'm sure but can you imagine what would have happened had he hit you?"

"Yeth, you'd be talking to yourthelf, without me there would be no reathon for Oh-Four to thtay any longer."

"Don't you even care?" Edward was surprised at the nonchalant way she viewed such a dire situation.

"I don't exitht, Edward Clark Maurithe, there ith nobody here to give me hugth and kitheth and thoon becauthe of what I have done I will theathe to be, you will have no memorieth of me. Tho what good would it do to care?"

"I couldn't forget you, how could I?"

"Forget ith perhapth the wrong word, it will be ath though I never wath. There will be nothing to forget."

"You're losing me; you can't just suddenly disappear from people's memories."

"I altered your Genetic mapping Edward Clark Maurithe and from that moment the potential variability of life changed."

"My life, yes, you said I wouldn't die young."

"No, everybody'th, a thingle change will thend out rippleth that will have conthequentheth beyond calculation." She said seriously.

"You're kidding, just because I'll live longer?"

"No, becauthe of what you will do with that life, but do not worry the world will alwayth be ath you expect it to be."

The night air was cooling as they stepped out into the shadow cast by the building, "Where are we?" Edward asked.

"In unknown land, whatever happenth now will never have happened before; we have neither map, no plan tho we mutht do only our betht."

"Excuse me?"

"Olivier Dagon, 'Winter of a Pathing Thmile'." Oo-neh replied.

"Who?"

"You don't know her, maybe you will, it ith a book she wrote. Do you like walking? It ith no more than forty minuteth if you don't dawdle."

Shortly after eight o'clock in the evening the doorbell rang causing Eleanor to cease staring at the magazine in her lap. If asked she couldn't have told you what was actually on the page, her thoughts were elsewhere. Standing up quickly she almost ran to the door. Slamming the door-chain back in its slot whilst simultaneously turning the key in the lock, Eleanor opened the door.

"Sorry I didn't have my key," said Edward as he stepped through the doorway, still dressed in his now grubby hospital attire.

Eleanor paused momentarily as she appraised her son for any possible injury then she wrapped her arms around him and gave him a big hug, and then she pushed him back. "You're alright, they didn't hurt you?"

Glad that there were no kisses accompanying the hugs he replied. "No, they just dumped me in this filthy office and left me. I don't think they have much in the way of social skills." He sniffed, then held his clothing closer and sniffed again, "Oo-neh was right I do stink."

At the mention of the girl's name Eleanor looked out into the late evening air, the street was empty. Closing the door and relocking it she told her son to go and get showered whilst she rang the hospital to advise them he had arrived home safely and that she would drop him off the following day. Then she prepared a quick meal for them both.

When Edward finally returned dressed in his own clothes he told her the details of what had happened and his subsequent rescue. "I am beginning to think she's really weird," he started saying. "I mean it's not normal to talk as though you will disappear and nobody will ever remember you've been here. Not likely we'll forget her is it? Then when you think things are getting back to normal and you're just walking in the dark she suddenly starts singing at the top of her voice, 'I love the night, I love the night, I love the element of danger and to feel pure delight'."

Eleanor smiled slightly recognizing the refrain from a golden oldie she liked, "What happened to the agent that took you?"

"Oo-neh said he'd gone home but that must have been after he wrecked this industrial lathe trying to kill her."

"If he's gone home as she puts it, then she will have put him down first, I saw her do it to the other one. If I hadn't seen it I would never have believed it. She's an athletic young lady that's for sure. But, young man, what I'd like to know is why you didn't bring her back with you. It is the least you could have done."

"I did ask, but all she said was that you would want to give me lotth of hugth and kitheth and she would be in the way,"

"Don't make fun of her Edward; she can't help how she talks. You should have insisted." Eleanor was irritated by her son's lack of thought. "Get your coat we're going to find her."

"What, at this time of night, where would we look? We know nothing much about her," protested Edward.

"I know where she lives, we'll start there. She's alone Edward, in a foreign country where she can't trust anybody. Just imagine how you would feel! You've just told me that she has given up everything to help you, why I have no idea, but what grates more than anything is that you never thought to give her a hug. I don't even imagine you said thank you, you're getting to be like your father and not the good parts either."

The car journey passed in silence, Edward stayed in the car as his mother rang the doorbell at Missus Wainscroft's Bed and Breakfast. She returned a few minutes later more irritated than before.

"She's gone; no forwarding address," Eleanor said glumly.

"Maybe she's gone because there's no reason to stay."

"Edward don't be flippant, I don't think she can go home."

"She can't, she said so, and she also said she has nobody, family I assume." It was only as he said the words did it finally dawn on him how truly selfish he had been, she'd told him but he hadn't heard.

"Those agents," Eleanor continued, "the ones that took you, have been hunting her; they wanted to take her back for stealing a secret file. She's here, alone in a foreign land without family or friends, she's probably here illegally and she's dying."

"Dying! Nobody said she was dying." retorted Edward.

"She said it to one of the witnesses I spoke to, her words were more to the effect that she had no expectations of reaching old age or anywhere close. I have to find her Edward, nobody should die alone and friendless."

It was after nine-thirty the following day when Eleanor passed through the main doors at Central HQ. The journey from the hospital where she had dropped Edward off had been slower than normal due to the many roads that had highway engineers or utility companies digging holes. Parking in the first available space she activated the central locking system, noting as she did so the larger number of vehicles than was usual that were parked up. She'd asked at the reception desk what was going on, but Sergeant White only shook his head in ignorance, saying only that something was going down upstairs. After the climb up the stairs to her office, which she had been advised was a healthy option, Eleanor stopped to catch her breath. On the landing a constable passed on the summons for her to go directly to D.C.I. Fairclough's office.

"Morning Eleanor," Fairclough started briskly, "I suppose you've already noticed something is going on around here?"

"Yes sir, hard not to," she replied briefly, awaiting enlightenment.

"The Drugs Squad has been up all night with that suitcase you brought in and since six this morning they've been drawing in men from the other divisions. It looks like they are going to make more than a few arrests."

"It was good intel' then?"

"They must think so. Officially I've not been told anything but I gather the storage units held a substantial amount of cash, forensics are going over it all now for prints. Good of the owners to wrap it all in plastic. I imagine it'll be commendations all around when the dust clears. You'll be a D.C.I. now whether you like it or not because I'll make damn sure those that need to know will be made aware of your role in all this."

"There's no need sir," Eleanor protested, "I did nothing but carry the case here. Sergeant Coltrain did just as much as I did," she continued, playing down her role.

"Yes, well he'll never make D.C.I., be lucky if he gets to be an Inspector. Anyway you inspired the girl's trust, enough for her to hand it over, says as much in the letter she left. Mind you there are not many I can think of that wouldn't have helped themselves to a few notes before telling us about it all. I imagine she did look in the units, there could be more of course and she's only told us about three of them. Pity we don't know why she gathered all that data; could be a reward there for her."

"All I know is that she's a researcher, her forte I guess but I have only spoken to her once and can safely say I don't know her, not by a long way," Eleanor was defensive and she knew it. "I doubt anybody will see my role as anything but as an intermediary, sir."

"It's all about perception Elle, what people see or imagine they see. I doubt D.C.I. Wright will be stingy with his praise, he knows, as he said himself, you deserve D.C.I. rank. Take the opportunity to fast track if it comes, you know you can do it."

"Yes sir, if they offer." The Inspector said in a subdued tone, promotion was just not on her wish list at present, she didn't feel ready.

"They will, I've already spoken to the Super'. I'll keep you posted if I hear anything else. Good work. Oh, by the way I think we can forget about the girl, let her go. I don't care if she's knocked off two hundred drug dealers; she's done us good here. Do you know if she's still got the weapon?"

"I believe not, I saw her put it on the agent's hand before he disappeared."

"Disappeared?"

"Did you see the video from the N.I. Police, the one at the swimming baths?"

"Yes I did as a matter of fact, very odd that."

"Well the last one I saw disappeared just like that right in front of me. Don't ask me how it happened but it did."

"Bit too X-Files for me that. Anyway if it's gone we don't have to worry about it further. Maybe you should keep that bit about him disappearing out of the reports, just say he was recalled or something equally vague."

"Very good sir," was her final comment before she left her boss's office returning immediately to her own. The sound of booted feet running down the stairwell told her that whatever was being planned was now operational.

"Morning boss," Detective Sergeant Coltrain cheerfully called out as she entered the open plan office.

"Morning Tony."

"Any idea what's going on?" he asked conversationally, leaning back in his chair to look past her towards the stairs.

"Not for certain, need to know basis I imagine," she replied without committing herself. Long experience had taught her that when something like this was happening bent police officers were occasionally scooped up in the process. Eleanor just hoped none of them would be from her team.

"I have the analysis results on the gun, it has Tobbit's prints all over it and the blood on the butt matches James Maurice's blood type.

Good news or what?" Sergeant Coltrain handed the report across to Eleanor.

"Good news? Most certainly; okay gather the files together, write it up a case of self defence, and then leave it on my desk to sign it off."

"What about the 'in possession of a firearm in a public place'? Do we just let her wander about with it?"

"Firearm? Nobody has come forward to say they heard any shots being fired and there are of course no bullet wounds on the body. I imagine it would be difficult to prove possession." Eleanor thought back to the hospital corridor. She remembered seeing the girl place the weapon, if that is what it was, on the body of agent Oh-Five as Oo-neh had called him just before he disappeared. "However I don't think we need worry, after all the pathologist was non-committal as to what had killed Tobbit or what kind of weapon - if any, had been used. True he had what might be a fine hole through what passed for a brain but can we know for sure she caused it or was it from some other long standing cause from his life-style? Should it of course be a weapon that is under secret development, I doubt we'd get far with it in court, the security services would shut the case down."

"Speaking of the Security Agents, what shall we say about them?"

"The truth; and that is simple enough. We have been unable to establish their identities or what organisation they belong to. Make a note that the evidence given in their initial interview has proven mostly inaccurate as far as we can ascertain. Whoever they were, I doubt we shall see them again."

"Morning boss," Detective Constable Hazel Wilson walked into the room. "How is Edward today?"

"He's good as it happens; in fact I'd go so far as to say I haven't seen him so cheerful for a long time, even after the kidnapping yesterday."

"Kidnapping! Nobody said anything to me," said Coltrain in surprise.

"No and that is my fault I'm afraid, the agents took him from the hospital and one of them, the one that did the talking here, met me there."

"What did he want?" asked Ceri who had just entered the office on the word 'kidnapping'.

"The girl as always, they wanted me to give her up to them and then they would go away, at least that is what I was told." Eleanor recounted.

"So what happened?"

"Researcher Oo-neh Maurice happened; I was standing in the corridor near the recreation area when she arrived. What I saw is hard to explain because I'm still not fully certain what it was that I did see. Suffice to say what happened to Agent Oh-Five was the same as happened to the one at the swimming pool."

Coltrain sat up straighter, "He disappeared? You're kidding?"

"Right in front of me, one minute he was there, the next there was nothing, except perhaps for a slight shimmering in the air. Oo-neh did explain but because of the way she speaks English she's hard to understand. I have no real idea what she was talking about except she termed it as a recovery. Whatever you do, do not write this up unless you want sectioning."

"Creepy," commented Ceri.

"And Edward was still in the hands of the other one? Why didn't you call it in boss?" Hazel frowned.

"Simple really, Tony do you remember when we were in the alley and the girl called me on my phone?" Coltrain nodded. "Well she said to me that the agents could hear what she was saying even though they were standing about fifteen plus feet away. Their senses, at least some of them are more acute than normal."

"Engineered do you think?" Coltrain asked, still pursuing the idea of genetic creations.

"Oo-neh said as much - keener sense of smell, better vision and hearing. All I can say is that she must walk very quietly because when he and I were in the hospital he made no indications that he was aware of her until she dropped her satchel onto one of the hospital trolleys."

"She obviously knows these agents or whatever they are," commented Hazel.

"So it seems, anyway, regarding Agent Oh-Four, she was concerned he might decide to take offensive action if he became aware of us arriving mob handed. Strangely Oo-neh didn't think they'd want to harm Edward, but as for everybody else, that would be a different matter. She volunteered to go after him and since she seemingly knew how to deal with them, I let her. Edward came home latish last night, smelly but otherwise alright."

"And Oo-neh?" asked Ceri showing feminine solidarity.

"Fine I guess, she never came in and I must admit that annoyed me. Edward showed so little in the way of gratitude which is not like him as a rule. I went to the B&B she was staying at but she'd gone; no forwarding address. And do you know it really pisses me off when she seems to have done so much, for who knows what reason and nobody seems to care about her." Eleanor knew she was getting emotional so she said nothing further.

The others felt slightly embarrassed until Coltrain lifted a sheet of paper from his desk. "Boss, the cup and plate came up negative for prints or DNA. The forensics on the gun showed it was probably a hand me around. Records show that it's been used in two shootings, where we've previously recovered bullets. Whether he was renting it or just acting as a courier we may never know but, and this is the interesting part, they found two partial prints on the bullets left in the gun. They appear to belong to one Charles Avery, and we have a file open on him as a person of interest."

"Avery? Not someone I'm familiar with," said Eleanor thoughtfully. "Hazel dig up what you can about him, who opened the file, who's interested in him etc. We need to see if it is one we can deal with or pass on. Tony call off the dogs on Oo-neh Maurice, she is no longer a person of interest to us, and make sure you note that during our investigations we came across the suitcase of research material she left us."

The desk telephone rang three times before Eleanor picked it up, "Inspector Maurice," she said briskly.

"Elle it's Alex Brightly, Oo-neh wants to see you," said the nearly breathless voice.

"Is she there now?" Eleanor asked her heart rate picking up.

"Yes."

"I'll be there in five to ten minutes." She said, dropping the phone into its cradle. Gathering her things together she dropped them into her bag.

"Everything alright boss?" asked Hazel slightly concerned.

"Yes, everything is fine; I'm going out to interview Oo-neh Maurice. I'll call in as soon as I know what my plans are. If you need me I'm on my mobile." Without further comment she hastened out of the office, and was gone from sight.

Eleanor walked with hurried pace to the cafe all the while wondering what she was going to say when she arrived. Whilst it was true that there were still a lot of unanswered questions, did they need answering now? Perhaps it would just complicate matters, and since the case was nearer to closure with each and every step, did it really matter if all the i's were dotted and the t's crossed? As her hand reached up to push open the door to Brightly's Café Eleanor finally made a decision, yes it did matter. The girl mattered, Edward mattered but most of all as she stepped through the door there was one over-riding thought in her mind, 'Why' followed closely by 'How'.

"Morning Elle, your usual?" asked Alex cheerfully.

"Yes please."

"The drink and cake are already paid for."

Eleanor resisted looking towards the table she knew the girl would be sitting at, she also knew the first thing Oo-neh would do and say. Was she so predictable or was it just the formality of her homeland, the must do formalities before any further communication took place? In some respects it unnerved her that this mysterious young woman seemed to know so much about her family while she knew next to nothing about her.

"Go and sit down I'll bring it across." Alex said turning to prepare the coffee.

Eleanor finally turned and looked to the far end of the room and there she was, smartly dressed as usual, this time in a green blouse and black jacket, her hair was red this time, shoulder length and framing her aquiline face. On the top of her hair was a green bow. The half smile was there as was the pair of shimmering glasses just as Edward had described to her. As for what she was thinking. Eleanor couldn't read the elfin face like she could some others, it was probably the glasses; the eyes told you a lot about a person. Eleanor smiled as she got closer; it was a genuine smile and not just for show.

Instead of stopping in front of the table she moved to the side, she didn't want this conversation to be formal with the table as a barrier. "Before you say anything," she cautioned, "Good Morning Inspector Maurice is acceptable in this society as is what I am going to say. Good morning Oo-neh Maurice."

"It ith?" the younger woman said.

"On my honour and my name is pronounced Maureese and not Maur-ice."

"Good morning Inthpector Maurithe."

"You see the world has not come to an end and I think you'll find if you call our host Alex she will not mind." Eleanor paused as she reappraised the source of so many questions. "Can I ask you to speak a little slower, I'm afraid the way you speak is sometimes hard for me to follow? May I call you Oo-neh and if you want you can call me Elle, most of my friends do?"

The facial movements on the girl suggested consternation. "I couldn't do that it would lack rethpect, and if you wish to be correct my name ith pronounthed 'Oo' which is a longer thound than 'neh' which ith brief"

"Oo-neh," Eleanor said by way of practice.

"It'th good," the little face smiled a little brighter.

"Well calling me Inspector Maurice would be formal and at this time I'd rather be more relaxed with you."

"May I call you 'Maw-her-vhor' it ith a name uthed to call an older wither perthon."

"Alright if you are happy with that, but I don't know about the wiser bit."

She stopped speaking as Alex arrived with the coffee and gateau, before she could speak again Oo-neh spoke first.

Almost conspiratorially, the elfin face drew closer to Eleanor, "I think I have upthet Prop." She stopped, remembered the earlier comment Eleanor had made, "Alexth, I told her she had a little mouth."

The inspector smiled, "Well it's better than being told you have a big one."

"No it'th only little, it ith under the cupboard by the sink."

Eleanor had to think a moment before she realised what had been said, then, speaking quietly in turn, "Oh, you mean a little mouse. Well she wouldn't be happy but it's better to know than not." She smiled briefly before becoming serious again. "Oo-neh, I want to apologise for my son's behaviour last night. His lack of gratitude, not to mention a total disregard of common courtesy especially after you went out of your way to bring him home, is unforgivable. Even more so since his health seems to have improved markedly since you injected him with that flu virus. So if you will allow me I want to thank you personally, from the bottom of my heart and if you'll allow me I'd like to give you a big hug which would be wasted on Edward."

What occurred next surprised Eleanor more than she could have imagined. As she leaned over and wrapped her own arms around the girl's small frame, with the intention of giving her a brief hug, she felt Oo-neh's arms embrace her in return but with an unexpected intensity. As she wondered what to do she felt the small frame close to her start to heave with an emotional outpouring like nothing she had experienced before. All she could do was hold onto her until the sobbing ceased, even Alex looked across with some concern but all Eleanor could do was shrug slightly, not knowing the reason for the outburst.

Without warning Oo-neh pushed herself away and rushed away into the rear of the premises where the washrooms were. In the interim period Alex came across, "It had to happen eventually," she said looking towards the rear corridor, "like I said she's homesick, and alone. Probably frightened to blazes with you lot after her. But that being as it may be, you looking like her mother may be making it harder for her."

"Then why did she ask me to come here?"

"Wasn't it the story of Pandora's Box that said when all the evils of the world had been released all that remained was hope?"

"Yes, but what happens if you don't even have that?" queried Eleanor.

On hearing the door latch click open Alex went back to the counter leaving the police inspector to put on a smile.

On arriving at the table the girl Oo-neh looked a little contrite, "Forgive me Mhor-her-vhor, I do not know what had overcome me."

"'Overcame me' would be a more normal pronunciation," Eleanor said trying to shift the emotional emphasis.

"It ith?"

"It is. Most people would say what I said. Look why don't we finish our drinks and go to my place? It's only about a half hour's walk."

"You are inviting me to your home?" Oo-neh said as though it was the last thing she expected to hear.

From the way it was said Eleanor could imagine the girl's eyes would be wide open in surprise. "Yes, you'd have been invited before had my son been more considerate. It'll be more comfortable and we can just talk about anything you want; for myself I'd like to get to know you better. After all you saved my son's life, possibly corrected a medical abnormality and stopped someone beating my ex-husband to death."

"Nobody hath ever invited me to their home before. I would like that." She smiled slightly more than usual.

"What nobody? Eleanor too sounded surprised. "Well it'll be a new experience for you then, okay now that's settled, finish your cake."

Fifteen minutes later Eleanor contacted her office to update them of her movements, and then together they left the café and walked at a steady pace for the next thirty minutes. The only interruption to their journey was a call from Edward to say he was being sent home. In reply Eleanor had told her son to get a taxi and advised him she should be home before him.

Eleanor turned the key in the lock of her front door just as the taxi drew up, on seeing Oo-neh, Edward showed some surprise after the failed excursion the previous night to find her.

"Don't stand there with your mouth open Edward it's unseemly. Here pay the taxi." Eleanor handed her son two twenty pound notes.

Stepping inside Eleanor hung her coat up on the row of hooks fastened to the wall. Turning back she saw her guest was still standing in the porch clinging to the satchel she held in front of her. The tip of her tongue projected between her lips.

"Are you alright? Eleanor asked.

"Yeth thank you." The girl replied.

Strange behaviour was something she had come to expect from this girl and the agents; they just didn't fit the normal pattern of individuals she was familiar with. But on the other hand she thought there may be a more rational reason why she hesitated.

"We don't have a dog if that's what you're worried about, there's just the two of us. So come in, we don't stand on ceremony. Through here, sit where you like."

"Mum," Edward interrupted, "a letter from Doctor Forbes." He handed over a sealed white envelope. "I'm going to get changed then I'm off to Darren's place unless you have any objections. I called him on the way back; we're going to do some revision, bat things about between us."

"No objections, that'll leave us free to talk. Have you anything else you want to say," Eleanor nodded sideways in Oo-neh's direction.

"Oh, right, yes. Oo-neh, look I'm sorry if I was a bit rude yesterday not inviting you in when you'd done so much for me. Honestly I seem to feel in over-drive at present."

"The 'Oo' ith pronounthed longer than the 'neh', your feelingth are normal now, they were not before. I thank you for your apology, I had thought it wath my thinging that upthet you."

"No, not at all, you have an interesting voice," Edward said diplomatically.

"If you're going, you'd better go; we'll see you later, we're eating at six, maybe six-thirty. Do you want a drink Oo-neh, coffee, tea, soft drink?"

"I like tea Maw-her-vhor, if it ith actheptable."

By the time the tea, milk and sugar had arrived, served up on a small cane tray covered with a small cloth, Edward had departed. Eleanor sat quietly for a few minutes wondering how to start her questioning.

"Did you come looking for me after Edward came home?" Oo-neh asked looking straight at Eleanor.

"Yes, I was so incensed at his bad manners, inviting you in was the least he could have done and we should have seen you home safely. We did go to your previous address but I found you had left. I think Missus Wainscroft was sorry to see you go. That's why I was so glad when you asked me to meet you this morning, first to apologise and then just to make sure you were alright." She noticed the girl's face tighten slightly.

"Oo-neh, this investigation I have been on since James Mason Maurice was attacked has left me with a lot of unanswered questions which, to be honest even if it's just for my own satisfaction, I'd like to know the answers. Would you mind if I asked you those questions?"

"No, I will do what I can to help you underthtand what hath happened more clearly, it ith my duty ath a thitizen." She sat up attentive.

"I'm not asking as a police officer, I'm asking purely for myself. I am glad however to say that you are no longer part of any investigation. As yet I don't know the ramifications of the material you gave me but others seem to find it of great interest, they want to thank you. In their stead please accept their grateful thanks. Now tell me," Eleanor smiled encouragingly, "what would have happened to you for killing the man who assaulted James Maurice in your own country?"

"It ith the duty of every thitizen to prevent an unlawful act, and aid anyone who hath been the subject of a criminal act, failure to act ith a contravention of the law, the thitizen can fathe a period of labour in a prison camp."

"Do you mean they wouldn't arrest you for the killing?"

"Not if I wath fulfilling my duty, they would make an invethigation to find out the detailth of the crime. In helping Jameth Mathon Maurithe who had been clubbed with intent to rob, I would be thanked and my help recorded. The robber would be freeze dried."

"Freeze dried, you mean literally?

"Yeth, it ith the way we all go eventually, criminal people die of the cold first."

"Sounds awful."

"It ith not intended I believe, to be an event to look forward to." Oo-neh said matter-of-factly.

"Why did you help my son Oo-neh. We don't know you or of you, and yet you seem to have deployed techniques that the doctors I've spoken with, simply don't have. Please help me understand, the why of it all and then how you can do it." Even to Eleanor her voice sounded like she was pleading.

"Have you a sheet of paper and a writing inthtrument?" Oo-neh said quietly, this was not the response Eleanor had expected.

When she came back to the living room with an A4 pad of lined paper and a clutch of pens and pencils she discovered that Oo-neh had closed the curtains and set up a light display on her electronic pad, filling the space against the wall with a pale blue glow. After setting the writing implements down on the coffee table Eleanor sat back in an armchair.

"I imagine that everything began with him," an image floated into the glowing field of light. It showed a man in his early to mid twenties wearing what appeared to be an academic gown; a golden trim went from the right lapel to the hem. He was standing in a room lined with books on one of the visible walls, and a table lay just behind him. On the wall directly behind him was a picture, beneath which was a clock-like display. "He ith my father," she said with what Eleanor interpreted as paternal pride. "Ioan Maurithe, twenty-three yearth old and newly a Doctor of Thience, qualified in Genetic Evolutionary Biology. He will become a world authority on the 'rubbish pile' of the genome or what many call the redundant gene pool. For hith doctorate he turned on an inactive genetic component in a DNA sample, creating a bald rodent that had the thkin properties of a chameleon - natural camouflage. He ith the only man alive I know who would think an invithible rodent wath a good idea. Ath time would tell that would prove a problem later in hith life and mine. He had the faulty gene Edward had, and that would kill him before hith fiftieth thelebration of birth. When I left, the progreth of his condition would allow him one to two yearth of life left, if he wath lucky."

Taking the pen from the bundle on the table Oo-neh, holding the instrument vertically wrote her father's name on the paper.

"You have an interesting writing style," observed Eleanor.

"My mother told me to write often to improve my hand-eye coordination; I kept a journal from my fifth birth thelebration. I wrote down everything that I had done and learned and on the fethtival of the darketht day, the day of my birth, I thent it to my grandmother."

"I'll bet she enjoyed reading it."

"I do not know, my grandmother never ever communicated with me. My mother told me my grandmother had travelled all the way from Cark to be at my birth but after theeing me she left. I don't think she can have liked me."

From her tone it was obviously a source of great sorrow Eleanor thought. "I'm sure that's not true, she probably only came to see you safe into the world. She probably has all your diaries on a shelf and gets a lot of pleasure from reading them. Some people aren't very good at writing down what they feel or think while some just don't know how to handle young children."

"I do not think you are correct." Oo-neh said, persistent in her belief.

"Well, maybe when you get home you can go and see her."

"I can never go home and even if I could, I could not travel to her, I do not have any paperth of identity but I will come to that. All the Mauritheth that have the mutant gene are Enith - and he died at forty-eight, Glyn Ioan died when fifty. Conrad Emar wath the firtht to try gene therapy, he wath thirty-three but he too died tragically before he wath thirty-four ath a result of the therapy itthelf. William, fifty-one he hath the record for longevity, Philip died at forty-four, death by hith own hand, he couldn't cope with either the mental or bodily degradation.

Thith ith a picture of one of their motherth, it took me a year to find it in the North Engle Archive."

An image flared into the air in front of them, it seemed to be part of a bigger picture but the focus of this picture was a woman in her mid to late fifties, dressed in a uniform emblazoned with two medals, she held a uniform cap under her arm.

Eleanor stood up and approached the three-dimensional display and examined the practically life like image. The quality amazed her. From her perspective it appeared to be taken from an old picture as it was crossed with an occasional crease and some of the colour seemed to have faded. "She looks like my grandmother, except that she wasn't in the police force. This lady is a superintendent, that's a couple of ranks above me. She must be a brave woman because that looks like the Queen's Gallantry Medal and that I think is an MBE – impressive!

"The medal, ith it a good thing?" Oo-neh asked trying to understand what she didn't yet know.

"Very much so, it is the third highest civilian honour I believe. She must be a very brave person, who is she?"

"My thixth timeth great grandmother." Oo-neh replied.

"That can't be right, two hundred years ago there was barely a police force, the uniform she is wearing isn't so different from that used today and the Gallantry Medal in this form didn't exist until the mid nineteen seventies. I'm sorry but your research is a bit up the spout there."

Oo-neh remained quiet for a moment, trying to decide her best course of action; she finger tipped the controls on her tablct, the image changed to show the full picture. The woman was flanked on her right by a young man appearing to be in his late twenties, on her left stood a woman holding an infant in her arms.

Eleanor's mouth almost fell open, "It's incredible, that young man could be Edward when he gets a bit older. Who are they really? They must be related to my family somehow or other."

The image on the screen split to show a family tree, Oo-neh pointed with her finger, and in a more rushed mode of speech than before she pointed out the names and her relationship with them. "Thith man Ioan ith my father, Enith my grandfather, Glyn my great-grandfather, Conrad my great-great-grandfather, William my three timeth great grandfather, William my four timeth great grandfather, Philip my five timeth great grandfather, Jameth my theven timeth great grandfather and finally the thon of the woman you jutht thaw, Edward ith my thix timeth-great grandfather." The image switched back to the group picture. "The woman in the picture hath her name written on the back with a date."

Once again the image changed, this time to a grubby grey white card. A black stamp at the top gave a photographer's details and set centrally beneath it was a hand-written notation and date. It read 'Superintendent Eleanor Maurice' and the day of her promotion.

"That ith a image of you, and that ith your thon Edward Clark, hith wife Clarith, and baby boy Philip."

"Oo-neh you are not making sense, it's not possible, and I'm not that old and have never been awarded any medals. Edward is too young and is not married." Eleanor turned perplexed to look at the girl.

Oo-neh stared straight back, "I wath born on the darketht day of the year in twenty-three-zero-four; thith picture will be taken fifteen yearth from now, pothibly."

"Possibly?" Eleanor queried, it being the only thing she could think of.

"I have changed Edward'th life and the future outcometh may change for him, but you might thtill get your medalth if they are good to have." Oo-neh smiled slightly brighter. "The girl in the picture ith a relative of the friend Edward ith currently meeting with, she ith two yearth younger than he ith."

"It's not possible Oo-neh, it really isn't." Eleanor voice was raised; she was trying to hang on to her own version of reality.

The picture switched back to the newly qualified Doctor of Genetics, "Look again, you thee the picture on the wall behind my father?" The image expanded showing the picture in greater detail.

"It's like the picture of the bridge at Barbridge, the one you gave Edward. Is it a copy?"

"No it ith the same picture," a second image flared next to the original one, "Thith ith the back of it."

To Eleanor the back had the look of age with faded stickers with some barely legible writing, then her mind flickered back to the art dealer and his experience with the girl, how she had insisted he check the catalogue number on the back with his records. She didn't understand at the time why it had been important beyond provenance, but now if what the girl was saying was true the numbers had to match. Or was she making it fit to support her story.

"My father will thell the picture a year or two after the image wath recorded, for a large amount of credit, he will never worry about money ever again, and with it he will create the Inthtitute of Evolving Geneticth."

"Do you want another drink?" Eleanor wanted some time to think.

From the kitchen, as she waited for the kettle to boil Eleanor looked back at the small young woman sitting and just gazing at the images in front of her. From the sad forlorn look she could make out, the police inspector deduced that Oo-neh was looking at images of someone close to her, possibly her parents. Eleanor shook her head; the girl looked so lost when she wasn't animated by discussion. What she wondered was what she was to make of it? Logically it made little sense, but why make it all up and in such detail? Then slowly her mind reflected over events that had brought her and the girl together, the weapons the agents had, the I.D. card shown to her. Were they in on this plot too? A plot, but with what goal? Then the way they had disappeared, how can anyone explain that unless this explanation was somehow true no matter how unbelievable. Then what about that wafer thin tracking display her son had shown her? What technology made that? Edward who was certainly up on such things had never heard of it. Finally the very device she was using to display the images; that really was the stuff of science fiction, not just the display method but the quality and sharpness of the image. And hadn't Oo-neh told Edward it was old technology. The girl at least believed it.

When she returned carrying a tray the police inspector saw her guest was as she suspected looking at the suspended images of a man and a red haired woman. One she knew was her father the other, a woman who looked so much like herself could only be Oo-neh's mother. She set the tray down quietly. "Are you alright?" she asked.

"I mith my home and father, I wish my mother wath here to tell me everything wath going to be alright." Tears rolled down her cheeks unheeded.

Sitting beside Oo-neh Eleanor placed an arm around the girl's narrow shoulders and pulled her closer, "Everything will work out Oo-neh, I find it always does eventually and sometimes in ways we least expect. They say it is always darkest before the dawn. Now dry your eyes, you don't want to look red eyed and puffy faced when Edward gets home."

Taking up the china tea-pot she started to pour the pale brown liquid into the matching cups. "Why can't you go home?" she toned her voice to sound curious rather than inquisitorial.

"There ith no way available now, what brought me here ith jutht a thmoking hole in the ground outthide Donderry. Even if it were pothible it would not be thafe for me to return.

Eleanor placed her hand lightly on Oo-neh's, "Why isn't it safe for you, what changed?"

"Everything, maybe nothing, I don't exitht." The girl said wiping her eyes inside the glasses.

"I'm sorry Oo-neh but I don't understand."

A new image flared into the air, a map. "That ith Engleire, my homeland," the fact Oo-neh changed the direction of the conversation was obvious.

"But that is The United Kingdom and Ireland."

"But it will become Engleire on the firtht of January twenty-two-forty-eight, a democratic republic with a Prethident and ruled by the military." Oo-neh replied.

"A police state - in England?" Eleanor said incredulously.

"A military thtate, one with lawth that prohibit the freedom of a perthon who hath no proper documentation, or one that will prohibit the exthithtance of any who fail the health regulation A10-BC."

"Eugenics by any other name," Eleanor observed, appalled to think it could happen in her country at any time.

"I will tell you from the beginning to give you contextht," Oo-neh replaced her handkerchief back into her pocket. "My mother wath born Margaret McLeod in Thcotia and graduated a Doctor of Biological Engineering, my father and she met at a convention where he read a paper on Evolutionary Redundanthy. They fell romantically in love, well I alwayth felt they loved each other very much. I imagine the chain of eventth that brought me here began with my mother having eight mithcarriageth in a row. No medic could give her a remedy, but what they did find wath a tumour on her brain. Treatment removed it, and then they tried again for a baby but thith time they determined on finding out why, if it ended in failure.

Five more mithcarriageth followed and they found out that the developing foetus wath making a protein that triggered a mathive antibody rethponthe. After that finding, my father put hith heirloom picture of the bridge up for auction to get him enough credit that would allow him to find a remedy. He told me that he wath beyond thpeechleth at the amount it fetched. It allowed him to buy the twenty-five thquare mileth of land, nearly all of it woodland, on which he built hith thentre of exthellenthe."

Another image floated in the air, showing what to Eleanor looked like a low two storey industrial building with a gently curving roof. It glistened in the daylight and appeared to be built entirely of glass. A lake could be seen on the left hand side and behind the main structure was woodland.

"It is very beautiful," Eleanor commented.

"Yeth it ith, my room ith the one with dark windowth," Oo-neh pointed it out energetically, "it hath a view over the lake and at night I would clear the Thilplexthigen above my bed and look up and thee the thtarth. It wath like I wath thleeping out in the open, but warmer and drier. My mother and father had a room nextht to mine at the rear. My mother and I would often take a blanket outthide and lay on the grath, jutht here and gaze up into infinity," she pointed to the lawned area behind the structure. " 'Oo-neh' my mother thaid to me, 'all thingth are pothible in thith world, all you have to do ith dream them.' The laboratory work and teaching roomth occupied the ground floor. A big metal fenthe went all around the land and my father had it dethignated a natural refuge. When I wath five they built the large Tholar Thea Array to generate energy, it wath an exthtenthion of the Man Barrage."

The map filled the image field again.

"That ith it here between the three islandth." She touched the tablet screen and the image sharpened and zoomed in to show more clearly what appeared to be a two laned road between the British mainland, the Isle of Man and the Northern Ireland coast.

"Is it just a road?" Eleanor asked peering closer as the image scaled up.

"No, along the whole length of the road, energy ith generated from lotth and lotth of tiny compression pumpth. Beneath the road are over one hundred turbineth that are driven by the incoming tide. The water flow coming in createth energy until high tide, when the vent to each generator ith shut, a hundred mileth thouth another thimilar barrage thitth, the incoming tide fillth the contained thea and at low tide when the water ith let out it createth more energy."

Eleanor could tell from the enthusiasm the young woman showed that she was more than happy to share what she knew, and it also showed her another side of the girl, a warm, happy, infectiously amusing personality. The image zoomed in further showing the long building with its reflective covering surrounded by woodland, and to the west she could see the solar collection arrays.

"What's this to the north and east?"

"That ith the training camp for new recruitth when they are called to join the military, after thixteen weekth they are appointed a plathe to therve for three yearth. They built it when I wath ten, an aquatic training camp wath added later with a big tank for deep water training."

"Conscription you mean, when everyone over a certain age has to join like it or not?"

"Yeth."

"Is that why you left, because you were called up?"

"No, they didn't know anything about me, which wath good. I wath thafe until they found out that I wath there without a record of my life."

"And they found out presumably?"

"Yeth, all becauthe of my father's camouflaged rodent. My mother alwayth told me that I should do nothing that I might regret in the future, she should have told him that." Oo-neh said without rancour. "Anyway my father found the active gene group that created the deadly protein production hidden away in the depth of the redundant gene pool. He turned it off, making it inactive which allowed my mother to have a perfect, really beautiful and very clever baby girl. That i'th what my mother told me anyway. 'Baby girl', she alwayth called me that, 'baby girl I loved you from the moment you opened your eyeth and I have never thtopped loving you. I could not have wished for a more beautiful daughter'. It wath probably at that moment my grandmother looked at me and ran away never to be heard of again.

My mother had her baby, my father had hith - the laboratory, all were happy. My mother called me Oo-neh againtht my father'th wisheth, she told me they had a frightful row about it, he lotht. She thaid he wath frightened I might not live and didn't want to get too attached, but I lived and gradually wore him down tho he came to love me ath much ath my mother I think."

Family images slipped into the air in front of them, from babyhood to young woman, her mother ceased being in the pictures for, as Eleanor had heard, she had died when Oo-neh was only eight.

"May I ask you a personal question?" Eleanor asked.

"Yeth it ith alright."

"You don't seem to have much hair in any of the images."

"No hair, never had any, never exthpected any, I'm am ath polished ath a sheet of Thilplexthigen."

"You've mentioned that before, what actually is it?"

"Thilplexthigen?" The image of the laboratory filled the airspace. "That building ith made of it, it ith a clear bendable five ply laminate, the top layer will let light through to the netht layer which ith made of a hundred micro volt generating thellth per thquare foot. The mid layer ith lattithed to add thtrength, the light getting through thtriketh the offthet fourth layer of more micro volt generating unitth. The fifth layer ith mirrored to reflect the light back up again, the top layer ith altho mirrored on the inner thurface to reflect light back until all it'th energy ith depleted. The fifth or bottom layer can be electro-actively coloured to darken a room to prevent people looking in or toned for ambienthe."

"High tech stuff then?"

"No, not really, it ith common enough, the really good type hath impact generation on the top layer to create energy from rain or even high windth. No point in using thuch material in thith building though, the woodland ith a barrier to the wind. Both typeth repel wet and dirt, it alwayth lookth polished, like my head. I only wear a wig to thtop people being dazzled by the glare. In truth I am a meth, no hair, eyeth that don't like bright light, I have bufferth in each ear and I talk funny not to mention a thkin condition which ith why I wear cotton gloveth all the time. I think my mother had wished for thomething better."

"I think your mother was very happy with the daughter she had. Do you know, all the people I spoke to during my investigations who met you, they all thought you were a really lovely girl? Mister Sinclaire at the gallery, I think he would even adopt you if he could. Alex likes you and so did your landlady Missus Wainscroft, so there's no need to think anything bad about yourself." Eleanor said by way of encouragement. "So how does the invisible rodent come into all this?"

"The war with the North African Federation wath the reathon thingth fell apart. It had been going on for eight yearth when the Europa Allianthe thtarted loothing ground. Rumourth thaid a meeting of the political hierarchy couldn't reach an agreement on how to thircumvent the outcome. Becauthe of thith political inability the military leadership entered into a thecret conclave. At that meeting, an unproven, undocumented, 'it never happened event', agreement wath made, to do the unthinkable. Shortly after the meeting that never took plathe Field General of the Allied Forthe, George Goth, who had more medalth than you could carry on a donkey, came to thee my father.

Enter the rodent; the paper he had written on how to create a camouflaged rodent wath read by Project leader Oberon Tyler-Wolfe. He had created the Drothophila Quinth two yearth before I wath born. Why he wanted to let everyone know he wathn't competent at gene manipulation ith a wonder. One failed exthperiment would have been enough, but five? Anyway he worked for the military in their covert technology unit, it wath he that brought my father to the attention of the General.

The Field General athked my father hypothetically whether it wath pothible to create a viruth that killed rapidly but left no trathe and had a defined life thpan."

"The agents said your father had created such a virus for terrorist reasons."

"No, it wath the military who athked for it, they needed to find a way to put the North African Federation down, conventional meanth were failing. It goeth without mentioning that Tyler-Wolfe wathn't up to the tathk."

"Was it legal?"

"No, not in any jurithdiction, the application of viral or bacterial agentth in warfare had been banned for a long time; any country that applied them would thuffer huge legal and financial penaltieth."

"Hence the secrecy; did your father do it?" Eleanor probed further.

"For the love he had for hith country not to mention the opportunity it prethented for funding and future thecurity, he did. It took two yearth to develop a variant of an avian flu viruth that could replicate at a rapid enough rate, be highly contagiouth and have a life thpan of three dayth before it destroyed itthelf. It worked by over-whelming the body'th natural immune reaction then it targeted the oxygen uptake of the body, many would die from heart attackth before they thuffocated. All that had to be done wath infect ath many people by direct injection into the blood thtream ath could be managed in three dayth. Military people were a priority target."

"Was it ever used?" Eleanor asked soberly - already knowing the answer.

"Oh yeth, the Alliance wath failing, a total defeat wath only two monthth away by thith time, they had little choithe if their way of life wath to continue."

"Did the war end, and if so with what casualties?"

Oo-neh was silent for a moment before answering; to Eleanor she seemed to be reliving the events. When she spoke the earlier bouncy enthusiasm had gone leaving behind a more sombre, sadder tone to her voice. "A week after the initial infection the war ended, although there are no firm figureth, it ith thought thirty-eight million died in one week, fifty million in ten weekth. The army of the NAF died, fighting came to an end. An invethtigation by the International Counthil could not find out how the outbreak began but that wath a long time after, with all the corrupt dead there were other pathogenic outbreakth that mathked the original event."

Eleanor was silent; death on such a scale was unthinkable, especially as a weapon of war. She couldn't help asking, "Was your father proud of what he'd done?"

"No, he wath very quiet for a week or tho after that, I think the numberth even bothered him. However I believe he thaw it ath the better of two evilth ath it became an introduction to what eventually led me here."

"Oh! And how did that come about?"

"Thince the development of the viruth had to be beyond thecret, before my father began work, the military checked all recorded documentation they had on every member of the laboratory workforthe, ath I had no thuch documentation I didn't exthitht. They needed to know who I wath and why I had no record of birth or life thereafter, I could be a thpy."

"Do you mean the State kept records on every person?"

"Yeth, from the moment you are born your whole life ith recorded, it ith the law. The birth of a child mutht be recorded, and the baby mutht be medically exthamined even if the child dieth. At pre-ordained timeth there hath to be further medical exthamination to declare the child capable of proper development and capable of living a full independent life."

"And if they can't?"

"They are removed from the family, freeze dried, crushed before being taken to the organic digethterth. There the remainth are fermented to generate gatheth to drive the turbineth which create energy. It ith what happenth to all the dead after due theremony and if you want you can convert part of the remainth to fairy dutht."

Oo-neh put her hand inside her blouse top and removed a clear phial, in the light it sparkled. "It'th really diamond dutht, you can have a little gem if you want, to put it into a ring, my father had a big one but I wanted the dutht." She held it out for Eleanor to see the twinkling particles before slipping it once more out of sight. "It ith my mother, I like to think the little thparkleth are her life forthe still with me."

"I'm sure she's watching over you right now."

"She told me before she died, that if it were pothible she would be with me, but if not she would go to thothe who had gone before where I would meet her in time. Do you think that ith pothible, I am with my anthethtorth now?"

"Truthfully I don't really know but I like to think there is more to life than what we sense around us and I have had some strange experiences which give me room to hope." Eleanor smiled, "Now going back a bit, are there no people with disabilities in your time?"

"Oh Yeth, the war hath made many men and women dithabled, but none are allowed to be born that way. There ith a guide that mutht be followed, any child with a genetic abnormality mutht go to the freezer, they don't want them pathing on to the nextht generation."

"How did your father survive, his illness is genetic, isn't it?"

"Yeth, but the cauthe wath hidden in the redundancy gene pool, not much ith known for sure about the conthequentheth of thothe geneth. Anyway he wath a healthy baby, it would only be in later life that it would it become a problem, too late by law to freeze him."

"I don't think I like the sound of your society Oo-neh. I gather then that your parents didn't register your birth."

"No, I think they were frightened they would lothe me ath I wath the result of genetic manipulation, which ordinarily ith banned in people."

"So your parents committed a crime to make it possible for you to be born and then risked losing you if the authorities found your genes had been altered. That's awful, but how did Tyler whatever his name was; get away with creating those agents?"

"He worked for the military, he created weaponth, they were not regarded ath people, they were an exthperiment to be got rid of if they didn't perform to a required ability level, their liveth were not their own. They co-opted my father to the Prometheuth Team to thee if he could correct the glaring problemth they had, but that wath after he created the viruth."

"Let's take a break shall we, have something to eat. While I do that I'll put some music on, I think you might like it. Just relax, I can manage." Before slipping into the kitchen Eleanor placed a CD into the player's drive and pressed the play button. She smiled as the song came to the chorus line for she could hear her guest singing out, 'I love the night, I love the night, I love the element of danger and to feel pure delight'. Back to her happier self it seems Eleanor thought, at least for the moment.

When she returned Eleanor found her guest half surrounded by the whitish glow of the tablets projection screen, every now and then an arm was raised and a finger pointed. Other movements suggested Oo-neh was dancing, her hip moved sideways, an arm shot up extending fingers cutting the air before a rotation and finally ending with an arched back and a high kick. The inspector could not be other than impressed; she wished she had that kind of flexibility.

"Oo-neh?" she called out. The light vanished. "Just help yourself to whatever you like." Placing the tray of sandwiches down onto the table Eleanor left to bring in the drinks. "What was that, a dance app?"

"No, it ith a military program that ith for training in fighting methodth, it hath a large choithe of terrain and townthcapeth. You begin by learning how to move fluidly before learning the bathic moveth of attack and countering. When you have acquired a good rating you move onto one-to-one fighting before competing againtht larger numberth. The higher your rating the harder it becometh. When you have a very high athethment you move to random variationth in topography and thituationth requiring good tactical thkillth. The pothiblitieth are huge."

"But you weren't in the army, were you?"

"No, they have to know you are alive before they give you the honour of dying for your country. I was given the unit ath a gift from Military Invethtigator Lieutenant-Captain Eric Gibb, he wath very kind, he ith now a Captain-Major and often tellth me how he ith progrething. I don't think he hath a family, tho I am like hith little thithter, which ith good. I think he knowth I am unrecorded, he will have checked."

"Well I must admit I haven't seen anything like it." As Eleanor continued to listen, her younger guest became more than enthusiastic as she described her tablet.

"Thith one ith nine yearth old, tho it ith out of date technologically but with a guaranteed life of thirty yearth, it hath many yearth of uthe yet. It ith a DL-104MG, diamond lattithe memory, nine kilo-yotta byte active protething with a tera-yotta lattithe – thecond generation, that'th enough to record the life of the whole population of Engleire for two hundred yearth. It ith military issue only, I shouldn't have it really but I helped Military Invethtigator Lieutenant-Captain Eric Gibb tholve a murder involving the military. You can have a go if you want to."

"That's very nice of you but I can't fight, at least not in a combative way."

Seemingly insistent of getting Eleanor to take part Oo-neh continued, "I have another one which ith very good, no fighting. It ith thet in an urban environment, you can choothe where you begin or you are put thomewhere at random and you have to take note of what ith around you in a timed period. At the end you'll be athked to report what you have theen, it might be the number or type of red thingth, how many people with a mathk. You can do that, it'th really, really not difficult."

"To you maybe, but I'll give it a go after we've eaten, as long as you don't laugh at my efforts." After a moment of reflection Eleanor continued, "How old are you Oo-neh? You could pass for a twelve year old if dressed right but sometimes you act like someone in their early twenties."

"On my latht birth thelebration I wath eighteen but when I arrived here it wath nearly four month out of thync with home, pluth three hundred yearth or tho."

"You must tell me more about that, I mean things must be so very different, it would be like me going back to the Elizabethan period. I know you were in Northern Ireland six months ago, but how long have you actually been here." As soon as she asked the question Eleanor realised that she was accepting the girl's story that she was from the future as being true.

"I arrived jutht over a year ago in a boggy field full of rabbitth outside of Donderry, that'th where they built Project RoToth. That will be information for them ath they weren't sure whether there would be thpacial dithtortion. All the crythtalth that are worn are locked to that primary location. It would track wherever you went from there."

"Pause there, what actually is this Project RoTos, what does it do?"

"It thtarted out ath a theoretical idea by Project Leader Dioth who ith captivated by the idea of time travel, he wanted to prove the nature of time. Wath it linear, where time moveth ever forward from patht to future. There are thothe who believe that all time ith now, the patht and the future happening together, while otherth think that there are infinite time thtreamth where the infinity of every pothible outcome will lead to different and infinite futureth. Another belief thythtem ith where time ith but an illusion where life ith like a dream and happenth in literally no time. Dioth wanted to know if going back in time wath pothible and if tho, could he watch hithtory unfold.

After pleading hith theoretical idea he wath allowed fundth to build a prototype. The actual thing ith made up of two rotating thircular plathma fieldth, mounted one above the other but offthet with one rotating in the oppothite direction to the other. Seen from above it lookth just like a staring eye. The whole thing ith unthtable, held in plathe by a powerful magnetic field; it ith the 'eye' through which you travel to get here. Being here ith not the problem it ith the when, even to Project Leader Dioth it wath an educated thtab in the dark. He worked out the recovery mapping with rodentth, but that told him only that he could get them back - not where they'd been or when. Hith thpotty rabbit wath a breakthrough, off it went and then wath recovered in fifteen minuteth, which wath good. What Dioth didn't exthpect to find wath the bonny giving birth two dayth later, it wathn't pregnant when it left. That meant the rabbit had been wherever for thirty-two dayth minimum during the period Dioth measured ath fifteen minuteth from going to recovery. He didn't know for thertain whether it wath thome kind of time dilation or exthpansion and the rabbit wath thpatially only in a field a mile away? Truth to tell a lot of hith little bonny'th didn't come back, thome did, but in bitth, having been attacked by an animal. DNA tethting showed it belonged to the dog family."

"It sounds more than a risky enterprise to me, so how did you get involved?"

"My father thought it wath a great idea."

"Your father, was he mad?" Eleanor sounded disbelievingly surprised, "The man who designed the camouflaged mouse? I hope you'll forgive me saying so but it doesn't sound like a good idea. Why on earth would he put your life so much at risk?"

"My father loveth me, all he wanted wath to put me in a plathe of thafety."

"I can think of a great many less hazardous solutions."

"Perhapth, but none that would work in the world I left behind. My mother left me a methage in the event of it being found that I wath not on record, she believed it wath inevitable. Do you want to thee it?"

"I don't know, it's private, but will I understand the language?"

"You can underthtand me, can't you?"

"With difficulty sometimes, the way you talk is more like you are speaking syllables rather than words. Then it's not like the language of the word you call me, maw-her-vhor, is it?"

"No, that's Thcotian, the language of my mother'th people, it ith my firtht language but it ith not uthed much in the broad population." Taking the tablet up, with her left index finger she slid the pages up, across, then down in the index system, before selecting a file. "My father gave it to me when it wath clear the authoritieth knew I had no recorded life."

The air filled with the figure of a woman; if life-size she stood about five feet ten inches tall, and of medium build. The similarities between the woman and Eleanor herself were not lost on the detective but with the one exception, Oo-neh's mother had naturally red hair. It seemed as though she was there in the room with them, the detail was frighteningly good.

"Hello my baby girl. How you must hate me saying that today; I imagine you're all grown up and a beautiful young woman by now."

The voice was soft and slightly husky and most certainly accented to Eleanor's ears, although the language was plainly English there was a different accentuation to the expression of the words. The vision was dressed in a plain green flowing dress cut in a style unfamiliar to her, the detective thought she looked tired but was doing her best not to look it.

"How I wish I was there to see you, to hold you, to see your funny little smile and to hear about all the things you've been doing. But alas I cannot be. I have thought long and hard what to say to you in this record I just hope it helps you. When we last met you were still so very young and even with your learning ability I doubt you would have really understood what I am going to say now. Anyway sweetheart your father will have given you this because he believes that the authorities will have discovered, or be close to discovering the fact that they have no records of your life. Something I hope your father will have explained to you before now. Although the administration of Engleire may have changed in the time between the time I speak from, and the day you are listening, which I doubt, I must prepare you for the worst of cases. Because there is no record of your existence there will be an enquiry and your father will have to explain why you weren't registered soon after your birth. I wish I knew for certain what the outcome would be but I feel that if they apply a strict reading of the law as it stands today they could seek your destruction.

Your father could of course appeal to the courts but even so the outcome is uncertain. Truly my baby I hope I am wrong, I hope things have changed, but I must guide you the best I can. That is why I hope you have done all I asked of you when we last spoke, you are my baby girl and you are so much better than the others. That you can and will survive I have no doubts, but you must do whatever it takes to get away from Engleire. Other States do not have the same strict regime, all you will need is an identity card for most countries, your father will organise that for you. He will try to get you passage on one of the Shuttle Skifs that have regular journeys to Scandia which you may find a bit cold but it will only be a stop-over. A better choice for you will be the Free States of Candadia. I have an aunt there, she has four children and I'm sure she will help you even if it's just to annoy my mother. Failing those options try to gain passage to the Australis Republic, but you will need to keep up to date with political developments as to which places you should avoid, things can change so rapidly.

I wish I could be there with you baby girl, I am trying to imagine what you will be like all grown up, hopefully you'll be a confident modern young woman. Alas I cannot picture you, for I don't know how old you are as you watch this. I have chosen to speak in the Standard language because I don't know if you have kept up with the language of my forefathers. All I would ask of you is to be calm, that way you can use your mind to work things out, and there will be a solution - there always is. Try and make yourself a valuable commodity to the State, it will help your case. After all if they can give documents to those psychopaths - the Drosophila Quins there is no reason why you shouldn't have one too. Whatever you chose, I will be with you in spirit. Don't worry about your father, as you will know by now his illness will end his life around fifty, unless he has found a cure. So you must get things sorted out before you lose his protection, either by gaining citizenship or leaving the country. If everything fails and you run out of options you must ask your grandmother for help, once she sees how grown up and polite you are, I'm sure she'll help you.

I love you Oo-neh, I always have and I always will, you were the best thing I ever had in my life, even better than your father; you were all I ever dreamed of. I know we went against the law to make you happen but I had to have a child. Yes I admit it may be have been selfish of me, and yes perhaps we should have registered you, but the thought of holding you, only to lose you again would have been unbearable.

Now listen to my last words and always imagine me saying them to you if you ever doubt what you must do. Do what you can, then do what you must to survive with my love and blessing."

The spectre kissed her curled fingers before extending them forward, and then the image faded leaving the room darker and more silent than before.

Eleanor felt a little choked up as she saw in the corner of her eye, Oo-neh kiss her own fingers and stretch them out.

Then without warning Oo-neh jumped up and put a dining chair in the middle of the floor.

"Come and thit here, it will be like riding on an open shuttle."

"What?" said Eleanor slightly disorientated from the sudden switch in events.

"The game! You thaid you would try it. I'll put it on the really, really thimple level."

Once seated Eleanor waited for a few seconds when she was suddenly surrounded by a cityscape, unlike any place she had ever seen. She couldn't help gasping. From her right peripheral view to that of her left eye all she could see were glass faced structures, or more likely she corrected herself - Silplexigen, the energy generating laminate. The buildings all looked new, no hint of any historical edifices, but equally no gaudy shop signs. She wondered if this clean urban setting was real or just a construct for the game play.

"Is this a real place?" she eventually asked.

"Oh yeth, it ith the capital thity of Engleire. That ith how it lookth in all the pictureth I have theen."

"You've never been?"

"No, I had never travelled beyond the perimeter of the Inthtitute land, but for one week five monthth before I left for good."

Eleanor thought about that for a moment before it fully registered what had been said.

"Are you saying you never went anywhere in eighteen years? No holidays, no visits to relatives?"

"No, why would I, everything I needed wath in my home. There were few living relativeth nearby that I know of, and the majority live abroad. Without documentation, travel wath out of the quethtion. Many thingth are different when compared to here, ath you will thee there are no private vehicleth in the view, that ith because none are allowed within any urban area. You will thee there ith a very efficient shuttle. It'th good, in fact you will ride on it. Now you mutht look carefully for children in red clothing, they can be either thide of you. The journey ith not fatht only three mileth per hour, you have three haltth along the way, are you ready?"

"No," Eleanor said honestly as the view started to move in what appeared to be real time. Initially she knew she was tensed up but gradually as events moved on she started to relax as though she really was travelling. At the end she didn't need telling how poorly she had done.

"It's absolutely amazing; you really feel you're there, London looks so different from today."

"It doeth, but that'th not London."

"I thought you said it was the capital."

"I did, but London theathed to be the capital in twenty-two hundred and ten, the new one wath built on what ith currently called Warrington. It ith in the North of Engleire, better thentred more thecure."

"On, you said it was built on?" Eleanor queried.

"Yeth, I believe it wath cleared entirely away for twenty thquare mileth and redeveloped."

"Why?" The whole idea of a town being levelled to build a new capital was hardly democratic, but then she reminded herself, the future United Kingdom plus Eire was not seemingly a democratic place.

"It wath decided to move the capital to where your enemieth couldn't get to it tho eathily, and there wath a lot of flooding that could not be managed. Your London ith a military bathe for the protection of the thouthern border as ith Brithtol. Do you want another try?"

"Yes, and now I have the idea I shall do much better."

An hour passed in no time at all as Eleanor made attempt after attempt to improve her rating until finally, after many hilarious denials and excuses both of them collapsed onto the settee.

"Maw-hesh that wath truly awful," Oo-neh said between giggles.

"I wasn't that bad, I got better, and improvement is always good. So don't go calling me names."

"I didn't."

"Then what does Maw-hesh mean young lady if it is not to ridicule me?"

"Did I thay that? Thorry it wath a thlip of the tongue, I wathn't thinking," Oo-neh sounded surprised.

"That's alright, so what does it mean, if it is not so very rude?" Eleanor asked starting to become intrigued.

"No, it ith not unpleathant, but I should not have uthed it, thorry."

"Then it shouldn't be hard for you to tell me its meaning, should it?"

"Mother, it meanth mother," Oo-neh said at last her lips losing whatever little smile she had left.

A silence hung momentarily over them before Eleanor finally spoke, "Then I take it as the highest of compliments. Your mother would be really proud of you Oo-neh, I mean that. I expect you have become everything she would have wished for, I'm sorry it never worked out for both of you."

As though nothing had happened Oo-neh suddenly switched the conversation back to the earlier topic. "The great idea my father had revolved around two thingth, the need for thecrethy and the need to know. He told me the plan and what he intended to thay to the Field General when he came calling. He would admit to making thmall changeth to my DNA tho that he and my mother could have a child, he didn't engineer a girl - that wath good luck. He would go on to point out the many advantageth of having an intelligent, loyal thitizen, who didn't exthitht. I could do thingth that were entirely deniable if I wath caught."

"Do you mean make you into some sort of spy?"

"Not quite, but he wath following my mother'th idea, that of making me a great benefit to the Military, tho that I wouldn't be immediately taken to the freezerth. It would altho give a time of reflection until other opportunitieth prethented themthelveth. In fact my father wath already thinking about Project RoToth, becauthe each exthperiment tho far involved little uncommunicative animalth."

"Do you mean your father was considering using you as a guinea pig?"

"No, they only uthed mithe and rabbitth in the early trialth, not a guinea pig in view they are far too twitchy."

"Okay no guinea pigs, so he was volunteering you as a test subject. Why not use pre-programmed robots, or cameras on the animals?" queried Eleanor, thinking it seemed the obvious step.

"They did, the camerath tended to have good imageth of grath and undergrowth and rabbitth running away when anyone came by, but no man-made thingth. The initial little robot they thent wath mobile but when it wath recovered it wath in a flattened thtate. Project leader Dioth had no idea what had befallen it. The one that followed, from the recording theemed to have been found by a child, ath the imageth after a period of darkneth showed a room coloured pink. The unit may have been on a shelf ath it manoeuvred and filmed the dethent at which point it wath recovered."

"So they wanted to scale up with a more reliable guinea pig?"

"Yeth they wanted a better way of viewing, but no guinea pig wath ever thought of."

"No, no Oo-neh, I mean a guinea pig in this sense is a person to take the part of an animal in an experiment."

"Not then, my father hadn't suggethted it, they were trying to think of a new idea, ath they had proven that they could thend and recover living tetht animalth. They were not sure of where or when they had been thent to."

"I think," Eleanor said after a bit of thought, "before you lose me completely, I know the sequence of events that led you here - stop me if I'm wrong. Now your father was asked to develop a virus to infect the North African States with who you were at war." A serious little face nodded agreement in her direction. "And, as a result of that a security sweep would be done on all the people in or around the compound. Presumably they discovered you weren't officially in existence which led to what?"

"I had been my father's helper and rethearcher for a year or two; he pleaded the cathe that to do what wath required he needed thomeone beyond reproach and who knew how to keep quiet about the work. That argument wath acthepted but the compound would from that moment be part of the military camp. I wath not allowed to leave, but ath I had lived my whole life there it wath not a problem. We made the viruth eventually, and the next talking point wath about it'th delivery.

It had been conthtructed to be pathed on by both contact and airborne inhalation, but the initial infection had to be by direct injection ath it wath by far the motht effective way to trigger an epidemic. It wath thought a good idea to thend the Drothophila Quinth to five different locations in one night. My father vetoed that idea ath he didn't think they were that bright or reliable."

"Do you mean because he thought like your mother, that they were psychopaths?"

"Partly, they were with time becoming more unbalanthed which could lead to them being captured and should they get caught there would be an almighty thtink. At thith point he put forward my name claiming I knew the viruth and how it should be adminithtered without any further training. If I got caught, which he felt wath very unlikely, ath being little I offered no threat and would be over-looked."

"And you could probably beat the crap out of anyone that tried, I imagine. Don't look like that Oo-neh; I saw what you did to Oh-Five, probably worse to Oh-Four. Not to mention the one in the swimming pool in Northern Ireland, so I know it is within your capability. Having said that you do look the least unlikely fighter I've ever met."

"I wath totally deniable, even if they checked every available record, including finger printing, eye thcan data, fathial recognition, and gait recognition. I didn't exitht. The military liked the idea; if thingth went wrong they could deny all knowledge of me and be thafe from a perthonal chilly end and an International outcry."

"How did you feel about it? You knew what the potential results of spreading the virus would be."

"It wath a way for me to be thafe, the NFA would not be a benefactor to any if they defeated the Allianthe. Although you may think the military of Engleire regime ith harsh, they do in fact act according to democratic lawth. Thethe are created by the one hundred elected memberth of the Counthil of the People. They are there to protect the whole population from harm. The NFA have no regard to rightth in law or otherwithe, if they won the war my life would be over in a very unpleathant way, ath I do not accord to natural life."

"Surely not," Eleanor was aghast. "Are there no International rules in warfare?"

"The doctrine of the NFA thayth if it ith right according to the law of their God that I should be born then it mutht be naturally. If it ith with the tampering of man it ith unnatural. That part of their belief ith applicable to anyone that requires any medical technique to get pregnant, it ith to be the natural way or not at all. If I prevent the NFA from winning I do not get burnt to death, the military are grateful and they don't freeze me and I have more time to plan my get away."

Oo-neh went on to tell Eleanor the details of how, under military escort, she was taken first to one of the Medi States, where her presence was neither acknowledged nor recorded. Her escort did not relate to her except for communicating the next night's schedule. She ate and slept alone in a locked room with only the bare essentials, it was her first journey away from home and all she knew. Each night thereafter when the dark descended she was taken to the departure point, given a satchel containing the phials of the infectious agent, from that point on it was her responsibility. Her briefing had included a list of what was considered to be the priority targets, mostly military or medical personnel. The first target site was the western most state, each night they would move easterly until the virus had been spread evenly across the North African lands.

"Weren't they worried you'd run for it or ask for asylum and report the plan?" asked Eleanor.

"Athylum in the NFA, are you mad? Anyone who thought that a good idea should be put in an athylum becauthe the NFA government do not protect their own people, foreignerth have no chanthe. No, there would be nowhere to run to and beyond doubt no protection under law for an enemy combatant. The combat team accompanying me knew where I wath, they had my tracking signal if I should need help."

"Ah, I wondered why you had that in your leg." Eleanor said as another piece fell into place.

"The military didn't put it in, my mother did, she didn't want me to get lotht. When I wath little I went out into the woodth at night, when she found my bed empty she wath really worried. I wath in a glade in the woodland when they found me, my mother gave me a telling off but I wath too mad to lithen."

"Mad, Why?"

"All the noithe they were making frightened all the rabbitth I wath watching, it made them run away. It took them hourth to find me, that'th why they put the tracker in. My mother told me much later it wath to make sure I never got lotht and they would alwayth know where I could be found for my own thafety."

"I imagine she loved you too much to risk losing you, especially after the difficulties she'd had getting a child."

A brief silence followed before Oo-neh continued to relate the events that took place in North Africa, how she was nearly caught on six separate occasions but managed to slip away into the shadows. Finally, duty done, she was transferred back to the only place she knew well, her home.

"What would have happened if you'd been exposed to the virus?"

"My father had checked me for any vulnerability, I had never been ill, and then he gave me the thterile form to allow my body to know it and be prepared, jutht in cathe."

"Was that the same one you gave Edward?"

"Thimilar, but the one I gave him acted ath a carrier vector to deliver the agent that would rectify hith faulty gene."

"So you knew what would happen once you'd given him it?"

"Oh yeth, it had been well tethted. My father even thought of giving the live version to the military around uth, to give me a way of ethcape if thingth turned out badly."

"You are joking?" said Eleanor surprised that the possibility was even considered.

"No, it wath an option, he would do anything to make sure I wath away from harm before he died. The life of my father wath coming to an end that I should live wath a priority in his mind regardless of the prithe?"

"He must have loved you very much too even consider such a thing, either that or you're both a pair of psychopaths."

"He loved me I have no doubt, he once told me that bringing me up had been a great joy."

"But weren't you frightened? I mean being alone in a foreign country on a war footing, at night, when the risks of being caught must have been high."

"Not really, it wath very dark, artificial light wath banned becauthe of the night raiding aerial craft. The NFA kept their illumination off or showing dark red or blue lighting only and I jutht love the night."

"Why?"

"The night ith quieter, you may not underthtand but for me the dark offerth freedom to unwind, daylight ith too rich and I like to get away from people. To lay with the bonnieth in a moonlit glade and watch the ever changing infinity overhead, then to feel the early morning dew clinging to my thkin."

"Yes that is something I can empathise with, but what's a bonny, you've mentioned them before?"

"A bonny ith a little rabbit, we had a great many of them in the woodland. The night ith my friend, the night will hide me and never betray me, I can move and act freely, be thomeone I can't be in the day."

"What happened when you returned home?"

"Everybody waited for the outcome; they didn't wait long before an initial report arrived. After a week, in which time the military had collated the data, I think even they were appalled. The death toll wath eventually recorded ath ninety-four point three perthent of the population, the North Aftrican Federation wath a wathteland. Neighbouring countrieth evacuated the borderland between them and the infection. Eventually the Allianthe non-military population became aware of it and although relieved the war wath over there wath a movement to aid the living and remove the dead. Thith was one event that nobody wanted to talk about or admit being a part of. Nobody worked out what had happened, it could have been an airborne pathogen of avian flu origin but after a week there wath not enough intact DNA to make a definitive claim."

"How did you feel about that?"

Oo-neh paused before she answered, "I didn't know them, they had no meaning in my life and they had too many dogth. I don't like dogth. All I have ever known are the people in the compound; they are all that had been important in my life, notably my mother and father who thought only to protect me. Everybody elthe would lay me in the chillerth or burn me."

"I imagine the military were pleased with you though."

"They were happy with the outcome naturally but that brought another problem. If it ever came out that I had delivered the viruth that had created the enormouth death toll I would be arrethted and charged with any number of international death penalty offentheth. Equally I would be a national heroine for ending the war that had killed ten million tholdierth from all the allied countrieth. The Government might like the latter but not the former tho getting rid of me wath thtill an option. Enter the thecond part of my father's plan, Project RoToth."

"Which was?"

"My father had a meeting with the military hierarchy, tho he told me later, in private. At the meeting he pointed out that they needed him to rectify the problem they had with their Drothophila Quinth. It had been made clear that a shot in the head would make that particular problem go away but my father, although agreeing, pointed out that it would not tell them why the problem occurred. If the program wath to be continued then the error in the DNA coding would have to be found. He went on to tell them that while he had every thympathy with their problem he wath not going to let them take hith daughter away for recycling."

"He must have been very brave or sure of his ground?"

"He wath raving mad; he wath blackmailing them, he knew it, and they knew it. After all having all the detailed record of the NFA infection revealed wath not appealing. He even went further to tell them that all would be revealed globally unleth my father operated a coding key at regular intervalth. He can be very believable when he wantth to be, after all people believed in the undoubted merit of hith camouflaged rodent. Anyway ath part of the gambit he put forward the idea that I would be ideal to be the firtht living heroine to travel on Project RoToth. I wath highly intelligent, extraordinarily funny, I could think fathter than motht rabbitth and therefore take full advantage of every event. Not to mention being articulate and very gifted in uthing technology. Ideal in fact, and should I die horribly by being torn apart by the plathma field it would thave money cooling the freezer. My father knew the people in front of him, vain, arrogant and gullible."

"Your father said all that?"

"Well maybe not the part about me being brilliant in every way, but he would have done if athked."

Eleanor smiled; this girl, who she had at first thought of as very serious, had during their time together shown this lighter funnier side of her character. She liked her very much. "Brilliant but not modest it seems."

"What ith modetht?"

"Well, we say someone is modest when they don't shout about how brilliant they are."

"Ith modetht good?"

"Can be if it's not false modesty."

"Then it'th good I'm modetht about how brilliant I am, I tell nobody."

Eleanor shook her head, "You are funny, but you have to admit it was a very big, not to say enormous risk?"

"The rabbit made it, well the one with baby bonnieth did. They would never let me be free onthe they really thtarted looking into my patht."

For the rest of the time Oo-neh outlined the induction she had had regarding Project RoTos. They couldn't tell her what she would experience because the rabbit hadn't told them but they reassuringly pointed out that the rabbit hadn't suffered anything deleterious as far as could be ascertained. Most of all it was instilled in her what she above all mustn't do, 'DO NOT DO ANYTHING THAT WOULD CHANGE THE STATUS QUO'.

"What was that warning about?" asked Eleanor.

"Well, becauthe they had no real idea what Time wath, jutht theorieth. They were worried about the outcome if anything got changed. For example if I killed a flea, I might prevent a global epidemic that would wipe out half the population of the world."

"Would that be a bad thing?"

"No, not in that example but what if it had been a wathp that would have gone on, had it lived, to thting a killer who wath trying to murder a good politician. The wathp attack made him fail and he got caught, in that event many other targetth would live on. By killing the inthect the killer ith not attacked and the good man ith killed thereby making way for a ruthleth dictator."

"How could you ever know the consequences of one simple act?"

"You can't, that ith the problem and why there should be no interaction at all. I wath only suppothed to arrive here, look about, record as much as I could before I wath recovered."

"But you changed something, that was your intention; you said that was why you were here?" Eleanor pointed out the flaw in Oo-neh's ruling.

"I came to prevent my father and his forebearth becoming ill, to thtop him dying young, but primarily to be in a hidden away plathe where they couldn't get at me."

"But if there are consequences of minor changes what consequences will occur as a result of what you did to Edward? Wouldn't those changes, which are quite big compared to a wasp, have huge ramifications?"

"Yeth, it meanth that the moment Edward'th faulty gene wath altered the whole of time up to my coming here would be re-written, it will be different. Even the man who will be your fifth generation grandchild will not be my father; the man I knew will be gone forever but the one who liveth will not be ill."

"How do you know these changes will be good?" Eleanor queried.

"I have no idea, how ith good and bad meathured? It will change Edward Clark'th view on life ath he will not thuffer recurrent ill health, and he will not be tho limited. How he will be different from the Edward he would have been, I do not know. Only hithtory will record whether he ith good or bad. What may be of interetht ith that hith attitudeth may be different and lead him in different directions, which may be better or may not when compared to what might have been. However nobody will ever know. Ath the change flowth down each generation the perthon born ath your five timeth great-grandthon will not carry the faulty gene and he may go on to do greater thingth."

"And you may never be asked to go to Africa."

"There may be no war but in all probability I will never be born."

"Why on earth not?"

"My father thtudied in the field of geneticth becauthe of hith genetic condition he wath driven to look for a cure. Without that drive he may never have bothered with the topic but become a painter. Therefore he would not manipulate my DNA making it pothible for me to be born. He may never know the woman who wath my mother."

"But, but that would mean you would never come here to change Edward's genes, so how can you be here now?"

"It'th a paradox, hithtory may record that Edward grew out of hith condition and there never wath a genetic problem. Depending upon who you want to believe, time will be re-written with each day or each moment that goeth by, in which event I will be long dead before my life ith over-written. If time re-writeth rapidly I shall thimply theathe to be, you will not remember me, and nothing I have touched will bear my mark. It could be minuteth, it could be dayth, I do not know."

"That's awful."

"Ith it? If I thtop being I shall never know, there will be no memory of my life. I shall never know the love of my mother and I shall never thee her again in the after-world. I never will have been."

A tear slipped silently from beneath Oo-neh's glasses.

Eleanor was appalled at the idea; she wrapped her arms around the little girl and held her tight. "People don't just cease to be sweetheart, they just don't, people have lives, and they have memories. I can't believe all that can be re-written away like some computer program. You are so very real as I hold you, so physically here."

"But that ith what will happen if time ith linear from patht to prethent to future. I have made a big change, the future will not be ath I lived it."

"But you said yourself it is only theory, nobody really knows. What would have happened if you had broken your crystal thing and been recovered after you'd done your job? What about Oh-Four and Oh-Five were they recovered safely? Because if the future you left no longer exists what has happened to them. What about Project RoTos was it ever made in the new future? Oo-neh we have no way of knowing. Please for your own happiness live each day, if you don't, you will always be unhappy, always expecting what might never be. We all live in expectation of dying one day, none of us know how or when, but you can't live life worrying about it. Now come on dry those tears because you might be in the ever present now, no past, no future. Or you might even have side slipped into another time line where you live a long life, marry and have lots of children. Can you be certain where or when you are exactly?"

"No," Oo-neh said wiping away a residual tear. "but it will be unlikely I will find thomeone who will love me and each and every fault I have. Nor will I ever have children."

"You don't know that sweetheart, things can happen that often surprise us, and you certainly did. So enjoy life, wherever you are is right for you at that moment. I know things are very different from what you are used to, but I imagine you'd have felt the same when you had gone out into the wide world in your own time. New things can often be intimidating but you'll settle down now since nobody is hunting you, that is unless they send some more agents."

"They won't, even if time ith thlow to re-write, fifteen thecondth or tho after Oh-Four wath recovered Project RoToth rapidly became a smoking hole in the ground. Neither I nor my father wanted a never ending purthuit. I am free now, free within my own limiting frame of mind, free for ath long ath I exthist."

"Free with limits?" queried Eleanor.

"Free to go and do ath I like but I will alwayth be a prithoner of what I am."

"Well I don't think it will ever occur to people to ask where you originated; I think those that even care will think you are just a moderately modest brilliant, extraordinarily funny, clever, polite and shy young woman who is good at researching things. So what was it like when you arrived here, for you I mean?"

"Are you making fun of me?" Oo-neh asked seriously.

"I only speak what is true. So tell me how we appeared to you."

"It wathn't very bad ath I had examined the archiveth for half a year before I came, that wath to make mythelf ath familiar ath I could with how people lived and talked. I watched every recording I could find, learned how people talked, but I think I needed more time ath there ith a lot I don't know, a lot of wordth I don't underthtand. I found people kind in the main, helpful when I wanted to find a themi-home."

"What's a semi-home, I've not heard that term before?"

"It'th a non-permanent home it can apply to a tent or a hotel."

"They probably thought you were foreign, and regardless of what you may hear, most people will help someone in trouble. I imagine the Drosophila Quins had it harder with next to no time for preparation."

"It ith hoped, their deployment had to be an outcome after they failed to recover me. There wath only a fifteen minute time event which equated to a month here. My father told me we have to prepare for the worth outcome and take every precaution we can."

"How did you stop them tracking you so easily?"

"I read up on the unit in my leg, it ith commercially available for tracking animalth and hath many inbuilt channelth which can be opted for by moving a weak magnetic field over it. I wath prepared to keep altering the channel if they locked on to me. However it turned out I didn't have to thince the active magnetic field around the rotating plathma field damaged the implant. It began to randomly thycle through every available channel. Onthe they locked on they could follow me until the channel moved to the nextht available one, the lock would be gone and the locator would then begin to look for the nextht available channel. Luck wath with me there. I think they will have interrogated every network at home, looked at every deleted file and archive requetht I ever made. They probably had an idea where I wath going and when but not why. That ith maybe how they found out about Project 01x, it would not have been difficult to weave a tale around it to account for them looking for me."

"Well I admit it was initially very convincing but like all good stories the facts must support the narrative. It became clear that the more information I gathered that the person they described wasn't the girl I was after. Oh damn is that the time, I must get on with dinner,

Edward will be home soon. How time flies when you're having fun."

"Edward Clark doethn't like me," Oo-neh said flatly.

"What? Nonsense, he was quite taken with you from the time he first set eyes on you."

"Maybe, but he doethn't care for me now," Oo-neh replied matter-of-factly.

"Why do you think that? Just because he didn't invite you in when you brought him home? Well apart from bad manners he was probably upset that it wasn't a squad of gun toting macho-men throwing flash-bang grenades and shouting for people to get on the floor that had rescued him. He could brag about that all day long, but to admit to being rescued by a girl, especially one as slight as you could ruin his street credibility for years. Don't worry about it; he has much to be grateful for since you came, I know I have. Now forgive me I must get on, you can come through if you want to talk or play some music, or maybe beat some bad guys up on your game."

When Eleanor had slipped out of sight Oo-neh drew up her legs and sat with them crossed and almost silently spoke a mantra she had spoken many times before.

"I am Oo-neh Maurithe the lawful daughter of Margaret McLeod and Ioan Maurithe. I mutht be of good appearanthe, be polite and well mannered, telling the truth at all timeth even though it may offend thome. Then I shall be rethpected. I mutht help the thecurity forthe at all timeth tho they will be aware I am a good and utheful perthon ath I blend in. Daily I mutht write my journal to have good hand eye co-ordination, noting everything I have done and learnt. Each day I mutht extherthise my mind and my body in order to be capable and flexthible in all thingth. I shall do what I can and do what I mutht to thurvive." A single tear slipped beneath her shimmering glasses, "I mith you my mother, I mith you my father with all my heart, I have nobody now who will love me."

Twenty minutes elapsed before Edward entered the kitchen through the rear entrance, "Hi mum. She hasn't bitten you then?"

"What on earth are you talking about?"

"Oo-neh," he spoke in a lower tone but not quite a whisper, "I think she's a vampire."

"You know sometimes Edward I fear for your sanity, you're not making a lot of sense."

"Well I've been thinking; that song she likes is all about vampires."

"I thought it was about a werewolf, you know 'the wolf that was raging inside'. Be that as it may you can't build an entire belief on her liking a song?"

"Not in itself, but when we were at that disused factory it was getting pretty dark inside and when were leaving she never tripped over a single thing. I practically broke my neck dodging half the rubbish on the floor. It's well known vampires, even werewolves can see in the dark."

"Are you sure you didn't fall and bang your head? Maybe she's just less clumsy than you."

"Do you remember when we got to the front door and she stopped? Well again it is well known that you have to invite a vampire in otherwise they can't enter your house."

Eleanor put down the knife she was using to cut the vegetables and wiped her hands before looking through into the living room. She saw Oo-neh sitting writing something in that peculiar way she had of holding the pen nearly vertical. Then closing the door she turned to her son.

"I thought you liked her?" Eleanor tilted her head quizzically.

"That was before I found out how creepy she is, she reminds me of Igor, you know one of the Terry Pratchett characters, he uses body parts to put people together."

"You are being very unfair Edward not to mention childish considering what she has done for you. Have you so quickly forgotten what your health was like before you first met her? The muscle aches, the headaches, the lethargy not to mention the occasional memory loss. It's amazing how quickly people forget things when everything is good." Eleanor could feel her anger rising, "Grow up Edward, vampires and werewolves do not exist. You know nothing about her, so don't judge her, her life has been anything but like the normal you would understand. And I told you before, stop making fun of somebody because of the way they were born; it'll all come back on you." Even she realised she was sounding defensive, protecting Oo-neh. Eleanor just didn't know why.

"Aw come on mum lighten up, even you have to admit she's hardly normal, I mean the way she talks for a start. The Mickey Mouse gloves not to mention that pink satchel she carries about with her. Have you forgotten she's a murderer?"

"Now you just listen to me, she has not been and will not be charged with any crime because there is no evidence she has done anything wrong, do I make myself clear? All she has ever done is to be helpful to you and the police."

"There maybe is no evidence but what happened to that even creepier guy that was holding me? She said he'd gone home, come on, his mother hardly called him in for tea. So what happened to him? Whatever it was he didn't go quietly judging by the mess he made of the machinery."

"Edward you can be really annoying sometimes, I have just spent nearly the whole day with her, and do you know, yes she does have a speech impediment but she is far more intelligent than most people I have come across, even you and she's only a year or so older. If you got to know her as I have you would really like her, she is so funny. Personally I have never met anyone like her before but that is not a bad thing, she is clever, polite, well mannered, and mature for her age and always well presented. Maybe you could learn a lot from her instead of being so petty - or is your problem, jealousy?"

"Jealousy, I'm not jealous of her," Edward's voice rose as did his anger.

"Keep your voice down, she a guest in my house and you will treat her with the respect you seem to expect as a right. Now go on in there, try and be polite and maybe she'll show you one of her games."

"That sounds fun, oh let's collect the lovely fluffy animals to gain points." He said childishly.

"I'll tell you what, go and pick a fight with her and see how long you last." Eleanor challenged.

"You're joking right, she's a foot shorter than I am and stick thin, she'd have no chance."

"Mister cocky is it; well when you're lying on your back aching all over just remember what I told you. I've seen her put down two men bigger and uglier than you with very little effort. Now go and try to be nice while I finish dinner."

Edward grunted but did as he was asked, he returned shortly after, "Where is she?"

"She was sitting on the settee when I last looked, she was writing, maybe she's gone upstairs." Wiping her hands on a towel she went to the stairs and called up, "Oo-neh are you up there?" There was no answer. Returning to the living room she looked around, no satchel, and no coat. "She's gone," Eleanor said crestfallen.

"Well she left you a note," Edward said holding up a folded piece of paper.

The folded letter was more like a piece of origami than a simply folded sheet, it read;

'Máthair mhér,

Today has been the best day of my life for a long while. I have enjoyed your company so very much. Please forgive me for leaving but I would like to remember this day with great pleasure, which I may not do should I stay. Thank you for your kindnesses and thank you for the good things you said in defending me, even though you may not have meant them all.

O|X.'

A feeling of intense sadness and disappointment washed over Eleanor as she slumped onto the couch. Edward stood almost lifeless, feeling somewhere inside he was partly to blame. Then as though a barrier had been released allowing light to illuminate half formed plans, Eleanor sat up.

"I'm going for D.C.I. rank Edward; I'm selling this house and taking the next available posting away from here."

"What?" Edward sounded what he was, surprised. "What about…"

"You; is that what you were going to say? That's easy; you can stay with your father, keep your normal friends, and stay in the same school until college. I divorced one selfish piece of crap, if you want to act the same, fine go and live with him, I'm sure he'll be the ideal parental role model. If you want to go with me, then sort yourself out."

"Is this just because of what I said about her?"

"She has a name Edward, in case you've forgotten. She's called Oo-neh and when she told you the price for putting you right, she wasn't joking. She has lost everything; she now has no home, no family, no friends and potentially no future. Compare that with what you have. It would not have hurt you; at the very least you could have tried to be her friend."

"She'll probably turn up, she did last time."

"You wish. Do you know what she said to me before I started with the vegetables? She said you didn't like her, I thought she was just misjudging you, but no she was perfectly right, you don't like her. Knowing that, do you actually think she'll come back? I have no idea where she'll be and I also know that if she doesn't want to be found she won't be. If you want any dinner, cook it yourself." Still holding the letter she moved out of the room and up the stairs.

Months later - 21st. December.
Police headquarters two hundred miles north.

Superintendent Charles sat at his desk musing over the flash drive he held in his hand, a knock at the door distracted his thoughts, "Come in," he bawled.

The door opened allowing the newly appointed Detective Chief Inspector Eleanor Maurice to enter, "You wanted to see me sir."

Charles slipped the memory stick into a small jiffy bag and tossed it onto his desk. "Yes, Eleanor I did. Sit yourself down. Nothing much, just wanted to make sure you were settling in alright."

"Yes, fine sir, I'm still familiarising myself with who's who and where everything is but everyone is very helpful."

"Good, glad to hear it, well anything you want just ask. Now I know you're taking leave as from tonight so I thought I'd give you a warning of what's to come your way after the holiday. We've had some issues with three or four drug dealers being killed and a couple of pimps. Serious crime took it over as they believed there was a gangland motive. Well they either couldn't find the motive, or the link, you know the who did what to whom or which gangs were in territorial disputes so they'll be passing the files back to us."

"Were they shootings sir?"

"No that's the odd thing the autopsies showed no reason for them being dead, apart from the absence of life, there was substance abuse of course but they could have gone on for a few more years."

"Maybe they tried some bad drugs that had just hit the streets." Eleanor suggested.

"No, not according to toxicology, as far as I remember there were traces of coke but little else. In fact apart from finding their bodies in some dark alley there was not a recent violent mark on them, very odd. Oh that is except for one of them, the report suggested that from the number of broken bones in his chest he'd been hit by a truck. Alone it is a possibility but if you consider he was found in an alley that you couldn't easily push a bike down it seems suddenly unlikely. Forensics say he died there and wasn't dumped - too much evidence to say otherwise."

"Well I'll get a better idea when I see the files, anything else sir?"

"No, I'll see you in a week, I'm sure you'll be glad to get back. I've always hated moving house. If it's not the packing it's the unpacking. You have my every sympathy."

"Thank you sir, but I think I'm organised this time." She started to stand, as she did her eyes flicked over the writing on the jiffy bag, she froze. "Sir, I know it may be a strange request but may I look at that package?"

"Yes, help yourself. It came a week ago; it was just left at the main desk. Tip it out."

Eleanor couldn't act fast enough, she first scanned the writing to make sure, and in her mind there was no doubt. Her excitement rose for the first time since her promotion was confirmed.

"That memory stick was all that was in it," Charles continued, "no letter, nothing. When you plug it in, I gave it to the techies before I did that to check for viruses, anyway it asks for a password. Not any password mind you but one with fifty-three characters in it. Now how am I supposed to know what that is? Anyway the geniuses upstairs couldn't crack it with all their paraphernalia. They reckon it's encrypted but without the resources to buy military grade decryption software they have no way of opening it up."

"They wouldn't be able to sir, not now, not anytime for a couple of hundred years, it's military encryption but nothing we can handle and it's for your eyes only."

"You know what it is?" Charles surprised sat up straighter.

"Not what's on it but I've seen the writing style before. Plug it in and then key in exactly what's written on the packet for the password."

"What about viruses?"

"It will be clean, the source of this has sent it to be helpful, and they believe it is good to help the forces of civilian security."

"Really, we could do with a few more like them?" Charles keyed in the script, 'Detective Superintendant of Police Louis Charles 17645'.

As soon as he pressed 'Enter' a secondary window flagged up - 'decrypting' it read, before a cascade of data poured down the screen. Five minutes later it stopped, the window vanished leaving an unnamed pink folder on the desktop.

"Now what?" Charles asked to no one in particular.

"I would open the folder sir; I'd be very surprised if there was any malware on it."

"Alright if you say so, but I still don't know how you knew what the password was." He clicked on the folder; it opened to reveal nearly a hundred images.

"That was easy sir; there would be no point in sending you a file you couldn't open, that is why the password was put on the cover where you could read it."

"But who would have thought to use that?"

"Exactly, hidden but in plain sight, in a sense the clue should have been her using what I take to be your service number, not usual when putting an address on something."

Superintendant Charles clicked on one of the images, the image browser opened, he just stared, his mouth opened slowly. "Jesus Christ," was all he said as he set the slideshow facility.

"Was it worth opening sir?" Eleanor asked watching his face and the attendant signs of incredulity.

"You have no idea." All through the image display he remained silent, until finally he opened the Excel file at the end.

Eleanor knew what would be on it without seeing it, but there it was for all to see the hierarchical map of who knew who, phone details and addresses.

"You know who sent this?"

"Yes sir I believe I do, we received something similar in the south but that was in a suitcase."

"Can you get them in here?"

"No sir, I have no idea where they are, it fact I was surprised to see the writing. If I were you I'd examine every frame for bent coppers, we had four in the first batch I acquired. We couldn't nail several of the key players before because they were always being tipped off from inside the force."

"Service, we are a service - no longer a force." The Superintendant said absently as he scanned the images a second time, "Yes I know what you mean. It's been the same with this man," he pointed to a face on the screen, "We've never been able to link him to anyone, no phone contact, no meetings, but we know he is involved somewhere in the chain. This picture alone will need him to come up with a really good reason why we shouldn't bang him up for twenty years. I'm really glad you transferred here Eleanor without you we'd still be looking at a silver widget not knowing what's on it until next Christmas."

"I have a feeling sir that you wouldn't have got this had I not been here. I just hope what I feel is not wrong."

"Leave, remember the term, I've got a lot of calls to make. I want some of these bastards in cells for the holidays. Enjoy your leave you never know when the next one will arrive."

"On my way now sir, have a good Christmas." Eleanor closed the door as her superior officer started to talk on the internal line. Quickly she moved back to her own office, opened the desk drawer and removed her private phone, flipped open the case and stared at the apparently clear strip stuck on the inside cover. Nothing, no small pulsating light, no illuminated blue markers, no indication the tracking signal was within a radius of thirty miles, but maybe it was just recycling she thought trying to convince herself.

Disappointed she slipped out of her office and walked without particular direction to the open plan office space used by the teams of detectives. Most desks were empty but four were manned by officers peering at computer screens or sorting through reports and case files. She turned to go back to her own office.

"Ma'am," a voice called out to her.

She turned and looked in the direction of the summons. "Yes," she smiled encouragingly as she moved to the person in question trying to remember the officer's name, "Yes, Sergeant."

"Sorry to bother you Ma'am but there's an Irish girl who wants to speak with you. I brought her up when I came in, but as you weren't in your office I kept her out here." Detective Sergeant Sian Thwaite's accent betrayed her own Irish roots.

"Irish?" Eleanor frowned trying to remember any Irish girls in her acquaintanceship, certainly none since she'd moved north.

"Yes Ma'am and a speaker of the old language, she leaves me standing with the Gaelic so she does. Speaks it beautifully, my grandmother would die to meet her; she's always complaining how the young never find the time to learn their own language. Mind you she lives on the West coast where there's more speakers than not."

Eleanor could see Sergeant Thwaite was a talker, not a bad thing if it wasn't nonsense, she probably relates with people very easily she thought. "What does she look like?"

"Oh, a red head, shoulder length hair framing her face, really smart, green blouse, black trousers, flat soled black shoes and she standing only about four and a half feet tall, slim build, a real pixie she is sure enough."

"Does she wear white gloves, have a pink satchel with her and talk with a lisp?" Inside Eleanor felt butterflies in her stomach; please say yes, she thought. Let it be her.

"So she does but the satchel's light green. You know her then?"

"Yes I know her, she's an enigma wrapped in a paradox tied up with a puzzle who goes by the name of Oo-neh Maurice" Eleanor smiled. "Where is she now?"

"She just trotted off to the loo just before you came in, she can't be long now. Forgive me for being nosey like, but is she related?"

Eleanor pondered that question a moment, "Distantly, how did she seem, was she happy?"

"Well she didn't seem one to smile much, lovely girl though, maybe a little pensive. She's not in any trouble is she?"

"No, certainly not from me anyway, are you sure she went to the loo and hasn't just made a run for it?"

"No ma'am she left her wee pink case just here, so she won't have gone far, and to speak of the devil and he shall surely appear in a manner of speaking."

Eleanor turned towards the opening to the corridor that led towards the stairs and lift. Framed in the doorway the petite figure stood feet together, clutching her satchel in front of her like a shield, as Eleanor had seen her do several times before. She could see Oo-neh's mouth held tight together, her knuckles seemed tensed as she gripped the satchel's strap. The half smile was missing replaced by the pensive looked the sergeant had noticed. She didn't seem on this occasion to know what to do. On later reflection Eleanor didn't know why she said what she did, under the circumstances it just seemed the right thing to say.

"Hello baby girl." Then throwing decorum to the wind she knelt down allowing Oo-neh to run into her embrace, where she remained for a few moments until the noise of approaching voices caused them to separate. Standing up Eleanor brushed her clothes and took hold of the handle of the little pink suitcase, "Come along let's go and talk in my office."

When the door was closed and the internal blinds shut she offered Oo-neh one of the visitor chairs while she brought her own chair around and sat facing her. "I've missed you Oo-neh, I just wish you hadn't left that day," Eleanor started. "I can understand why you did though. Any way where have you been since we last met?"

"I went to Ireland to see some of my mother's forebears, they were nithe but I didn't tell them who I wath. After three weekth and two dayth I came here and did thome rethearch while I waited."

"Waited? What were you waiting for?" Eleanor studied Oo-neh, noticing the bubbly side of her nature was no longer there.

"For you to buy your houthe near the moorland," was the cryptic reply.

"How on earth did you know I was going to come and live up here?" Eleanor was more than surprised.

Oo-neh rummaged in her satchel and removed her tablet device, after flicking through a few screens she turned it around. On the screen was a faded colour picture of Eleanor standing by the gate of a cottage, the name clearly visible on a sign affixed to the white fencing.

"I found it when I wath thearching the North Engle archiveth," she said by way of explanation. "It ith a nithe house and there ith no light much to stop you theeing the starth if you lie on the grath in the back garden." Oo-neh went quiet as she sucked her bottom lip.

Eleanor looked at the image; yes it certainly was the house she had recently bought but she looked older than she currently did. "Why would this be in the national archive, it just looks like a family photo?"

"It wath within the thecurity archive; mostly about you and your career up to your getting the medalth, I think they were proud of you. I found the property tranthfer document that wath athothiated with your data it gave me the date you acquired it. Tho here I am."

"Why have you come to see me now Oo-neh, you could have come to see me at the old house. I would have liked to have known you were safe or at least not on your own. I supposed because I could think about you it meant you were still somewhere."

Oo-neh removed two black bound books from her bag and held them out, the gold lettering on the top right corner said – Diary and the current year and the second book had last year's date. Taking them in her hands Eleanor looked questioning at her six time great grand-daughter.

"They are my journalth, it'th the day of my birth. Would you like to read latht yearth and thee what I have been doing and all the thingth I have learnt?" When Eleanor didn't respond immediately she continued, "I bought them from a shop, it'th good becauthe before I had to write on thingle sheeth and fasten them together." She stopped, waiting expectantly.

In the silence Eleanor had remembered what she'd been told before. Oo-neh's mother had told her to write everything she'd done down, so that her grandmother would see how she was growing up and to exercise her hand-eye coordination. Alas in that instance her grandmother had never taken any interest it seemed. "Oo-neh, I don't know what to say, I am deeply touched you should ask me. Of course I'd like to read them."

"You would?" Oo-neh sounded surprised as a slight smile crossed her face.

"Yes I would, I would very much like to read them. I'd like to read them to see exactly how you coped with moving here and what you learnt." She bent over and kissed Oo-neh on the cheek.

"Maw-her vhor, my mother told me if I ran out of optionth I should athk you for help. Will you help me?" Oo-neh's voice was quiet but rushed sounding like she was almost desperate and trying to get something out of the way.

Eleanor knew that wasn't what Oo-neh's mother had meant; she wondered if the girl was so desperate she was getting confused about their relationship. Was Oo-neh transferring her emotional attachments from a yet unborn mother or grandmother to her only living equivalent ancestor? Psycho-babble, Eleanor thought, but maybe Oo-neh did see her as the grandmother who had rejected her for no obvious reason. "Help you; of course I'll help you, whatever is the matter?"

"I'm thtill here and I don't know what to do any more." Oo-neh plaintively replied.

Eleanor pondered that for a second or two and it occurred to her that this brave, courageous yet very emotionally fragile girl had accepted the greater possibility that she would disappear from sight and memory. That she would survive hadn't been the most significant possibility in her thoughts. She must have hoped of course, but the consequences of continuing in a foreign and more primitive place cannot have been deeply considered. Now detached from all the family and all she had ever known, with no hope of returning to them, the reality of her situation was starting to dawn on her. It's wasn't really surprising she was finding it difficult to cope she finalised in her mind. "Oo-neh what did your mother tell you to do when you relate with people?"

"My mother told me I mutht dreth well, I must be well mannered and polite and pleathant. I mutht meditate to learn how to hear only what people near me are thaying and be attentive. Learn what ith happening in the world about me, as that will give me a perthpective. I mutht try to keep my tongue in my mouth ath that may offend if I do not. Above all I mutht watch other people and imitate good behaviour tho that I might blend in."

Eleanor drew breath, "Well the good news is you are doing very well, the bad news is simply this, you will never blend in Oo-neh. You are you; you will always stand out in a good way."

"I will?" Oo-neh said almost disheartened, and then suddenly brightening up she said enthusiastically, "I work all day, trying to talk well tho that people will not notice the funny way I talk,"

"And you do that very well when you speak slowly and choose your words. Listen sweetheart in a little while I'm going home, I have a week off work over the Christmas holiday, how would you like to come and spend it with me? It might mean helping unpack, cleaning the house and putting up the decorations but if you want to, you can."

"Really?" Oo-neh said, straightening up on hearing the offer.

To Eleanor, Oo-neh's face lit up with real pleasure at the unexpected invitation.

"Yes really, just the two of us. Edward is with his father so we can do as we please. We'll talk and sort something out for your future. So bear with me, I have one or two things to do, will you still be here when I get back or do I have to handcuff you to the chair?"

Oo-neh laughed softly, "No I won't run away. I'll sit here quietly hearing the world outside."

As soon as Eleanor had left the room Oo-neh slid her hands up behind her ears before closing her eyes and reciting her mantra. "I am Oo-neh Maurithe the lawful daughter of Margaret McLeod and Ioan Maurithe. I mutht have a good appearanthe, be polite and well mannered. Telling the truth at all timeth even though it may offend thome, I shall be rethpected. I mutht help the thecurity forthe at all timeth tho they will be aware I am a good and utheful perthon ath I blend in. Daily I mutht write my journal to have good hand-eye co-ordination, noting everything I have done and learnt. Each day I mutht extherthise my mind and my body in order to be capable and flexible in all thingth. I shall do what I can and do what I mutht to thurvive. I mith you my mother, I mith you my father with all my heart, I have nobody now who will love me except grandmother who will let me go to her home."

At the doorway leading to the main corridor Eleanor stopped and turned, she saw Sergeant Sian Thwaite look up; waving her over she put a finger across her mouth to tell her to keep quiet. Moving further down the corridor they met up at the small kitchen area.

"Ma'am?" Sian said wondering what it was about.

"Are you busy?"

"No, I've just finished collating the data I was working on. Is there something you want doing?"

"Well the fact is, today is Oo-neh's nineteenth birthday." The expected response came.

"Nineteen! And there was me thinking she was much younger."

"Do you happen to know if there are any cake shops around here?"

"Sure there is, just up the road by the butchers, its nought but a five minute walk." Sian answered.

"Would you mind nipping down there and getting a cake, doesn't have to be extraordinarily special, fruit or sponge. See if they have a big silver nineteen if not icing will do and the same number of candles. I doubt they'll have time but if it's possible have them ice 'Happy Birthday Oonex' on it." She wrote it down on a piece of paper.

"I thought you said her name was Oo-neh."

"It is. That's how you spell it and 'O|X' at the bottom."

"Do you need that?"

"What? Hugs and kisses, yes she likes plenty of hugs and kisses it seems."

"Oh right, then it's just 'O X' you'll be needing."

Eleanor looked at the sketch she'd made on the paper in her hand. "Why did you ask if I needed that?"

"No reason I just thought it was an abbreviation for her name that's all, do you see if you split the characters up, O – one – x."

The D.C.I. just stared at the letters, her mind flickering back over the many things she'd heard since the girl had come into her life. She considered the many things told to her by the girl herself and the agents even what Oo-neh's mother had said on the video. Finally what Oo-neh herself had said were her dead mother's instructions for her. "Shit," she finally said out loud before silently saying to herself, 'I missed it, it was there all along. She's open, truthful but can never admit the truth to anyone. The agents were never after any file called Project 01x, they were always after Oo-neh they just didn't know she was Project 01x. Oo-neh was wanted for one simple reason, the reason her mother had said on the recording, 'you are better than they are'."

"Ma'am is everything alright?" Sian asked at the sudden change in her superior's mood.

"What? Yes, sorry, something that's been puzzling me has just shifted into focus." Eleanor drew two notes from her purse. "Okay here's thirty quid that should more than cover it and see if you can get a card, fluffy bunnies if possible. Oh, one last thing, do you know what Maw-her vhor means?"

"Maybe not the way you pronounce it but it sounds like the Gaelic for grandmother. Right I'll be away, I'll be as quick as I can."

On her way back to the office Eleanor stopped to have a word with Inspector Sandra Windle and to tell her where her Sergeant was. Finally at her office door she drew breath and walked in to find a less than happy looking Oo-neh.

"Why the long face?" Eleanor said.

"Have you changed your mind?"

"Now what makes you think that?"

"You're more rigid than before, you walk differently. What hath happened to give you conthern. Can I help?"

"Ah! So we have a student of body language, full marks, something has happened, something that hadn't made a lot of sense has finally come to make a lot of sense. Do you know what that was? Well I couldn't understand why your mother would always seem to be encouraging you to strive to be good, helpful, polite, and above all to blend in. I couldn't grasp why your father would be willing to take the chance of you dying on some risky scientific experiment, if he loved you as much as you say. I suppose I wasn't even certain your story was true, yes you may well believe in the delusion but is it fact? Perhaps it was some scheme, for whatever reason, so that I would take pity on you, I don't know. But there is a way to be certain." Eleanor paused as she closed the external window blinds before taking her seat in front of the girl. Taking both of Oo-neh's hands in hers she lifted them up and kissed them, before she looked squarely into the oily moving lenses.

"Oo-neh I want you to think about something. Soon you and I are both going to go to my new house in the countryside where we shall spend a week getting to know one another. Maybe we'll have a lot of fun and laughs. Is that alright with you?"

"Yeth that would be nithe, like the day we thpent together and maybe we will lay on the grath and look into the night."

"Just like that day, but it might be a bit cold for lying on the grass at this time of year, but maybe we can wrap up well. You'll have your own room that looks out onto the moorland. Now what I want you to think about is this, I would like it very much if you decided to stay permanently, to make it your home."

Oo-neh was silent, her face unreadable.

Perplexed Eleanor finally said, "I thought you'd be pleased."

"Maw-her vhor," the girl finally said before lunging forward and wrapping her arms around Eleanor's neck and sobbing her heart out.

After a while Eleanor eased Oo-neh away, "Come on now baby girl you'll make your eyes red, people will think I've been beating you. I promise you I will always be there for you; I will help you through this time and see you settled."

Finally Oo-neh pulled herself away, sat up and slid her small handkerchief under the rim of her glasses; she smiled in a way that made her seem slightly embarrassed.

"Good, that's better, now I have a little surprise for you but until that moment arrives I want to ask you something. Is that alright?"

Oo-neh sniffed, "Yeth."

"Now Oh-Five mentioned a file called 01x, he told me he was sent to recover it, failing that then he wanted you. You told me that your father had deleted the file and encrypted the residue. So why do you think they wanted you when the file no longer existed, which the security forces must have known." Eleanor looked directly at Oo-neh.

"A hothtage, tho they could make my father tell them what wath in the file and how to conthtruct the genome to create a thtable, viable entity. Ath well ath, what changeth they mutht make to the genome to remove the problemth with the Drothophila Quinth."

"Okay, then perhaps that is why your father wanted you somewhere safe, somewhere they could never get to you. I imagine the military wouldn't shrink from ruthless practices to get that information. But if it was important then they had to know why the file was important, in fact I must assume your father did more than create a theoretic paper. I think he put the theory into practice. Would I be wrong?"

"No, my father worked on it before I wath born."

Interesting thought Eleanor, "Did he ever speak about it to you? What did he in fact create?"

"I remember once we were together on a bench watching the moon climbing through the treeth, he had hith arm around me. It wath then he told me he had created an awful little monthter, all red and making an awful racket. He told me he felt ashamed and regretted what he had done. He didn't know what to do with it tho he handed it to my mother and shortly after the noithe thtopped."

"There must be more to the story Oo-neh nobody spends resources to recover a failure."

Eleanor watched as Oo-neh's mouth tightened, "My mother found out the reathon for the yelling, the baby had hearing that wath more acute than normal, everything wath too loud and frightening. She put the monthter in a quiet room and all wath quiet again."

"Similar to the Drosophila Quins, they had good hearing, you told me so yourself."

"Yeth, but they didn't have the range in the higher or lower order," the tip of her tongue slid slightly out of her mouth as she finished speaking.

"What happened to her?"

"I didn't thay it wath a girl."

"No you didn't but you didn't have to. Your mother never struck me as the sort of person who could be so unkind as to treat this tiny, defenceless baby with ill intent. I think your mother came to love her very much, of that I have no doubt. I'm sure she knew how difficult things would be. I think that's why she encouraged the little girl to practice and practice being as normal as possible. I think your fathers' creation was far superior to the creations of Tyler-Wolfe. I believe that is what your mother said on the video you showed me. That is why the authorities wanted her, to find out how to create a weapon that didn't have the faults and limitations of the Prometheus Team. A weapon that had skills that could out-manoeuvre the enemy, slip in and out without so much as a stirring of the wind. Somehow I don't think they realised, until it was far too late just how superior your father's little monster was."

Oo-neh said nothing.

"And your mother, well she wasn't having her baby girl named like a laboratory experiment, that's why she changed the pronunciation. I guess your father was still unsure at that time, that's why they argued about it. As for your grandmother - well what can have upset her, maybe the constant screaming? Possibly she didn't like you sticking your tongue out at her."

Eleanor watched the tip disappear back into Oo-neh's mouth, the young girl smiled slightly.

"I doubt it was because you were hairless, many babies are bald, a lot of babies have skin rashes I doubt that would have upset her, so what was it? I think you'll remember when we first spoke to one another, how you told me how much of a mess you were. That was really clever because we, as a people don't like prying into others' disabilities; we avoid such things because it makes us feel uncomfortable. Then later you told me why it would be dangerous to attack Oh-Four since he would have established a sound-scape map and possibly a scent-scape map of the area around him. But if your father's creation was superior then what was the full scope of her senses? So the question arises, what if I had misunderstood what you had said, or that you had in fact misdirected me. What if, in reality, they weren't disabilities?"

"What ith a Hobbit?" Oo-neh suddenly said, distracting Eleanor's mental thread.

"A Hobbit?" she frowned, "Well it's a character in a fantasy fiction book about magic and dragons and weird things. Why?"

"Ith it good to be called a Hobbit?" there was no levity in her voice.

"I think perhaps it would not be a compliment. Has somebody called you one?"

"Detective Conthtable Brian Bane enquired of Inthpector India Wellth who the Hobbit wath in your offithe."

"When did he say that?"

"Forty-eight theconds ago, she wath angry with him and she ith going to put him on the nextht diverthity courthe, he argued he had already done it. Thith time she thaid, she hoped he would thtay awake and pay attention. Detective Thergeant Sian Thwaite hath jutht come out of the lift, she ith in a hurry."

Eleanor was speechless, "How do you know that?"

"The change in air pressure from the lift doors opening drove her thent particleth into the outer room; I imagine she hath bought a cake with waxthy candleth. I heard the converthation about the Hobbit. I told you I had a buffer in each ear, it ith how I filter the volume and frequenthy of thound around me."

Eleanor in all her guessing and fitting things together had woven a tale even she found hard to believe, but now there was evidence. Her mind flickered back to the time Oo-neh had stood motionless on her door step, it wasn't as Edward had suggested that vampires needed to be invited in. No, she was doing exactly what Oo-neh had said the agent Oh-Four had done, she'd been building a sensory map of the house. In the time Oo-neh had waited for her to come back to her office she'd probably done the same here.

"Oo-neh, will you do one last thing for me?"

"What thort of thing?" the girl asked warily.

"Will you take your glasses off?"

Then as though something had re-animated Oo-neh she opened up her satchel, "I am a real perthon now, which wath going to be a thurprise, I wath going to tell you. Now I have a regithtration of my birth." That she was happy was self evident by her sudden shift in enthusiasm. "Yeth I exthitht, now nobody can put me in the freezer. Look at thith, it'th good it hath my picture in without glatheth. They thaid you can't thmile so it'th not very good, I look like a thtartled frog. Had I thmiled I would have looked like an embarethed frog." She handed over a passport.

After looking at it, "So Miss Oo-neh Maurice is a subject of the Republic of Ireland." Eleanor flicked to the page containing the photograph, "Well don't feel too bad nobody takes a good passport photograph, especially in those booths. How did you get this, I hope you didn't pay for it."

"I went to a Government building in Dublin with my photograph thigned by a man of probity and character, my birth regithtration form and money becauthe they athked for it. I filled in a form and waited a long time before they called for me and gave me thith. I wath really happy; I can now go where I like and if anyone wants to know who I am I give them thith and they will not want to freeze me."

The image of Oo-neh's smile, Eleanor thought, would stay with her for a long time, she was evidently so very happy. "Well you have green eyes and they are beautiful eyes. Didn't you tell me that's what your mother fell in love with?"

The next step Eleanor wasn't really happy about but she must take the step; the passport couldn't have been legally obtained unless she really was Irish. "Now Oo-neh imagine I stop you and want to know who you are. You give me this; I open it and look at your photograph and because people look different in sunglasses I am going to ask you to take them off just to make sure it's you."

"You are?"

"Yes I am, so please take off your glasses. It's not bright in here so if your eyes are light sensitive it won't hurt you." Almost immediately the face opposite hers lost any hint of happiness.

"Pleathe grandmother, pleathe don't athk me." What had started as a simple plea rapidly became almost panic, "You'll never want me to thtay with you, pleathe don't athk me, pleathe." Oo-neh started trembling, "Grandmother pleathe," she cried out her pleading starting to turn hysterical.

So there it was Eleanor said to herself, what had seemingly endeared Oo-neh to her mother had frightened her grandmother so much she ran away never to be heard from again. If only she had known what she had missed out on, if only she had bothered to read the diaries. If only she had sent even one card on Oo-neh's birthday. How different both their lives would have been, but had that been so, perhaps today I would not be holding the little gloved hands of a girl I would be proud to call my daughter or even grand-daughter if I must.

Gripping Oo-neh's hands tighter Eleanor tried to calm her down, "Oo-neh, it's alright calm down, it's alright, it's not important anymore. Listen to me," she squeezed the small hands she held. "You and I are going to spend a week together and we are going to have a wonderful time getting to know one another. After that if you want to live with me all the time then I would be very happy. I told you before your parents would be very proud of you for what you have done and the courageous way you have done things. It must have been hard enough in the secure home you had, but to be thrown in the deep end into a backward and chaotic society like this, well that takes real courage. The only people who know are you and I, and we aren't going to tell anyone how unique you are. So when you feel you can trust me totally, then you can be yourself in my company."

There was a knock at the door.

"Yes," Eleanor said.

Sian Thwaite put her head around the door, "Ready when you are Ma'am." She covertly pointed at the card she held in her hidden hand.

"Okay we shall be right there." Holding out her hand she took the card and moved to the window ledge to sign it. On opening it she found several signatures already there from a couple of the teams, a thoughtful touch she considered.

"Ith it a thelebration?" Oo-neh asked out of the blue catching Eleanor off guard.

"As it happens it is, a very special one. Come along you might enjoy it." She slid the card back into its envelope.

When they entered the main room ten officers were gathered around one of the tables upon which sat a cake with several lit candles.

"It's amazing how many police officers turn up when the word cake is mentioned," Eleanor said only to be applauded. "First of all I'd like you to meet my baby girl Oo-neh." She looked down; her eyes met those in the turning head below hers. "Now Oo-neh all you have to do is take a deep breath and blow out all the candles and make a wish."

"Why?"

"It's good luck on special days, days like today, now go and look at the cake and you will see why."

As she did so, the little girl looked at the writing on the cake, realised it was for her and although not fully understanding the reasons she blew out the candles in one breath to the cheers of those around. Eleanor gave her the birthday card and kissed her cheek as the cake was cut.

Oo-neh was very happy and as the song 'Happy Birthday' discordantly rang around the room the only sound that echoed around her head was that so recently spoken by Detective Chief Inspector of Police Eleanor Maurice, 'my baby girl Oo-neh'. She remembered her mother saying so long ago that when the time was right they would be together again. Turning she looked at Eleanor who physically so resembled her mother they could be twin sisters and smiled brightly, everything was going to be alright now.

2304 A.D.

Time re-written.

Oo-neh Maurice had cured Edward Clark Maurice by replacing the defective genes that were causing his bouts of illness. The result of that one single change would have consequences – the future outcomes would reflect that change.

The bright autumn sun cascaded down on to the oval shaped stadium, now past noon, the one hundred and fifty foot dive tower sent a short shadow backwards for forty feet before it climbed the vertical wall. The tiered seats that formed a horseshoe around the dive pool itself were now filling up with spectators for the last dive of the final event of the World Quadathlon Aquatic event.

The northern stand was mostly populated by men and women of the military but more noteworthy was the fact that they all wore the light blue dress uniform of the Guardian, an elite force that guarded the most secure compounds throughout the United Islands.

Twenty feet up, set in the eastern rank of seats was the media centre from where all national and international media broadcasts emanated.

"Welcome back to this final of Quadathlon Aquatic event," began David Gilmore the front man for C9 Media, "and it promises to be a day to remember. You may recall that earlier today I was given the opportunity to stand on the dive-board and look down into the pool; I don't mind telling you I was terrified even with a safety harness on. How the men and women who take part in this event make that dive I just cannot imagine - they are in a class of their own.

You may have noticed as the recorder scans around the stadium just how many of the elite Guardian force there are here today. Do not worry though that our secure places are left unguarded, they are not, as these few represent but a small fraction of those worthy warriors that guard our nation. You might be forgiven for thinking that they are here today to cheer on one of their own ranks but you'd be wrong. They are here to support a civilian, which in itself is a record because the next competitor is the first ever, non-military person that the battalion has sponsored, and today the Guardian expect to break another record.

Just listen to that applause; I wouldn't be surprised if they can hear it as far away as the Italia States. That greeting is for their girl; and there she is, dressed in a powder blue costume she acknowledges her sponsors as she makes her way to the carrier that will take her to the one hundred foot board. While she is being carried to the top of the tower let me tell you a little about this aquatic marvel and a little is all we know, because so far nobody has been allowed to interview her. Her military escort tells me, and you do not argue with these soldiers, that she needs to focus. As she is of a somewhat shy disposition they do not want her distracted. However if she pulls off the impossible today the public will demand to hear and see her. So what do we know? Silvana Maurice, she prefers Silva, was born sixteen years ago in the Elsfast Province. Her parents are Marine and Ewen Maurice both of whom run the Centre for Genetic Archaeology a private research facility adjacent to the highly secure SeaSolar energy farm. Their near neighbours are the Security Forces Training Unit and it is they, who are for some reason, known only to themselves, sponsoring this talented young woman.

If you have been following this event from the beginning it will not be difficult to guess that reason. The image you see now is of her and her trainer, he stands six feet and one inch and at four feet seven inches tall she looks tiny besides him. Only those of us who have seen how easily she has pushed aside the taller, stronger competitors will realise she is exceptional. Her achievement thus far is beyond expectation, and today to take the King's Crown all she has to do is get the minimum of points.

I say all she has to do but that involves diving from that plank thrusting out one hundred feet above our heads into the dive tank beneath. Swim the twenty-five feet to the bottom and pick up just one ring and return to the surface. Make no mistake this is a difficult if not a dangerous event, one error in striking the water could prove fatal for someone as seemingly fragile as Silva. The swim down to depths where the water pressure is trying to force the air from your lungs is, according to earlier contestants, painful, during and after. She must hold her breath long enough to pick up any one of the ten rings scattered randomly on the pool bottom and then return to the surface and place it in the net. The dangers of this event cannot be overstated, and that is why you will see four divers in the pool, two at the halfway mark and two on the bottom. They are there to render help should they see a contestant in trouble. If you saw the first dive of the day you will have surely seen them in action, fortunately the competitor from the China State will suffer no long-term injury.

As Silvana makes her dive the travelling cameras will follow her all the way down to the bottom of the tank and back again. There it is, the warning buzzer has sounded, and the hopes of all here are with this young woman as she approaches the end of the board in her usual way, at a run. The stadium has fallen silent and everyone is holding their breath.

She leaps into the air and bends forward into a triple roll then rotates vertically before performing three backward flips. She hits the water, unlike most divers she is facing away from the dive tower. As the tiny figure arches her back she straightens out mere feet from the bottom. She swims hard now to the nearest ring. SHE'S GOT IT, SHE HAS GOT IT." His voice suddenly screaming, before the anchor man's voice suddenly went much softer, as if in total surprise he continued.

"No! She's trying for another one; she can't possibly do it before her air runs out. Doesn't she realise that if the divers help her she will have lost?

SHE'S DONE IT, SHE HAS THE SECOND RING, and now she's pulling hard for the surface. The divers are moving close just in case, but she gives them the vertical index finger signal, everything is alright. What is this girl breathing? The applause and the stamping of hundreds of feet are absolutely deafening. A sea of blue uniforms rises up from the curved seating as their heroine breaks the surface and drops the rings into the catch net. She has done it, for the first time in fifty years The United Islands has won the Quadathlon Aquatic event, and it will probably be another fifty years before anyone comes close to achieving the same record breaking finish.

The crowd is going wild, Leading Instructor Karl Gibson is there by the pool side, and he takes her by the wrists effortlessly lifting her from the water before wrapping her in a towel and hoisting her up onto his broad shoulders for her admiring supporters to see. Now he's taking what seems a leisurely walk around the dive tank so that everyone can see her. Let's just watch that amazing dive again. The crowd is ecstatic."

After the public display of the security forces champion, Instructor Karl Gibson took the new World Champion out of sight for the mandatory blood testing, skin scrape analysis, urine test, lung analysis and finally a brain scan. All the results would be compared with samples taken at the commencement of the week's trials to see if any illegal interventions had been used. The latter two tests were health checks to make sure the ordeal had no long-term consequences. Under the gaze of her chaperone, Major Rodetski, a woman appointed by the Sporting Committee to ensure all rules were abided by, Silva changed out of her wet swimwear. The test results usually took about fifteen to thirty minutes; afterwards her chaperone would be discharged and the heroine of the day would be taken out for the presentation ceremony. Facing the wall she towelled her short hair before replacing her mirrored glasses.

When two strong hands gripped her shoulders she automatically thrust her head back so that she could look directly at the person behind her and see who it was. What happened next would depend on the person gripping her. This time she barely got a glimpse before hot breath washed over her lenses steaming them up.

"Grandma," she cried out in great joy as her face lit up in a bright smile, "you came." Then twisting around she wrapped her arms around the uniformed body in front of her where she received a kiss to the top of her head. "Did you see?"

"See? See what? Did something exciting happen?" enquired General Abigail Conrad with a poker face.

A scowling face looked up.

"Aw its miss grumpy time is it? Of course I saw you silly, I wouldn't have missed it for the world and so did the President and his lady, and they are thrilled. You'll meet them tomorrow as they are to hold a special dinner in your honour back at the training facility officer's mess."

A half hour later the door clicked open, allowing Lead Instructor Gibson to enter, he saluted his military superior.

"The results are in." He handed the sealed letter to the chaperone. He didn't salute her.

The sound of the seal being broken by the unsmiling guardian of the rules seemed to echo through the now silent room. "All clear," she announced in her accented Slavic voice, handing the letter back and regaining her smile. "Congratulations Silva, may I embrace you?"

She could and did, finally kissing Silva on both cheeks. Gibson signed off the release notice as did Major Rodetski, witnessed by General Conrad before salutes were exchanged and the Major left the room.

General Conrad turned back to her granddaughter, her face now a stern visage.

"Now listen to me carefully my sweet, today you have done something incredible but equally very dangerous. You have become a national icon, and as such will be required to travel around the country and perform duties of which you have no experience. As we speak the President's agents will be finding out just who you are so he can be prepared when he speaks about you. Are you following me?"

Mirroring the same serious demeanour her grandmother had, Silva nodded.

"You have no record, you have no identity and that is going to be an issue for you and the Guardian." A knock at the door caused her to pause, "Yes?"

"They're ready for the presentation," a voice replied informally, the speaker not knowing to whom he spoke.

"We're ready, just coming," the General said, and then to Silva, "As soon as this is over we are taking you straight home." Turning to Lead Instructor Gibson, "General Saviour probably already knows the outcome but better communicate with him as soon as possible he'll need time to co-ordinate his plan. Until then keep close. Has the package arrived?"

"Yes Ma'am, outside," Gibson replied.

"Bring it in," Conrad calmly ordered before taking up a position behind her granddaughter. The door opened, "Your escort."

Silva paused for a fraction of a second before running towards the door, "Mama," she cried out before wrapping her arms around her mother. "I didn't think they'd let you come."

"Well neither did I. They wanted to keep me another day but the Guardian Skif parked on the hospital front lawn was a mind changer. I arrived just in time to see you trip over your feet on the board but you recovered well so I don't think anybody noticed."

"I didn't trip."

"Didn't you? Looked like one to me, it looked more like a fall than a dive, well I guess it must have been the angle of the recorder then. What do you think Instructor Gibson?" Marine Maurice's face was as wooden as she could possibly make it.

Silva glared in his direction.

"Me Ma'am, I think we'd better move, the presentation and the audience require the champion. Oh! Silva, try not to trip on the steps." He smiled slightly at the frosty look he received from his protégé.

"He is right we must go," Marine said as she kissed her daughter on the head. "I am really proud of you, so is your father. He watched it with everybody at the Centre. I was talking to him at the time on an open communication channel so I could hear the cry that went up when you put those rings down. They'll be celebrating tonight, Dada said to give you his love and he'll meet us when we land. Now come on, I've never known you stay in one place for so long."

The journey to the podium was through corridors packed with well wishers from every country and Silva hated it. She was not used to so much attention preferring to stay on the periphery of events - or at the very least amongst those she knew and trusted. Her life had been spent within the confines of the Centre's perimeter fences and beyond that the encircling military presence. There were no strangers that weren't vetted, no people calling to see her. Her education was conducted entirely through the medium of educational media channels approved by the State with assistance from her parents particularly in her early life. She didn't mind because she had lots of friends, lots of people she could talk to within the Centre itself and the military compound outside. Lead Instructor Gibson had warned her there would be a great many people around her but she had not realised until this point that she could not avoid them like she could at home. Being flanked by her mother and grandmother helped her feel safer, Gibson followed behind and an armed duo preceded them all. Fulfilling her dream had its price.

An hour can seem a long time if you feel threatened but once aboard the troop transporter Skif, amongst familiar people Silva relaxed as she showed off the winner's medal to her elite escort. The hum of the horizontally mounted wing engines increased as the craft lifted vertically off the hardened ground. The pale blue triangular shaped craft swayed slightly in the force five winds before the rear ram drives pushed it skyward. The rear nasal exhaust turned incrementally nudging the accelerating troop carrier on a bearing of two hundred and fifty-four degrees – homeward.

The journey time took less than an hour from leaving the ground in one place and settling back to earth in another. The engines were winding down as the ramp doors dropped down from beneath the fuselage. As one the military force stood first, with weapons held across their chests and they evacuated the craft and formed up defining the exit path leading away from the plane. Marine Maurice and her daughter followed next, wrapping their clothes around them as they felt the cold westerly wind. General Conrad and Lead Instructor Gibson followed after. General Saviour, Commandant of the combined military facility stood waiting. The moment Silva stepped off the ramp the soldiers stood to attention their weapons held in salute, the stamp of boots startled her but with a gentle push from her mother's hand she walked forward. Even the aging General saluted her.

"Welcome home Silvana Maurice, on behalf of the men and women under my command I salute you," Saviour said formally. Then crouching down he said less formally, "You have made us and the nation very proud, make no mistake we will not forget that. Your father is over there, you and I will speak later." He pointed towards one of the many anti-missile hangers.

Looking round Silva saw the figure of her father waving, causing her to break into a run, the sound of the troops being dismissed echoed behind her. Before Silva ran into her father's well built frame he reached out and grabbed her, swinging her up in an arc before drawing his daughter's small frame and kissing her on the cheek.

"Is it still alright to kiss the nation's aquatic heroine?" he asked.

"Only because it's you," she teased in return.

"I'm glad you're back, you've no idea how depressing it's been around here since you left." Ewen Maurice said with sincerity.

She placed her mouth close to his ear, "Is mother going to be alright?" she asked quietly.

His hold tightened slightly. "The doctors say she's going to be fine, but they'll be giving her regular checks so there's no need for you go worrying for nothing. She'll be fine, especially now you're home to take her mind off things. So what are you going to do next, what is your next dream? Hi there baby." The latter comment was directed towards his wife whom he kissed as she moved in closer.

The sound of running booted feet caused the trio to look round in the direction of an approaching figure, who was dressed in camouflage grey combat fatigues. On his belt were two compact personal protection side arms mounted in quick release clamps on both hips, two bladed weapons being set in open sheaths behind them. Strapping across his chest held pouches of additional ordinance, there were no badges or patches to indicate rank, military unit or even which country he belonged to. Standing around five feet ten inches tall; his solid frame betrayed the amount of exercise he took. Stopping by General Saviour he saluted, "Sir, permission to speak with Silvana Maurice." His voice was both monotone and coarse.

Saviour could feel his skin crawl as he looked into the dead matt grey eyes of the man in front of him. In all the contacts he had ever had with Team Phantom he had never seen any hint of emotion but then that made them good at what they did he reminded himself. Regrettably it had been reported several members of this experimental group were showing signs of instability, and the last thing he wanted was one unstable psychopath let alone seven of them.

He returned the salute, "Permission granted Captain Siven," even as he said it he wondered what might have happened had he denied permission. Saviour looked across at the rest of the waiting team who stood silently staring in his direction; even from that distance the stare was unsettling. Although not clones they had remarkable similarities and they all scared the crap out of him.

Siven like a man in a hurry moved quickly towards Silva who was now standing on her feet near her mother and father, "Sir, Ma'am may I speak with Silvana?"

"Of course Captain," Marine said smiling, "are you being deployed?"

"Yes Ma'am, I don't have long." Then crouching down he beckoned Silva to him. "Hello little sister I'm glad you returned in time, I wanted to talk to you and this may be the last opportunity."

"You're coming back, aren't you?" the young woman said softly.

"I don't think so, not this time, we have outlived our time. We all sense a growing anxiety with those we come in contact with, even

Project Leader Tyler was not being honest with us at the briefing today. His body was giving all the wrong messages. Especially when he was telling us about the anti-virus and how we are to inject ourselves before we leave the southern base with the serum your father gave us. He said it was to reinforce the previous course of treatment but he was lying, his stress chemicals were flooding out. I believe they are terminating us." His grey eyes rarely blinked as he looked steadily at Silva, his tongue periodically flicked partially out then in again. "Your father prepared the serum phials, have you heard anything?" His voice was pitched low; even a man with normal hearing would have to be touching him to have heard his words.

Silva leaned forward, she had no fear of Siven, and his steady unblinking gaze never caused her a moment's concern as she wrapped her arms around his thick neck. Pressing her mouth close to his ear and speaking very, very quietly she said, "Siven, if my father gave you the serum phial directly into your hands take it before you embark, he does not wish you harm." She backed away again.

Captain Siven examined the girl before him, he sniffed a couple of times. "I will do as you say little sister, and now take this just in case. It will open my lock-box at the barracks everything is yours, do you understand me?" He held out a square, clear, electronic key.

"You're coming back, tell me, tell me you're coming back by the sun setting on the third day from now." Her voice betrayed her feelings.

"Shush now, I will collect this from you before the sun sets in three days time, just hold it for me, yes."

"I will hold it for you and that is all." She said firmly.

"You did well at the games, but do not stop there, you can do more, you know that, and if they had enough sense they would know that also." He brushed her cheek with his index finger, "One day you will emerge into the light and you will make us proud but please little sister, never, ever allow them to control you." He turned his head slightly as though hearing a soft wind-blown command, "Now, I must go, they are waiting but if I may offer one last piece of advice, learn to relax that way you will be in control. I think you panicked a little and let recent events control you. Good-bye." He stood up in one fluid motion.

"Captain Siven?" said Ewen Maurice, Silva's father.

"Sir?" his head turned in one move the grey eyes fixed on the speaker.

Ewen held out his hand, "My daughter is expected to travel around the country; she will need someone she trusts to watch out for her."

Clasping the extended hand in return, Siven said, "Look around you, there are five thousand well trained soldiers here who will guard her safely."

"But not one understands her like you do." Then much quieter, barely hearing his own words, "Get back as soon as you are able, but do not use the military transports to return from the Medi States. Good luck."

Siven gazed unblinkingly at Ewen Maurice, his face a mask of unreadable signs, he let go of the hand he held, saluted, turned and ran back to meet up with the team he commanded.

"Uncle General," Silva said, "where are they going?"

General Saviour watched the departing squad his face held a grim expression, without turning he answered, "I cannot say - they are covert operatives. Like all their missions it is a secret, and not without hazard. Now if you'll excuse me I have things to discuss with your grandmother." He nodded to Silva's parents before walking away to join General Conrad.

The following day Doctor Maurice and Project Leader Tyler sat quietly in the conference room, Tyler flicked idly through some notes on his display pad whilst Ewen Maurice updated some notes he had started earlier. Drinks and buffet food were available at the dispenser should they have required them.

The door slid open allowing General Saviour and a tall man, unknown to Ewen, to enter the spacious room. "Doctor Maurice may I introduce Major Calvert, he is from the investigations section of the Office of Scientific Funding and Audit."

"Major," said Maurice politely. He knew of the section but had had no previous dealings with them, he didn't have to; he could fund his own projects.

"Doctor Maurice," the auditor said in a voiced pitched higher than you'd expect from a man his size, "A pleasure to meet you, I have read most of your papers on gene management and order."

Maurice smiled, "Then you are two things Major, one, more than a military man and two, a military man with too much time on his hands."

"Quite so," Calvert laughed, seemingly sincerely. "I am a Bio-engineer by training but I like to read around subjects that we currently fund, just so I don't look a complete idiot when I discuss projects."

"Gentlemen, please be seated." the General pressed an icon on the table top. "For the record this conversation will be recorded in all formats, copies will be available to any of you who require them. Master copies will be forwarded and retained in the archives of the Office of Scientific Funding and Audit. Major if you please."

"Thank you General. The purpose of this meeting is to discuss Team Phantom. As you know OSFA has funded this project since its inception seventeen years ago and from the very beginning Doctor Header was the mandatory case management officer. However he has recently retired and I have inherited his oversight role. For information's sake Doctor Header was the person who originally gave the go-ahead for Project Phantom.

Doctor Tyler has recently advised us that the current project is being concluded but has requested more funds for developing a second phase. I have requested the presence of Doctor Maurice as an advisor since his specialism is in this area.

All information and material associated with this discussion has a classification level of 'Ultra', so although you may have copies of the record of this meeting for legal purposes they cannot be published in any format. Any questions before we begin?"

As there were none the Major continued, "Very well, Doctor

Tyler correct me if I am wrong. According to my predecessor's file notes, your work started with, quote, 'as an idea based on my investigations into what I call the hidden genome', unquote." In fact you wrote a paper on the topic expressing your belief that man's complete evolutionary history is held within redundant or inactive units within the genome."

"Yes, in twenty-two-eighty-four if my memory serves me."

"As you say and I have the very paper here with just you as the sole author. Now I have searched the databases and the complete university archive and I find no research or unpublished papers associated with you as the basis for that theory."

"Excuse me major but I was under the belief that we are discussing the current project." Tyler bristled.

"We are, but having looked through your initial application, unlike my predecessor I have seen no foundation work upon which your theory was based. If I am to consider a further grant of funding I must satisfy myself that it is going to provide some sort of benefit to the State and not just fund a personal project. You see Doctor the annual reports that you were required to file with us, are not as frequently received as specified in the original contract. In my analysis of the ones you did manage to file, there appears to be a disturbing lack of any detailed information regarding the current project's development."

"Are you suggesting that the project has had no benefit or that my reports are in some way intentionally misleading?" Tyler was getting redder with each word; he wasn't used to being challenged; after all wasn't he the Project leader?

"Misleading, hmm, an interesting choice of words if I may say so, not one I would have used. General perhaps you could address that point, what do you see as the benefits?" Calvert turned pointedly to Saviour.

"Team Phantom is beyond doubt made up of good, no, excellent soldiers. They have a one hundred percent mission success rate; they do not appear to suffer from Post Traumatic Stress Disorders. This is especially noteworthy since they have been constantly in the field for a number of years. But and it is a big but, although within the team there appears to be a close camaraderie, with outsiders there appears to be a lack of social interaction. That alone, should the need arise, makes it difficult to integrate any of them into another team. From what I am told by my officers nobody is comfortable with them. Their lack of the normal visual clues as to how they might react is definitely a handicap as it makes them unpredictable. Strangely enough the only time I have noticed anything remotely emotional about them was yesterday when Captain Siven spoke with Doctor Maurice's daughter Silvana."

"Interesting," observed Major Calvert, "but would you say they are safe. Do they always observe their instructions or orders for instance?"

"I have heard nothing from my officers to suggest any problems in briefings or training programs. When given orders they follow them to the letter without hesitation and so far as I know they have not appeared in any way aggressive towards any man on the base." The General reported.

Tyler cleared his throat.

"Yes Doctor, you have something to add?" Calvert turned to face Tyler.

"From the psych' tests we perform regularly, they are showing signs of increased instability with time. It is my opinion that if they were not engaged in combat roles for any period they would become a danger. That is why I chose to end the program. All of them show the traits of a high spectrum predator, they need to kill, it is their raison d'être. How they would cope in isolation from each other I have no idea but I suspect it would not be well."

"So what you are really saying is that your original choice of genetic modelling was flawed?" Calvert challenged.

"It is not an exact science, even after three hundred years we still do not fully understand how the two percent of the genome is controlled by the majority. What is less understood is the area of expertise upon which I wrote my paper, the inactive genes that were once part of our evolutionary growth. The last sixteen years has taught us a lot we didn't know before."

"Doctor Maurice?" Major Calvert swivelled in his seat, "do you have an opinion on this?"

"I cannot agree or disagree with Doctor Tyler as I have had no access either to ongoing physical or mental assessments or indeed any of the files linked to this project."

Tyler interjected, "It is of course a military endeavour and Doctor Maurice is a civilian as you may know Major Calvert."

"However," continued Ewen Maurice, "I feel it is wrong to terminate the project on the basis of on an opinion which has, as far as I have observed no evidence to support it. Has an independent assessment been performed on the team members? If not, then the analysis of Doctor Tyler may be brought into question. After all he may intentionally or otherwise have misinterpreted the data as he may himself have personal issues with the team. I do not believe all, if any, of the members of Team Phantom, are lost to us, especially Captain Siven who holds the others together; he is the alpha of the group."

"Have you had any opportunity to examine the genome of all the members to see if there is any way to put right the failings both Doctor Tyler and General Saviour have indicated?" asked Major Calvert.

"Regrettably Doctor Tyler has not seen fit to provide me with the appropriate data, however I have acquired my own samples with the acquiescence of each team member and constructed their gene model. They had a right of refusal but they chose not to."

"You've done what?" burst out Tyler. "How dare you? This is unbelievably unethical, not to mention a breach of security protocols. You do not have the security clearance or authority to replicate my work."

"I am not replicating your work," replied Ewen Maurice. "I am merely examining what you have already created, which as Major Calvert has already pointed out, is flawed. You forgot to mention that your prototypes are seventeen years old, nearly the same age as my daughter in fact and yet they look ten years older. They are in fact aging roughly twenty percent faster than the average human being. General Saviour mentioned their resistance to stress disorders, that doesn't mean they have none. They just do not exhibit the usual signs. That quality has been used as a reason to put them on more missions than normal. I believe it is that, that may have created the instability Doctor Tyler speaks of.

On the other hand because they are predators, being in the field may not be stressful to them. These men have been treated like experimental animals so don't be surprised when they act like them. Another point you made General is their lack of social skills. First of all the military must take responsibility for that, for it was the military that has directed their social or moral compass. All their lives they have been trained for one thing and one thing alone, to infiltrate and remove a specific target. They do it well, they are loyal and I believe that provided you do not attack them, they pose no threat. Any awkwardness in interactions could be due to the responses they get from others. After all every man on the base knows what they are and what they do, it's only natural some may be afraid. Maybe somebody should take them out for a beer and see how they respond. Finally I do not believe Project Leader Tyler has their confidence and because of that I believe they are less than forthcoming about their situation."

"Thank you Doctor Maurice, General, where is the team currently?" Calvert asked.

"In the field, I have been advised they were deployed late last night under the direction of the Allied Command." Saviour replied.

"Then there is no immediate chance of recall?"

"None Major, not one chance in hell, and I do not believe they will return from this mission."

"Because?" Calvert said disturbed by this admission.

"I am sorry Major but I cannot discuss the mission details even with the President, suffice to say it is probably the most hazardous mission of the war. An easy way to dispose of things that embarrass you," Saviour looked sharply at Tyler.

Major Calvert sucked his lip considering his options before speaking, "Doctor Tyler in view of the large investment the State has in this project I find it more than a little disconcerting that you decided to terminate it without prior discussion. However we may yet see the team members return since they have a sufficiently good record of survival."

"You won't," Tyler said more rapidly than he would have liked.

"Won't what?" Calvert queried.

"You won't see them again. Their mission involves entering a bio-hazard zone; they have no protection against what may be in there."

"Doctor," General Saviour spoke with a commanding voice, "I was led to understand that they would be inoculated against possible contamination. In fact it was you that told me that when we discussed this mission."

"I did, but a military base is not always the best of places to keep secrets. If they had known the treatment they received was merely a placebo and they were potentially going to their deaths, do you think you could have controlled them? I doubt it. You may have five thousand troops here but none of them are as skilled at killing as Team Phantom. They have no emotional or moral checks and that makes them far more ruthless than any you command." Tyler sounded like a man self-satisfied with his creation.

"Then you haven't considered the fact that they may have a more resistant immune system than the average man?" Doctor Maurice took no pleasure in stating what should have been obvious to Tyler.

"What? Absurd! You can have no possible reason for believing that." Tyler looked aghast at the idea.

"Doctor, you have, in re-creating their genome, activated sequences that we do not fully understand. Haven't you considered that their more acute senses, low emotional responses and totally dispassionate mind set is more in keeping with one of our primitive pre-human forebears? If you consider that then ask yourself do reptiles suffer from the same viruses we do?" Ewen nodded his head as he noted Tyler was beginning to see where he was going. "You have monitored them all their life; tell us, do they ever get sick?"

All eyes in the room focused on Doctor Tyler.

After some thought Tyler swept his upper lip with his tongue, "No, no they don't, they get bouts of lethargy but I don't recall them suffering any of the usual illnesses even as children."

"Dear God," muttered Saviour.

"What are you saying Doctor Maurice?" Calvert had trouble following the full implications of what he had heard.

"What he is saying Major," Saviour interrupted, "is that Team Phantom may well return and when they do they are not going to be to happy should they learn they have been lied to. If they think Doctor Tyler tried to kill them off or at least made no effort to protect them on this mission then whatever faith they have in him will be gone. We become another enemy and then who knows how many men we will lose."

"But you have their tracking beacons," a flustered Tyler said trying hard to prevent the inevitable.

"They do not have infinite range; it's only about thirty miles so within that range we can track their progress."

"Then you could send men to stop them?" When all else is gone all that ever remains is hope even for Tyler.

"Why is it that men like you always think the military should do your dirty work for you?" General Saviour was angry and he didn't have to or want to hide it. "These men may be feared by a lot of the troops around here but they are more respected. I would think most would have great trouble executing their own brothers in arms. If I were you doctor I would find somewhere far away to conduct your work and I wouldn't leave it too late."

"Doctor Maurice," Major Calvert wished to change the topic to something a little less charged with emotion. "What did you find Doctor, I mean with the gene models you constructed for Team Phantom?"

"Well let's say the genetic changes that were made are not ones I would have chosen. In my opinion Doctor Tyler was very lucky to have any viable individuals." A draught of air passed into the room causing Doctor Maurice to look round, the door was just closing and Doctor Tyler was no longer there.

"How so?" Calvert continued, seeking clarification and ignoring Tyler's lack of presence.

"Major, the more we learn about how the genes work the more we fail to comprehend. Scientists have been looking at the human genome for three hundred years and a great many successes have come about in the medical field. However in the field of Creative Genetics we are still groping in the dark. To really know the outcomes of any alterations we must create a living organism and many would say that is unethical, it's too risky. They are probably right. Even after years of study and experimentation it is unlikely, unless you are very lucky, that you can recreate the associations within the genes that nature took millions of years to achieve. I think Doctor Tyler was very lucky, based on the work he did and his understanding of the field to get even seven functioning outcomes out of the original fifty

"I agree," Calvert began. "I could find no recorded experiments or papers on his theories beyond the one I spoke of. So he either conducted illegal and therefore unrecorded experiments or he never did any. What I find interesting however; and why my predecessor never saw this I do not know, is that your paper on the theory predated Doctor Tyler's by three years. I even found a record of a discussion paper on Project Xenon. A most detailed work in which you proposed the possibility of creating a human being with enhanced sensory characteristics. Characteristics which once served us well in our evolutionary past but are no longer required in our more sedentary existence."

"That was a long time ago Major."

"True, but Doctor Tyler must have read it and plagiarised it before he made some intuitive steps in fulfilling the idea."

"Probably little better than guess work." Maurice said without rancour. "You see the whole basis of my theory was that hidden in our genes are markers, dormant genes that show us our hereditary journey from simple organism to what we are today. Characteristics, senses that we once used to survive were shut down and archived when we evolved; newer perhaps more efficient systems taking their place. Of course those newer characteristics may have been more limited in scope since we no longer needed the strength or power we once had. Once our lives became more sedentary, settling down and building strong defences to protect ourselves, we no longer needed such acute senses to detect approaching threats. Nor the physical strength to fight them, we could make weapons and fight at a distance. Mankind just hid behind his walls. In short we could afford to be weaker physically even mentally since we replaced that internal strength with an external one. The more technology advances the more we can retreat from the world out there, into a fool's paradise.

However you can't just switch these dormant genes on per se because the dominant management genes do not work in isolation. They work in teams, often in what appears to be unrelated components. Without all the constituent management genes, there could be one, two or many, to guide the gene processes you may not get what you expect. Plus you have to consider not just potential physical attributes, but the mental ones also. After all if you effectively create the neural links of what were once our ancestors you cannot necessarily expect them to think as we do."

"Is that why the members of Team Phantom seem, shall we say, so alien?" asked Saviour.

"It has to be a consideration. Tyler is not an idiot but he hadn't thought through the implications of his modifications. I don't think he can have explored the meaning of the gene sites he used."

"Is that why you never followed Project Xenon through?" Major Calvert pursued.

Before Ewen could answer a knock at the door caused him to pause.

"Come in," yelled Saviour.

The door swung outwards.

"If I had followed the path I had theorised I could have ended up with….."

"Silva," the General said, smiling as he did so, "what can we do for you?"

"Hello Uncle General," she saluted smartly, "as I was passing I just thought you'd like to know Dog-in-a-box is due just after twelve hundred hours and Doctor Tyler has just left. Since he was taking a lot of badly packed cases I don't think he will be back any time soon."

"And you came by this intelligence how?" Saviour enquired further, a benevolent look lit up his face.

"To the former, I asked someone why they were tidying up outside of the normal schedule. The latter I watched him go. If it helps he was sweating a lot, his heart rate was elevated, in short he was in a state of panic." Silva smiled continually.

"Then gentlemen I must leave you, no doubt my aides will think of informing me of this intelligence one fine day."

Major Calvert stood as Saviour moved away from the table.

"Major, can I ask what your recommendation will be concerning Doctor Tyler's request for further funding?"

"General, I cannot in all honesty, in view of his past record consider his application in a positive light. Not to mention the cavalier attitude towards disposing of the subjects before an inquiry was held into Team Phantom's current mental and physical state. I shall be recommending his position here be terminated."

"Should Team Phantom return; what happens then?"

"General, if that happens I believe they should be taken from active service and properly assessed before any further decisions are taken."

"Very well, when you've written your report make sure I get a copy. If you require anything further ask my staff by all means but I will be engaged for the rest of the day. I expect Doctor Maurice and Silva will help you sort out Doctor Tyler's files; they'll have to be impounded. I suggest you talk to Captain Morris in Intel' if you have trouble accessing the data retrieval system in the laboratory. Good day."

Calvert saluted the departing General before saying "We live in interesting times."

"We always do Major, most people just don't see it," observed Silva.

"While you are pondering those words of wisdom, let me introduce my daughter, Silva."

"Who has I believe done the impossible," Calvert replied holding out his hand.

Silva looked at the hand. "Not impossible Major Calvert, not beating them would have been impossible."

Calvert froze allowing the words to sink in, and then he smiled broadly. "Well it is none-the-less a pleasure to meet you."

Silvana finally decided to shake Calvert's hand a studied expression crossed her face.

"You must be very proud of her Doctor." Calvert looked back to Doctor Maurice.

Maurice placed his hands on his daughters shoulders, "I have always been proud of my little girl, as is her mother, she's worked hard to achieve everything she has. Entering a world-class competition has been her dream for as long as I remember and I have done nothing to put her off. However without the intervention of Leading Instructor Gibson it would probably have remained a dream."

"How so?" enquired Calvert.

"Gibson spotted her ability by accident." Ewen pointed out simply.

"I got caught using the trainee dive pool one night," Silva added candidly by way of a deeper explanation.

"Ah!" acknowledged Calvert.

"A happy accident but then after consulting with General

Saviour," Doctor Maurice continued, "Gibson took her under his wing and then after seeing her abilities they decided to sponsor her which was really beyond our expectations as it made the process a lot easier than it might have been."

"Oh, I thought that the General was already close to your family, what with Silva calling him Uncle General."

"General Saviour has known Silva since her was posted here about ten years ago but I don't think he was aware of her swimming abilities. My daughter is not one to brag about how good she is."

"At least not while I've got you to do it for me," said his precocious offspring.

Calvert smiled, then looking down from his position one foot seven inches taller than the girl, he asked Silva, "What will you do now, now that you've achieved your dream?"

Silva frowned and screwed her mouth up, "I have a dream or two left but for now I shall continue being an analyst for my father."

"Analyst, forgive me but Doctor I thought I heard you say Silva was nearly eighteen."

"So she is."

"Not quite seventeen," Silva interrupted.

Maurice continued, "She has been my wife's assistant for nearly two years. Don't look so surprised Major, her intelligence register is within the top zero-point-five percent of the standard model. She has very good pattern solving capabilities which make her good at what she does. However she does have a few problems."

"Such as?"

"To be honest Major, if I started now you'd be twice my age before I got halfway, Oof." The final comment was caused by a rapid expelling of air due to a sharp elbow being jabbed into his ribs. "She also has violent tendencies, but I love her dearly." He wheezed as he bent over slightly.

Calvert smiled at the easy going relationship the parent and child had, he wished he'd been so lucky. "Well duty calls, reports don't write themselves. I'll put Tyler's lab on lockdown for today: tomorrow I shall go through his files and interview his assistant. Should I need your aid may I call upon you?"

"Of course, should I be unavailable Silva can, I assure you, be of use to you. You will certainly need her when the team returns."

"You believe they will?"

"Major those men are survivors. Yes, most certainly they will return within the next three days. They like Silva so she'll be able to reassure them everything is as it should be, that is as long as people don't go firing weapons in their direction. Don't look so worried, they have no reason to harm you. If they arrive when you're on your own just talk to them as normal people, tell them who you are and what has happened with Doctor Tyler. Have a coffee, ask them how it went, believe me the worst that will happen is they'll just look at you."

"Not very reassuring, anyway I'll speak with you later." Calvert nodded to Silva and turned to go. Silva released the hold she had on her father allowing him to gather his things together.

Having picked up his equipment and fitted them into a satchel Doctor Ewen Maurice turned. He was just in time to see that Major Calvert hadn't left as intended but was approaching the turned back of Silva, his hand descending onto Silva's shoulder. Time seemed to slow as he saw his preoccupied daughter suddenly sensed movement behind her. Then her back and head arched backwards, almost by reflex Doctor Maurice dropped his bag, thrusting out his left arm as he reached for Silva's rapidly rising leg. Just in time he grabbed his daughter's ankle as her instep was passing over her head. Her shod foot stopped barely an inch from the bridge of Calvert's nose. The Major froze when his brain told him what was happening, adrenaline pumped into his system from the fight or flight response. He sucked air, in one rapid intake of breath. Calvert was pale, bordering on white as the blood was withdrawn to his leg muscles. Events had happened so fast he hadn't had time to move, and then he blinked. Maurice held his daughter's foot, firmly talking to her; reassuring her Calvert was not a threat. Eventually Maurice looked up; assessing the Major, noticing the colour was once more starting to return to the man's cheeks. He also noticed the laboured breathing and the shaking caused by the excess adrenaline as it was used up.

"Better sit down Major before you drop. Look I'm sorry about that but I forgot to mention that my daughter doesn't like being surprised or touched by people she doesn't know."

"The surprise was all mine I assure you." Calvert replied as he breathed raggedly, the shock to his system still apparent. "I'm sorry; I just wanted to ask what 'Dog-in-a-box' meant."

"The State President, he's a Dog-in-a-box." Silva said candidly.

Calvert looked blank.

"My daughter read a book when she was ten; it was called simply, 'Dog-in-a-Box'. You could call it an allegorical work that had more than a couple of levels of intellectual interest. The storyline was centred on a dog, literally in a box, having to experience the world without seeing it and deriving conclusions about the way it worked from what it otherwise sensed. The book was about exploring what we perceive as reality, both in a personal way, you know, what we are, where did we come from etcetera, and the external reality. On another level it was really a metaphor. The box represented restricted perceptions or closed minded thinking and how the reality of the world and life in general was affected by those perceptions. Should you change the belief system, then the reality in which you live alters. Was the box a prison or a secure place from horrible experiences?" Maurice explained, all the while observing the serving officer.

"Hardly a book for a ten year old," Calvert said trying to control his breathing, "and the relationship with the President?"

"He's like the dog analysing what it senses, trying to appease the many conflicting ideas mostly without success, to gain some idea of the reality of the world. The very ideas he has create more insoluble questions than answers. So to resolve the conflicts he should adopt only one of them initially and see how it fits what he believes." Silva just looked at Calvert then her face crumpled into a wide smile. "I'm sorry, you caught me off guard."

Placing a hand on his daughter's shoulder her father said to Calvert, "May I ask if you've seen active service?" He pondered the dilated pupils, the sweating brow and the skin that was likely to be clammy to the touch.

"Yes, several times in the field, the last two occasions were a nightmare, we lost over fifty men. I was lucky to get away unscathed."

"You didn't get away unscathed, Major; you know that as well as I. What medication are you on?"

"Trilevanse patch daily, I'm down to median-five strength now."

Maurice winced, he knew the drug, and that the man seated in front of him was walking a tightrope because of it. He just hoped the shock he'd just had didn't trigger any anxiety issues he was restraining. He removed a packet from his case, and expelled a wafer from a slim cassette inside, "Here put this on your tongue, it'll slow you down a bit but you'll be back in control."

"Thanks," Calvert said starting to breathe more steadily as the fast acting chemical wafer dissolved. "Silva's reactions are fast."

"Yes, her reaction time is less than half yours or mine. When you're ready Silva will go with you to the lab. Don't even think of arguing, she'll look after you better than your own mother and she'll clear any obstacles out of your way with Tyler's staff should they occur. It's the least she can do."

The staffroom was full of commissioned officers when General Saviour stepped through the door. Silence immediately fell over the assembled men and women as they saluted as one. With a brief salute in return he passed to the front before turning to face his audience.

"You will probably already know the President is soon to be our guest, regrettably I doubt he will be in a good mood. The recent success of our mascot at the games has triggered an enquiry into Silva's life history. This is because when he talks, the President likes to speak factually about things, just so he doesn't sound stupid. As a politician he hasn't yet realised the impossibility of that task."

He paused as a ripple of laughter ran around the room.

"Most of you, if not all, will probably already know that Silvana Maurice has no official record of her existence. Her birth was never recorded and so she has never had the mandatory medical checks in her life. The only records that exist we hold here and they pertain to Silva's educational achievements since she passed through the school with the other civilian staff's children. The lack of information is going to cause the President a few worrying thoughts.

So be prepared to answer any and all questions he or his staff put to you without prevarication or dishonesty. In short tell the truth, it might save your careers. I'd be surprised if any of you have not come in contact with Silva. You will have seen her about the base and those of you who have stood sentry duties will have had her company from time to time. You might recall her pressing you with questions about where you come from and what it's like there. She's friendly and exceptionally curious about the world beyond our perimeter. The reason for that is simple, until the games she had never set foot beyond the wire."

A ripple of questioning comment passed around the room, he let it flow before eventually holding up a hand.

"She doesn't officially exist and therefore has no identity card that will allow her to travel, that is the Presidential dilemma. How can she travel our country to inspire others without an I.D? If you ask her though she'll tell you she has no interest in such things, she's happy here. There's the woodland and lakes on the Centre's estate and the work she does for her father keeps her occupied and with your support she achieved her dream. So be truthful we have nothing to hide, tell it as you find it. Thank you for your time."

Saviour saluted and left the gathering that soon dissipated as they went back to their duties.

The pale blue Presidential carrier rotated in the air over the landing zone, its photovoltaic skin sucking in sunlight energy to drive the engine set beneath the fuselage. The blades' rotation increasing as the nearly silent, horizontally set drive, took over from the twin forward thrusting vertical fin engines. The dust swirled as the air currents blasted downward onto the photovoltaic pressure pads, allowing the sleek vessel to settle slowly and gently down.

No sooner had the wheels touched the ground than the Presidential honour guard trotted out double time from the hanger to the entrance ramp that slowly disgorged from beneath the hull, forward of the engine. The President's personal guard detail exited first, their keen eyes scanning the immediate area, a pointless act given they were walking within the confines of one of the most secure military bases in the Republic. That is unless they thought a coup was likely, in which case the act was equally pointless, six men against five thousand are not good odds. The President himself followed closely behind, the moment his face cleared the obscuring hatch the honour guard snapped to attention their high-energy compressed air weapons held forward, their barrels pointing downwards. General Saviour stood in his dress uniform, pale blue with dark belts and gold chevrons cascading down his sleeve. Medals emblazoned his chest showing a lifetime's achievement in his chosen career. They were there to send a message to an ephemeral political bureaucrat. He saluted before shaking the extended hand, his eyes trying to read those of the elected Head of State.

"Mister President, welcome to SeaSolar."

"General," his voice was taut, "I think we need to talk."

After that communication was brief as the base commander guided the political elite to his office. President Able Dawson-Wells may not have been the only holder of his post with the most inappropriate Christian name - that honour belonged to Capability Wallis but he was not far removed. He was a career politician, greasing his way to popularity by appeasement. True he had an easy manner that helped give him the air of a man who cared about his 'subjects' far more than himself. He had the manner of a salesman but all he really cared about was the bottom line, his bottom line. And not unlike like the many men and women like him through the centuries he would have to face reality sooner or later. For him being at the centre of the country's most secure military base, surrounded by thousands of soldiers, half of which were veterans of years of war, was not the safest of places. The Guardian fought and died for their country not the politicians that ran it, they knew their duty, and you annoy them at your peril.

Once in the General's office and after accepting the proffered drink, the President sat down opposite General Saviour mulling over what his best approach would be. He had noticed the medals not just on the General but on the honour guard as well, even for someone as self-centred as he was their significance was not lost on him.

"General, ever since your girl won the championship," not knowing the name of the nation's most recent heroine was not a good start.

"Her name is Silvana Maurice," Saviour interrupted helpfully. He didn't like to see a man dig his own grave too early or too fast.

"Quite so, ever since Silvana showed the world what young people are capable of, I have had her background looked into, so that we may advise the public about her with honesty and clarity."

Difficult words for a politician to understand, honesty and clarity, when much of what those in office say came nowhere close to either of those descriptions, thought Saviour.

"Surprisingly, despite their best endeavours my security staff has found practically nothing about her with the small exception of her academic achievements which were filed under the military education program. I wonder how this fact, that she has no record of her life since birth has skipped your attention."

"It hasn't." The General said directly.

"You mean you are aware of it? For how long?"

"I have known about Silvana from the moment I took up this posting, my predecessor advised me of her status, he was here when she was born."

"And you personally have taken no action." The President was slightly astonished at the response he was getting.

"On the contrary I have taken a keen interest in her; she is a most intelligent young lady as the files on her education show. She is polite and has never been any trouble to anyone, probably quite the opposite."

"You must surely be aware of the laws that make the registration of a birth mandatory, not to mention the stipulations in health monitoring for the first five years. There are no exemptions. We cannot allow the medical problems caused by uncontrolled genetic inheritance to return. All citizens must be assessed without exception."

"I am well aware of the medical history of our nation, and the current state of this country's health. So far as I know Silvana has never been sick in her life, all the childhood diseases passed her over. She's never even attended the base dentistry centre. At the risk of repetition, her intelligence evaluation is higher than most people running this country."

"Be that as it may, the law is the law, if you allow one person to dodge the rules where will it end?" The politician blustered.

"Fine, her parents failed to register her birth, officially she doesn't exist and that Sir is your problem. As I see it you have a few choices, drag the parents through the courts and levy a hefty fine, then take Silvana out to the marshes, shoot her in the head and leave the body to rot. But alas you can't do that, after all the public have a new heroine, someone to take their minds off this protracted war. You remove her and your life will be measured in minutes, if that."

"Are you threatening me General?"

"Absolutely not Mister President, but the public will not stand for an attack on whoever is their current darling. You could kiss goodbye to any re-election, even your party may end up in the wilderness for years, if not decades. Before you act too hastily I suggest you meet her and her parents so you can make a sound judgement on how to proceed. You will see her value I'm sure."

President Dawson-Wells swallowed his indignation with the drink he held in his hand. It momentarily crossed his mind it could be poisoned but he reminded himself Saviour was a soldier and soldiers don't do that sort of thing. They just shoot you.

"Very well, arrange it but you have no idea the difficulty you have all put me in. Already my office is being bombarded with requests for information about Silvana and they want to know why there is no public information available. Then there are interested parties who want her to travel the country promoting the achievements of the young and those that want her to inspire the same group. People want to see her; but without documentation she can't travel. How on earth has she travelled about anyway?"

"She never has, before the competition she had never left this base."

"What, never?" said the President aghast.

"Never, not once and when she went to the games she travelled with a military escort."

"Then she's little better than a prisoner."

"Well sir isn't that what you want her to be, under the law of the land? However Silva has never shown any interest in seeing the world or the country. She works for her parents at the Centre and so far as I know she has never ventured near the main gate. Not once has she tried to run away."

"Remarkable."

"She is Sir in every way; now if you would join me for lunch in the Officer's Mess I shall arrange a visit to see Doctors Maurice and Silva this afternoon."

The meal was standard military fare, even the President could expect no frills on this base, even so it was better than some meals he was forced to eat at dignified functions. "Have you ever heard of a Professor Dios?" The President asked once the table had been cleared.

"Not to my knowledge, should I have done?" General Saviour asked easing back his seat.

"I don't expect so, he's an academic with a seat at Scotia Universal, specialising in high energy physics. He's applied for project funding."

"Oh, and what is he proposing?"

"Believe it or not he has applied for State funding to build a pilot experimental facility to investigate the reality of time. It will involve creating two rotating plasma fields through which he believes we can move back maybe even forward in time."

"Sounds like he's been in the sun too long," Saviour quipped.

"Perhaps, but my advisors say that initial examination of the plans suggest it could be inherently unstable. Unofficially they say it could end up an expensive smoking hole in the ground."

"With little in the way of strategic merit I assume."

"Absolutely none so far as I can see, just an exercise to clarify theoretical beliefs. There are of course some quite frightening considerations, if it were possible."

"Such as?" Saviour asked politely even though he wasn't particularly interested. As an engineer by academic training he could work out the ramifications himself without the help of this political dunderhead.

"Well imagine if you went back say a hundred years and killed off my ancestors you wouldn't have me for President, possibly even not my Party."

"I thought you said there was no strategic merit sir." Saviour said dryly, a slight smile on his lips.

President Dawson-Wells stalled in his mental tracks, and then he smiled the smile of a politician, "Very good General, very good."

"I shouldn't worry sir; I doubt if you'll build it, after all if it was constructed and it worked surely someone would have left a message to say so. I can imagine the media headlines from way back, 'Men from the future tell us to change our ways otherwise we'll be at war for ten years with AfCon.'"

"Speaking of which have you heard anything from Trojan?"

Trojan was the code name for the current operation against the African Confederation, which involved Team Phantom.

"No sir, we do not expect to hear anything from our men before the early hours of tomorrow if at all."

"Meaning?" the President turned a concerned face towards the General.

"It is a highly hazardous operation sir, and there are those that do not believe we shall see our men again."

"Are you one of them General?"

"No sir, I know these men and their capabilities, they'll be back here before the outcome is known. That is unless someone doesn't want any witnesses left alive."

"Would that bother you, after all it is for the benefit of the Country?"

"Yes Mister President it would bother me, it would bother me greatly and I'll tell you why it would bother me. If Team Phantom makes it back and finds out someone put out a kill order on them they will not forget or more importantly forgive. They are very good at what they do, they enjoy the hunt and I wouldn't want them hunting me. So if I was in your position and such a request came forward I wouldn't put my name to it. You don't need a time machine to get rid of a President who is prepared to kill those who serve their country."

Dawson-Wells cleared his throat and shifted awkwardly in his seat. He was saved further discomfort by an aide, who came to advise General Saviour that the Maurice family had arrived.

It was early evening before the Presidential flight took off, watched by the Maurice family, General Saviour and Silva's grandmother, General Abigail Conrad. For most of the afternoon Doctors Ewen and Marine Maurice had explained the nature of their daughter's conception and the subsequent genetic manipulation that had been instrumental in allowing her to develop and be born. Questions had been asked and answered. Silvana had been presented by her proud parents to the top political dignitary, who had, on meeting the new national heroine, made the usual predictable comments on her victory.

By the time the meeting had ended President Dawson-Wells knew he was trapped. Even having looked the young Silvana Maurice in the eye he knew there was nothing he could do to avoid what may be the inevitable. The girl's steady gaze had unnerved him. Looking at him without her glasses made him feel he was under the microscope but at the same moment it was the first time he had felt personal fear. Even with his bodyguard standing feet away outside the office, he hadn't felt safe in the room with her. Why was that he wondered, it wasn't as if she had made any threatening movements, quite the opposite in fact she'd been very friendly. It was as though her, her disability was of no significance. He wondered if that was what frightened him, her total acceptance of what was and her undeniable confidence that she could deal with it. As General Saviour had pointed out he couldn't make her disappear, the Guardian wouldn't like that and neither would the people. But then they hadn't seen what he had just seen.

He knew of course he couldn't reveal the nature of Silva's genetic history, to do that would be to have her win in the games made null and void. His country would become the laughing stock of the world, they would be called cheats. As a politician he knew how to win the political games, taking risks was part of it - getting caught wasn't. There would be risks too in letting her roam the free world as his country's sporting ambassador. It would only take a single slip for someone to see her without her glasses. What if? What if? That was the one single thought he had hammering away in his mind. What if he hadn't been told everything and there were other things? He didn't feel reassured.

Why his chief aide General Conrad had said nothing before about her granddaughter he did not know for certain. All he could assume was that it had to do with family loyalty but that same loyalty had put him in an invidious position. Dawson-Wells wondered what he might have done had this slip of a girl not won the swimming events.

That scenario was irrelevant, as he undoubtedly would never have come to hear about her, he told himself. The Guardian would have protected her as they had always done. The problem for him was that he didn't know why.

The aircraft levelled out after its initial climb, the noise level dropped as the lifting drive slowed down allowing the rear thrusters to push the vessel back to the capital. He had time to think. Weighing up his options he knew one thing above all others, he was not going to commit political suicide. Yes he was trapped but he had been offered a way out.

02:00hrs South Europa

Camp Titan – United Islands Military forward base.

"Incoming," shouted the Impulse Radar operator.

The attendant officer looked south across the Mediterranean Sea through his night vision long-range lenses. "What is it?"

"Sir, looks like a small surface skimmer, heading straight and true for the harbour wall, three miles and closing."

Lead Officer Kent triggered the alarm system for the two guard positions either side of the harbour entrance. "Attention, attention, we have an incoming small surface vessel heading for the harbour wall." Kent's voice was clear and audible to the guard forces having linked his own audio communicator with the main system.

"Any communication signals coming from the craft?" Kent asked his signals and communications tracker.

The operator looked at the read-outs from the all band high frequency audio scanners, looking for any emanating signals. "Nothing sir the airwaves are clear, even the traffic on the other side has almost shut down."

"Since when?" Kent asked, his curiosity peeked.

"I noticed it first around twenty-two hundred, it's been getting progressively quieter since. Do you think it's coming sir?" The operator looked up at his superior, every man and woman in the forces was expecting the knockout blow to fall soon.

Kent considered the question and looked out across the dark sea, finally making out the foam bow wave of the incoming vessel, "Not with a four man skimmer it's not." He switched back to broadcast, "Forward surveillance can you make out anybody on board that vessel?"

"No sir, heat patterns signify only emissions from the electric drive." The lookout reported back.

"Very well, power up the pump action. If no life is spotted at seven-fifty yards we must assume it is an explosives run at the wall, destroy the vessel."

"Acknowledge, at seven-fifty yards if no signs of life are observed we are ordered to destroy the incoming craft," the forward observation officer reported back.

From his higher position Lead Officer Kent saw the infra-red trackers swivel around to point directly at the speeding vessel, at the same moment the high compression pump action guns locked onto the incoming target.

"Thomas, start a seaward sweep of all sensor arrays out to four miles, let's see what is under the water. Comm's, contact air support request drone launch with sensor arrays in quadrants four through eight and twelve through fifteen," ordered Kent.

"Two miles, target speed and bearing constant," reported the forward surveillance operator.

"Sir the sensors indicate the only movement sub-surface is a single target, possibly a dolphin chasing something by the erratic nature of its motion. Nearest shore position is Delta-nine."

Kent scrutinised the illuminated map display before communicating with the ground forces spread out along the coastal strip to request a sweep along the beach looking for possible intruders. He had barely disconnected the link before several two man hovercraft left their hard hangers. One man worked the machine the second man studied the sensor data that streamed in from the underwater inshore arrays.

"One mile," announced the operator on the harbour wall. "There are no signs of life, no broad spectrum broadcast received and no deviations in speed or direction. Prepare to fire."

"Target acquired, target locked, safety keys off." The gun commander reported, his eyes watching the digital readout of the proximity signal steadily move down to the seven-hundred and fifty yards mark, at which point the guns would automatically fire. Their combined discharge of four hundred, explosive tipped darts would shred the incoming boat and everything on it to pieces.

Eight hundred...seven hundred and eighty...seven hundred and sixty..

The barrels hissed loudly as they discharged. All eyes scanned seaward, those with night vision equipment had counted to nine before they saw the skimmer disappear from view. In the overlooking outpost the Impulse Radar operator scanned his displays, eventually after a half minute she confirmed the data. "Target no longer visible sir."

Kent turned to Thomas who reported, "Multiple small targets sinking and surface detritus sir."

"Comm's contact the drone command, check to see if there are any mobile inbound contacts," ordered Kent. In his mind this event made no sense, after five years intermittent service in this command zone he had never known this type of attack take place. What was its purpose? Distraction perhaps? Unlikely he thought, it just wasn't big enough. Maybe just a probing run to see if we are awake he speculated further.

"Sir, Drone Command reports debris in the water but no moving targets on the surface as far out as fifteen miles."

"Very good, contact the beach patrols and see if they have anything to report. It's beginning to look as if we just shredded a perfectly good skimmer."

Further reports added nothing to the lack of intelligence; it would be a further half hour before the small floating mines would explode further to the east. As all attention moved in that direction a dark figure slipped ashore and moved rapidly inland. Even though multiple sensor arrays were triggered, nobody had a visual sighting of the near invisible intruder.

Black Flight One-Zero sat silently on the launch pad as the final plain, uniform boxes were loaded into the racking that extended along the length of the fuselage. The Black Flight squadron existed for the sole purpose of repatriating the dead to their homeland and their loved ones. It was so called because of the sombre colouration of the outer skin. They flew only at night, almost silently traversing the night sky so that few would realise the extent of the attrition on the Allied forces.

Load Master Monroe, a career Warrant Officer locked the final casing into place before checking the roster and recording acceptance of his kinsmen in arms who had so recently died. He handed the record pad back to the delivery agent after removing the copy data file block from the side. They nodded to each other and parted company.

From his position at the rear entrance he turned to look along the racking, so much loss, and so much waste he thought to himself. "Nav," he said into his radio to the only other crew member, the Navigator pilot, "racked and stacked, closing outer doors."

"Check that," a feminine voice replied in his ear piece.

Monroe turned once more and moved to the control panel that operated the closure mechanism. He was half way through the turn when he suddenly became aware of a figure standing on the ramp. He shivered slightly, although not a superstitious man he hadn't heard any sound as this one had approached. He drew his tongue across his lips. The figure before him was dressed in grey, dark belting and pouches adorned his body, a reserve bag was held in his hand. What troubled him most wasn't the wet clothing but the almost fixed stare from eyes set in a face that looked as though it should be in a body bag. There were no rank markers, in fact there were no indications of name, rank, and regiment not even the country the figure was from. Monroe's mind pondered how that could be in such a heavily militarised zone.

"Are you okay," he finally said, "because you look like you're in need of resuscitation?"

"I feel like I'm beyond that kind of help," the stranger replied in a flat monotone. He held out an identification cell.

Lead Master Monroe had seen plenty of them but never one quite like this, he'd heard of their existence but they were so rare as to be part of military mythology. He took it and posted it into his register; the readout made his eyebrows rise, not only was the cell a myth but so was the holder. "Nav, could you please come down to the cargo bay. It's urgent." He pressed an icon on the panel to activate the door closure routine.

A few minutes passed before the tall figure of Navigator Isla

Quaker dropped from her control eyrie to the cargo deck. As she approached she examined the solitary figure besides her Load Master, "What's up got one that doesn't like flying?" she asked cheerfully. When she got closer the smile disappeared from her face even before Monroe passed her the register.

"Captain Siven?" the surprise she felt marked her speech. Then she looked at the readout which read 'Render all available assistance'. "You look like shit."

"So I believe; it has been a long day. I need transport to the SolarSea."

"Better come top side," she handed back the identity cell. "Our flight plan is for Donder, you'll get transport from there easily enough."

Leading the way the navigator led Captain Siven past the rows of coffins, stopping briefly to retrieve a green overall before climbing a short ladder to the control deck. At the top Quaker indicated a doorway on the right, "It's tight but you can wash up in there, you can put this on while your stuff dries out. Chris will sort you some food out when we're in flight. We heard a rumour earlier that a kill order had been issued on your team, the Red Stripes picked it up."

The Red Stripes was the name given to the Balca Regiment from the eastern provinces on account of the red stripe they wore on the left sleeve.

"You didn't think to collect a promotion?" Siven asked.

"They didn't give me the order. Besides we carry enough of our own dead without creating more, especially veterans like you and your team."

"Any word of the others - we were split up?"

"No I'm sorry, we tend not to be in the loop what with flying nights and the cargo we carry."

Siven nodded in quiet understanding then pushed through the small door into the tight cubicle. At the controls Isla Quaker setup the automatic flight plan and radioed in to flight control for clearance. She didn't expect a refusal as there was no other traffic that night. By the time she had initiated the flight checklist on the automated systems, Load Master Monroe had arrived on deck sealing the pressure door behind him. It wasn't necessary to pressurise the cargo bay.

"You know that guy?" he asked quietly.

"Only in passing, I was Navigator about three years ago on a run to the Greco Islands, his team were the cargo. I only know his name because he introduced himself."

"Is it true what they say about them? Monroe asked furtively.

"Well that depends on what they say, they are covert op's that's all I know for certain, so nothing you'll ever hear about them is likely to be true." Isla Quaker slid her finger across the initiation key as the checklist completed its action and the engines vibrated as they powered up. A moment later a white light flashed on the control board. "Starting flight," the navigator said into her microphone as she initiated the autopilot that would control the flight systems from that point forward until the black skinned craft landed.

"Well he sure as hell doesn't blink a lot that much is true." The Load Master grumbled more to himself than the green clad figure that stood silently behind him.

"He will when he drinks your coffee," the Navigator retorted.

The sky in the east was brightening when Black Flight One-Zero rotated on its axis before settling down onto the hard ground at Donder Aerial Base. From the cockpit windows she could see the activity around the base as heavy lifters and small drone systems were readied for operational use. Once the flight plan completed its actions Isla Quaker shut down the power systems. Shortly after the ground crew entered the cargo bay and with due reverence to the dead, they set about retrieving the mortal remains of men and women they may have seen going the other way. A separate team drew up outside to re-power the batteries, ready for the return trip. Standing on the ramp Load Master Monroe felt the cold morning chill from the north-easterly wind; it felt good to be back he thought. A grey coloured military vehicle came to a halt at a respectful distance. Monroe felt a hand slap onto his shoulder; he turned rapidly at this unexpected assault to see the almost anonymous passenger, now clad once more in his grey uniform and black belting.

"Don't believe everything you hear Load Master, I and my men are soldiers, we kill the enemies of our country, that's what we're good at. Give it a couple of days and the war will be over then we can all go home and forget the things we have had to do. Thank you for the ride." So saying he stepped confidently down the ramp to the waiting vehicle, he saluted smartly as the driver got out. "Good morning General Conrad, General Saviour got my signal I assume," he said.

"Captain Siven," she said returning the salute. "You look like death warmed up, get in I'm taking you to the Centre."

Once inside the sheltered environment of the military personnel carrier they secured their strapping. Conrad initiated the autopilot that was programmed to take them to the SolarSea base. Setting off south-easterly they travelled along the currently quiet military road.

"Any word from the team, Ma'am?"

"Deuce made it into Gib' at zero-four hundred, Nano stole a flight home from the Italia islands at zero-four-thirty. No word yet from the others, don't worry they'll make it one way or another." General Abigail Conrad tried to sound positive.

"There's a rumour the Red Stripes have picked up a kill order on us, do you know anything about that Ma'am?"

She turned to look at her passenger, "You're joking, and no I most certainly don't." Her mind, reeling, considered the possibilities.

"I think it may be a cleanup operation due to the nature of our last mission, total deniability if there are no witnesses," Siven intoned.

"I'm sorry Captain but I don't know the nature of your deployment this time and that in itself is unusual. I'll ask around to see if I can find out anything. Might even ask the President himself," she noticed Siven sit up as he paid closer attention, "he was here yesterday having discovered Silvana's lack of documentation. He's coming back with a decision on how best to deal with the situation, let's hope for his sake it's the right one. Doctor Maurice wants to check you over when you arrive so better catch up on your sleep. I'm sure it will help if you start looking more alive than dead."

The guard duty officer had just taken over from the night guard when the camouflaged grey vehicle drew up to the gates; he bent over to look through the side window.

"Morning General," he said cheerfully, after saluting he recorded the vehicle and occupants on his scanner. "Captain Siven, glad to see you back again sir, the word is Noona is on her way back by freighter into Doblen."

"Thank you Lieutenant; and the good money is on who currently?" Siven asked. He knew from experience that when the news had got out that Team Phantom was not expected to return from the mission a sweepstake would be set up. On this occasion he expected the bets to be on who came in last. Strangely he liked the custom; the soldiers may fear his team, some he had heard even thought they were unnatural godless creatures but in his mind if they took enough interest in them returning, then that at least showed acceptance.

"Elvin sir."

"Tell me Lieutenant Marcus how can you bet on the odds of Team Phantom returning when you don't know the nature of their mission?" enquired the General.

"This is the most secure base in the military Ma'am, but inside there are few secrets." He passed a sealed envelope to Siven. "Doctor Tyler left in a bit of a hurry, he's been held at the Barrier until we're certain he is carrying no official or sensitive information that may be useful to an enemy."

Siven broke the seal on the message, looked at the close script and the signature before folding it and placing it in one of his pockets. Marcus stepped back as the gates rolled open and the steel centre post slid into its sheath. The vehicle moved forward taking the left hand road towards the Centre research centre.

Doctor Ewen Maurice took an hour to finish and collate the myriad of tests on Captain Siven.

"Well Captain all things considered you look in good shape but I'll need another blood sample at eighteen hundred hours and every twelve hours until I tell you otherwise just to monitor your progress."

"Progress sir?" Siven asked without emotion, just a mono-tone enquiry.

"The drug I gave you all to take before deployment wasn't to protect you from the virus although it will have helped. The serum was in itself a sterile form which I used because of the way it propagates throughout the body. Doctor Tyler made what I consider to be some ill considered judgements when he worked on constructing your DNA."

"Is that scientific talk for saying he didn't know what he was doing?" Siven didn't smile, there was no intended humour, all he sought was clarification.

"Something like that, anyway the serum is an attempt to incrementally put right some of those errors. I admit it is experimental but if all goes as I hope, it will remove some of the sensory blockages you all seem to suffer from. It should also, all being well, slow down the aging process."

At that moment Marine Maurice entered the room.

"All done?" she asked.

"For now," replied her husband, "all the tests are positive. Have you the blood work results?"

"Yes," she glanced at the pad she held, "the virus is dying off now as it was programmed to do. Captain Siven your body has shifted into overdrive to clear out the remnants, so I expect you'll be just about back to normal by this time tomorrow. Quite impressive, I imagine that is down to your enhanced metabolic response, but it may be something to do with the current gene remapping. I understand your recovery rate from injury is quite good."

"Yes Ma'am, we don't stay down for long."

"Right I'll need to check your genome daily for the next week." Unexpectedly she threw a ball at the seated captain; he snatched it out of the air before it struck him. "As you can see there is already an improvement in your reaction time and hand-eye co-ordination."

Siven looked at the ball in his hand, considering what had just happened, never, as far as he could recall, had he responded so flawlessly. Usually in such tests the ball practically hit him before he caught it; there had always seemed a delay between him seeing an object coming towards him and his reaction to it.

Marine Maurice smiled at his uncomprehending look, "It will get better yet, the changes have only just started to take effect."

"What I don't understand Doctor is why you are involved at all, Doctor Tyler has always been in charge of the project. We, the team that is, had the distinct impression he wanted rid of us, we never expected to return. But you knew that, otherwise you wouldn't have replaced our injection packs."

"To the latter question, yes we believed that was his intent. He was concerned about some of the psychological test results; it suggested to him that you were all becoming unstable, less controllable." Ewen Maurice watched as a barely discernible look of puzzlement crossed Siven's face. "I don't know for certain as his records have never been available to us. That may change however as his new funding supervisor has found a few irregularities in the original plan and follow-up supervisory oversight. As to the why we're involved, that's simple enough, Silva asked us to be. She was concerned about something, she never said what specifically. Do you remember her asking you for some swabs off the record?" As the question was rhetorical he didn't await an answer. "Well to do anything I needed to see your gene map and since Doctor Tyler wouldn't release the data I had to start from basics. The alterations we engineered were based on the gene mapping from those samples."

"The work can't have been authorised without his knowledge?"

"No it wasn't, but then I don't answer to anyone for the work I do. It'll come out of the research budget initially, after that I'll stop Silva's pay for the next thousand years to recover it." He smiled slightly but saw the humour may have passed the Captain by. So he added, "I can afford it Captain, my daughter thinks you're all worth it and if it makes Silvana happy, well I can hardly refuse her. Plus it will also help me in developing a new technique that may ultimately help a great many other people in the future."

"We will be in your debt sir."

"Maybe but let's see what happens first, if we've got it wrong the long term results may not be as beneficial as we may hope. Like I said it is experimental. Now as Mari said the effects you are feeling should subside in the next day or so, in between time inject one of these in the morning, one late afternoon if you continue to feel rough. However if you feel okay don't bother."

General Conrad and Silvana waited outside the door, when the examination was finally over they looked expectantly at Ewen Maurice.

"He's all yours Abi," Maurice said to his mother-in-law. And you young lady needn't worry, things are looking good."

"You mean he isn't dead?" Silvana said harshly.

"Ow," Ewen said holding his chest, "such a calumny. What a vile, ungrateful daughter you are, your mother is no doubt proud of you."

Silvana frowned, then she turned her attention on Captain Siven, "You'll be lucky not to be hopping around like a frog come tomorrow. All I wanted was a slight correction to a stigmatism in my left eye and look what I got." She lifted her glasses up.

"Now Silva don't tease the Captain; at ease Captain." said Abigail Maurice as she placed a hand on her granddaughter's shoulder. "Captain might I suggest I return you to your barracks where you can get a shower before presenting yourself at the Officer's Mess at twelve hundred hours for the President's address."

"Yes Ma'am."

"Captain, when you return to barracks you may well find a Major Calvert in the Assessment Suite. Just remember he has a right to be there and he may well need your assistance in accessing Doctor Tyler's files especially if Tyler's assistant Dawkins is unhelpful. Dress uniform I think Captain Siven, and if your comrades return in time they are to attend, that's an order. Best to show a united front in these troubled times."

As Captain Silva turned he felt a slight pressure against his palm, when he looked down he saw his lockbox access key block. He looked at Silvana, "Was I back in time?" He asked simply.

"It wouldn't have mattered if you'd been a little bit late," she replied.

The gathered officers stood to attention when the President arrived. The double doors swung closed, leaving his bodyguard outside, as he made his less than stately way to the top table. As soon as he took his seat the assembly followed suit.

President Dawson-Wells didn't look at the Maurice family sitting to his left; he preferred not to think about the cause of so much personal discomfort. He looked up as one of the doors reopened allowing entry to three men and a woman in their bottle green full dress uniform. Other heads turned to see who it was and then almost as one the gathered officer corps stood and saluted the newcomers, who in turn saluted back. With a noticeably sour face Dawson-Wells leaned over to General Saviour, "Who are they General, they seem to be given greater honour than myself?"

"Four members of Team Phantom Mister President, there are seven in total."

The officers applauded.

"And the others, where are they?" The President continued.

"On their way home as we speak sir, they are exceptional soldiers beyond doubt. Few had any great expectations they would make it home from their last mission. Shall I introduce you?" enquired General Saviour.

"Yes, I think so; it would fit in with some news I received on the way here. I'll go to them if that's alright." The President forced a smile onto his otherwise austere face as he stood and walked towards the group of soldiers he had heard about in briefings but had never met.

"Mister President," began General Saviour standing at his side, "may I present to you Captain Siven, Captain Deuce, Captain Nano and Captain Elvin."

In turn the President shook each hand, placing his left hand over the top of the others, an overt piece of body language that suggested an attempt at control. He realised as soon as he looked into each pair of implacably, cold, staring eyes that control was not in his hands. When he tried to release the grip he had on Captain Elvin's hand he soon realised he couldn't, he looked down at the grip then rapidly back up. With his other hand Elvin removed from his pocket an electronic pad, the President recognised it as a logbook that all soldiers carried; it held a record of all orders issued.

"On my way back here a squad of red-stripes tried to kill me Mister President, one of them carried this." Elvin's voice was flat and gave you the impression each word he uttered had been roughly sandpapered before it was spoken. "Read the last order, it was received two hours into our recent deployment."

President Dawson-Wells tried to remain calm as his eyes scanned the small display. The text, written in the universal military script was unequivocal; it was an order to terminate the seven listed subjects. A photo image and description was attached to each name with a note advising extreme caution.

"I know nothing about this," he said perhaps too rapidly to be convincing even though it was true. With his free hand he scrolled down the page to see the authorising details; by order of the Allied Command. When he looked back up at Elvin and then across at the others who stood watching him closely, "I swear as God is my judge I had no knowledge of this."

"If I find you had any hand in it I'll get to you before your God does and when that happens I shall cut off the hand that I hold."

"Captain Elvin," said General Saviour firmly.

"Sir?" Elvin replied briskly to his superior officer.

"I think the point is made, the President knows what actions he has to take."

Dawson-Wells felt the iron grip release; he immediately removed his communicator from an inside pocket. After selecting a secure contact he spoke rapidly to his communications officer. "Toby, I want you to send a message immediately to General Gos at Allied Command under my name, make it state with immediate effect he is to withdraw the kill order issued against Team Phantom. Immediately - do you understand? Just make sure he understands that if he fails to respond there will be one issued on him. Just stress, that if that happened, it wouldn't be withdrawn." He paused as he listened to some recent intelligence received by his office, his face paled. "Then send it to his number two, and all other of the Allied Commanders," he snapped. Then he broke contact.

He paused as he took several deep breaths, finally wiping his mouth with a clean handkerchief, "It seems General Gos and two other members of Allied High Command were killed two hours ago and as yet nobody knows who did it." The President pocketed his device before turning and walking back to his seat, his face betraying his innermost fears. The lull in activity on the African coast was to cover a strike on the command and control of the allied forces. If this was the big push then they were doomed. Once back at the table he turned to face the assembled soldiers.

"For those of you that didn't hear it, a quarter of the A.H.C .were killed recently, General Gos was amongst them. So far details are lacking but searches are being made for possible insurgents. It seems there was a distraction earlier today, which may have allowed a small team to get ashore. If true the long expected advance may be imminent, the next day or two will tell." In his unsettled state all thoughts of 'Project Trojan' had vacated his mind.

Brushing aside his earlier feelings he continued. "Now to hopefully happier things, today is the first time I have met any of Team Phantom, from your earlier salutation you seem to be more aware of their exploits than I. Suffice to say much of what they do is covert and perhaps nothing will ever be said of their work or sacrifices when the history of this war is written." He paused then continuing like a true politician, "One thing is beyond doubt they do not deserve what I have just been appraised of, their name on a kill order. They have served this country; doing the dangerous if not the nearly impossible tasks few men could perform. You know; that is why you so honoured them on their arrival, whereas I, an outsider knew nothing."

As he spoke he thought of something another General reportedly said long ago, in different circumstances - but it had a resonance he felt. 'I don't know what effect these men have upon the enemy, but, by God, they terrify me."

Pausing, more to judge the effect of his words on the officers than for any other reason he took a sip of water out of a glass on the table. "The other day, and in many ways it seems like a long time ago our country rejoiced in a major athletic success. This young lady," he paused again and with a sweep of his hand indicated Silvana who sat with her parents on a nearby table, "entranced the nation by her pursuit of the championship."

Silvana looked up as the door opened slightly, she smiled at the grey clad figure in black utility belting, two standard issue personal immobiliser weapons hung upside down on their vertical straps. She heard the President stall in his eulogy, his breathing becoming rapid once he saw the 'Phantom' was armed. General Saviour registered the new entrant as he quietly closed the door, acknowledging Captain Forten's presence with a raised forefinger wave: another Phantom had returned home. When she heard Forten's voice Silvana was expecting it, audible only in the low frequency range where most adults couldn't hear.

"Hello little sister, keep calm you are starting to look flustered. We are here with you and for you. He will go on to say what we all know but it will all be to vindicate the choice he has made, or at least he has convinced himself it's his choice. Everybody in this room knows differently. So just relax and enjoy the experience, Dog-in-the-

Box is sharing his own distorted version of reality."

"His fantasy," she barely whispered smiling.

Siven spoke in turn and the others smiled, "It's what we all do sister."

As the President continued unaware of the silent conversation, Siven spoke sub-audibly to his newly arrived comrade, "I'm surprised the President's guard let you in armed."

"It wasn't their first thought, nobody said it was a dressy do."

"And their second thought was?"

"No idea Siven, I'll call by the infirmary later and ask them."

"Have you heard from Zwansi?"

"None stop all the way home, was she pissed when we found out about the kill order."

"The President has just said three of the Command structure has been assassinated." Siven kept his eyes forward no hint of interest in his voice.

"Really," Forten sounded very slightly surprised, "they can't have found the other three."

"Where is she?"

"I left her in the barracks. You know her, she won't show up until properly showered and her head polished but she'll be here, after all there's free food fit for a President."

"After this is over you, Zwansi, Noona and Nano have to report to the Centre for a medical. Doctor Maurice wants to check out the progress of the serum he gave us."

"Where's Tyler?"

"He ran, but he only got as far as the barrage, he is held pending inquiry. Major Calvert wants access to the records but so far he can't get access to Tyler's personal files."

"I'll sort that out later; I don't imagine Tyler's assistant is being helpful."

"Not yet, he needs Tyler's permission blah, blah, blah, to show anyone his notes. When this is over we'll test his solidarity."

They stopped talking as the President arrived at last to the nub of his problem.

"This is probably the most secure base in the United Islands," he stopped as a hand rested on his arm.

"Forgive me Mister President but there is no 'probably'," said General Saviour.

The room erupted in applause.

The base Commander continued, "Just before I left my office I received the news that for the tenth year in succession no team has been able to gain access to the trophy tower without apprehension. As you may well already be aware, this year we have had the greatest number of teams from every military unit in the country and nobody got anywhere close, nobody failed being detected by our systems. You may pass on my congratulations and thanks to all your staff. Forgive me sir it seemed an appropriate time to mention it."

Dawson-Wells's face lit up, even though he hated interruptions or anyone else sharing his moment of glory. "Of course General, now where was I? Oh, yes I was mentioning THE most secure base in the country."

The room erupted once again in applause and some laughter.

"That there are secrets here is beyond doubt, however perhaps your greatest secret has been our new heroine. From the day she first graced this world with her presence no record of her existence was ever made. In fact the only indication she existed at all were the records of her education within the confines of this base. You all know her, and those that have been here for some time may also know about her lack of identity. In fact you have all been complicit in a crime as the law says all births must be recorded and all infants must undergo regular and rigorous assessment. This has never happened in Silvana's case, the reasons have been explained to me and I can quite see the parents' perspective. But the law is the law, without records there is no citizenship and no rights.

Why you may ask has this come to my attention. The reason is simple, I, like the rest of the country wanted to know about our new champion. My office has been inundated with requests for information about Silvana Maurice because there is no public record, and they want to know why. Secondly without documentation she cannot travel to the many venues that have requested she visit them to inspire the young people of today. In fact if she left the confines of this base, if you did your duty properly she could never get back in again."

The room was very still.

"You, yes you, all of you have put me in a very invidious position because this country has produced a star athlete and I have to stand up before the world and say sorry. Sorry because the military sponsored winner is not in fact a documented citizen of the State of the United Islands, some would even question her right to life."

President Dawson-Wells stopped dead in his tracks as he noted the figures lined up along the back wall stand up straighter, there was nothing remotely like a smile an any of their faces.

"I however do not subscribe to that belief," he hurried on, "nor do I believe that to court-martial you all would serve any useful purpose. In fact that in itself would only serve to weaken the citizen's belief that you are here to serve and protect them from all harm, without fear or favour. General if you please." The latter comment was directed at his General Abigail Conrad his chief aide.

The wall display lit up bathing the room in a pale blue light.

"To amend the glaringly obvious omissions my security staff has worked through the night to prepare this." All eyes swivelled to the now documented display. "It was posted last night in the public domain where the media have access. As you can see it gives a resume of your protégé, Silvana's educational history and achievements, including her interests. Most of the content is gleaned from the family but I suggest you read it and memorise it just in case it doesn't accord with your knowledge of her, and that includes you young lady. Of course it is not totally factual nor is it complete. To excuse that and the fact that nothing was previously within the public domain, we declared that the family and their premises are within the military jurisdiction of SolarSea. You know the rules, if it is not in that release," the President pointed to the display, "it never happened."

Dawson-Wells took a sip from the glass on the table.

"I must be doing well, there's no poison in it," the President exclaimed.

"Yet," a voice called out from the floor to everyone's amusement, even the President smiled if a little wanly.

"When I spoke earlier to General Saviour I was surprised to learn that Silvana has lived her whole life within the compound. In fact the only time she has ever left was under military escort to the Championships. That is extraordinary to me; this young woman has been kept under what can only be called house arrest her whole life and for what crime – being alive? Or is it that she is different? Silvana would you please come here?" the President extended a hand in Silva's direction.

Silva didn't move, she feared neither woodland nor water but to stand before this gathering of people she knew filled her, for some unknown reason, with terror. Even her mother's hand touching her arm and the encouraging words that went with it could not free her mind. She had lived her life mostly within the known confines of the Centre and then the military enclosure. Within those enclosing fences she felt safe. Even the recent swimming events, being surrounded it seemed by the uniforms of the military cast had not been as daunting as what was being asked of her now. She didn't want to be free to roam the outside world that was filled with people who were 'normal', people who didn't understand her. Then a hand touched hers even that, the lightest of touches caused her to jump. She looked up; the eyes that looked back were like polished glass, the radiant yellow filaments set in the grey iris that surrounded the black, oval, vertically set pupils seemed to glow even in the daylight. Captain Zwansi cocked her head slightly, the light glistened on her shaven scalp, she didn't smile, it seemed an unknown concept to her, as she drew Silvana out of her seat. Slowly they moved together, no words passed their lips. In her mind Silva thought only of Zwansi who was so different from what was the accepted norm, tall, shaven headed with eyes that suggested only indifference to any other living thing. So different but yet so confident, the smaller woman wished - wished so much that she could be like her.

Dawson-Wells cleared his throat as Silvana Maurice finally stood before him, if for no other reason than to mask his own fear. He had met most of Team Phantom earlier but this new one was something all together different. He almost dare not look at her in case she would see his fear. Little did he know he didn't have to; she could smell the reek of it in every drop of perspiration he exuded from his pores. He wished she'd go away having done her duty and brought the girl before him but she didn't.

"Silvana you have become an icon, an inspiration to the people of this country, and they want to see you, to meet you. My office, which is the only point of contact the public has to you, has been inundated with requests for you to visit places in every corner of the United Islands. It is one of the prices you must pay if you are a champion I'm afraid. However as things stand you cannot fulfil such an obligation, you cannot travel, if you stepped beyond the fence by law the soldiers could not let you back in, even to your own home." He paused as he fished inside his double breasted half coat.

"Today it is with great pleasure that I present to you this token, on behalf of the people of the United Islands."

The President held out a translucent rectangle, gold artefacts glistened within crystalline structure. Silvana took it noting the differences with the standard version of a citizen's identity.

"These are your identity scripts defining you as a citizen of the Republic of the United Islands and they will allow you to move without let of hindrance within its borders."

As he finished the sentence the assembled gathering of officers stood and applauded, even the members of Team Phantom nodded, the right thing had been done. After a moment the President raised a hand for silence.

"Abi would you mind?" he said to General Conrad his chief aide, who was also Silvana's grandmother.

Bending down Abigail Conrad took back the identity card from her granddaughter whispering as she did so, "Well that didn't hurt did it?" as she kissed Silvana on the cheek. "Welcome home Captain Zwansi, just in time it seems." No reply was given, none was expected.

Once placed inside the reading unit the coded contents of Silva's new identity card were displayed onto the wall.

"As you can see Silvana," the President said, "your identity pass has some military encoded content about you on it. This will allow you to exit and enter this particular base, but it also has other differences you will not find on the normal civilian display. Here for instance you will see a flashing warning symbol. If for any reason you are in need of assistance all you need do is present yourself and your identity cell to any government official, and I stress the word any. The presence of the warning symbol states simply this; by law the official you approach must assist you in whatever way they can. This is not by any means a common amendment, so do not abuse it." He faltered again having realised he must have said the wrong thing. The stillness that suddenly filled the room was tangible. "Which I am sure you won't," he quickly added before clearing his throat.

"Another addition to the standard content is this item here, in essence it gives you the historic 'Freedom Status', which means you can enter any Government or Public building and use the facilities available freely without interruption or explanation. You can, should you be so minded come and sit in the observation gallery as the Government debates the issues of the day. Not to be recommended even I try to get out of that one."

He paused to allow time for the laughter, which never came, to die down before he continued, "Finally this separate item is your passport to travel outside of the country and return without hindrance. You are free young lady to go anywhere you want in the free world." Recovering the identity pass from General Conrad he placed it and the passport in a case and presented it to the young woman. "Now you have no excuse not to call upon your countrymen." He smiled, she didn't.

General Saviour stood at that point and made a few congratulatory comments to Silvana and some of thanks to the President before dismissing everyone so they could partake of the buffet style food. After that the tone of the event changed, becoming more relaxed especially so when the President finally left, having outstayed his welcome. Silvana was still the centre of attention but being attended by her family the fear she felt before didn't return. She was pleased that her grandmother had stayed a little longer than intended, as it helped a great deal.

The messenger arrived three quarters of an hour later with a packet for the attention of Doctor Ewen Maurice.

"What is it?" enquired his wife.

"No idea," he replied turning it over, "but it's from the conservationist." Breaking the seal he emptied the contents into his palm, to him the object appeared to be a rectangular form cut transparent stone with a glyph enclosed within its shiny surface. He read the enclosed note, tilted his head and examined the crystal once more. "The Conservationist has started on the painting; this was apparently under the backing board fastened to the frame."

At that moment General Saviour came across and having spoken briefly to his token niece looked over at her parents. His eyes were drawn to the clear object that Ewen Maurice was holding up to the light. He blanched visibly.

"Where did you get that?" he asked trying his best to sound conversational.

"Strange as it may seem, it was hidden in a picture frame. I don't know if you recall the painting, it's the one hanging in the living space on the wall opposite the windows. It's of a stone bridge which in fact still exists today, on the western edge of the solar arrays. The picture itself has been in the family since it was first painted about three hundred years ago. In that time however, we as a family have neglected it and it has suffered a little, so I was having it cleaned. This little item was apparently fixed to the frame under the backing board which as far as I know has never been removed since it was originally put in place."

"May I?" Saviour asked holding out his hand. He pursed his lips as he examined the object then finally he came to a decision, "Come with me will you?" He didn't hand the crystal back but clenched it firmly in his fist. In the hallway outside the room his journey was interrupted by a security detail, the senior officer saluted.

"General," the detail commander began, "the President has lodged a complaint; three members of his security detail have been assaulted by a member of Team Phantom."

"And you are about to do what, precisely?" The General asked without much interest.

"Take him into custody for examination sir."

"Which one is it?" Saviour enquired further.

"He is currently dressed in grey fatigues, it's the only description we have sir."

"Captain Forten. Very well, but I suggest you do two things first before you pass through those doors. One, get more men and two, make sure your affairs are in order, he's not alone. Has the President gone?"

"Yes sir, five minutes since take off."

"Then forget about it I'm sure you have more important things to do than commit suicide. I'll speak with Forten myself later. Now if you'll excuse me I'm busy." He didn't await a reply only briskly saluting before walking to his office.

Once inside the totally enclosed secure space he locked the doors and activated the Faraday cage built into the walls and the audio barriers that surrounded it. What was said in his office stayed there.

"Please sit down both of you. Have you any idea what this is?"

The two doctors looked at each other.

Marine merely pulled a non-committal face, "No idea," said Ewen, "I have never seen anything like it as far as I know. Why what is it?"

"It's impossible that's what it is. You say it is three hundred years old?"

"As far as I know, the conservationist remarked on the backing when he first examined it. The original catalogue number was on it, with the proprietor's label and the original screws were in place seemingly never having been removed."

Saviour entered the one time algorithmic code to operate his safe security system then, after using a separate voice activated encoder; he pressed the skin resistance and magnetic resonance scanner unit on to his palm. Finally he keyed in the timed analogue code of the magnetic resonance generator onto the digital keypad alongside the locking handle. The safe opened and from the spacious interior he removed two objects both enclosed in separate boxes. From the smaller of the two he removed an object and handed it to Ewen Maurice, it looked very similar to the one now resting on Saviour's desk.

"That object is the latest in secure technology and will soon be released as standard issue to all officer ranks. It is called a diamond lattice secure configuration and that unit has the capacity to store the data of every person in the land. Without placing it within the encryption decoder you can't read it, and that coding is made up of several layers of complex algorithms, making it impossible to crack or copy."

Marine Maurice looked at the diamond memory block she now held, the similarities were remarkable, the same uniform cut and although different in shape the embedded cipher looked right, in context. "But you say this is new, the latest in technology, then how can the one from the picture be the same? I mean if the conservationist had stolen this new technology he would hardly give it back, at least not in this way it's too much of an aberration."

"Well there is one way to find out," the General said after recovering his new gadget.

The second box when opened contained a decryption unit, nearly three-quarters of an inch thick it possessed a clear flat screen. Taking the newly discovered block he inserted it into the side of the unit, amazing Saviour thought, exact in size and shape. He pressed the activation key, the screen glowed pale blue as it booted up the software, seconds later it did the unthinkable. The screen read 'Decrypting – Reference 0|X – secure data protocol F98xx'.

"What's happening?" asked Ewen.

"The impossible doctor that is what's happening, the data on that thing has been encrypted using the latest top level security protocols. Nobody should have any way of using it outside a select few at the development facility; the actual program to do it hasn't even been released from 'Ultra' yet."

The screen stopped processing, blanked then displayed the message 'activating external display'. Almost immediately the air around the table glowed pale orange before a figure came into focus in clear sharp detail. She, the figure, appeared to be young female sitting at a desk behind which was a blank wall containing but one thing, a picture of a bridge. Almost immediately the figure spoke.

"Hello, my name ith Oo-neh Maurithe and you are reading thith becauthe you have not only dithcovered the memory block but altho developed Diamond Lattithe technology and the Formiere multi-layer military grade algorithm."

The office was suddenly very still.

The figure that floated in the air held up a calendar and pointed to a black-circled date.

"I am recording thith file today, thith ith the date and it ith intended for the five timeth great-grandthon of thith man." A picture rose up next to the talking figure. "He ith Edward Clark Maurithe, he wath born in London, England ath it ith currently named, on the fifth of May two thouthand. Hith mother ith Eleanor Maurithe and father Jameth Mathon Maurithe, he lives in London at thith time and she lives outthide the Leedth conurbation, that ith where I am recording thith methage.

Thith ith my family tree, my father wath Ioan Maurice, both he and my mother were genetic engineers and my date of birth wath twenty-firtht of Dethember Twenty-two-eighty-three. My thtory ith a long one, I shall be ath brief ath I can. I have included in thith memory block fileth and imageth relating to my early life and my current life here. Included ith a textht of thith monologue. I apologize if you have trouble underthtanding me, I have a thpeech defect and ath you will hear in another file, thith ith not the language of my birth and there are a lot of wordth I do not yet know how to thay properly but I am getting better."

It was over an hour and a half before the audio-visual file closed, only once was the replay interrupted when Marine Maurice asked for it to be paused as Oo-neh Maurice removed her glasses. Her only comment was that they were the most beautiful eyes she had ever seen.

Her husband turned to General Saviour "General can you give me a decrypted copy of all the files on a wafer drive; I'll have to check out the facts as given about my family history. I admit some of the names are familiar but some I do not know. So far as I know there has never been a genetic disorder within my male line of descent but if what she says is true then she will, by her actions have changed history and the world she knew never came into being."

"Then how does she still exist?" asked his wife. "After all if our ideas about time are correct any change she made will affect the future outcomes. By curing her ancestor of a life threatening disorder her father, the man she knew would probably never be born. If he hadn't been, then neither would she be. I'm assuming of course there is some scientific fact here and not just some time travel fantasy."

General Saviour cleared his throat, "Maybe not and I say that in absolute confidence. I'll send a copy over tonight but right now I have to speak with the President."

Back at the Centre a few days later, the Maurice family watched the file from beginning to end, after which Silvana produced from her copious files of family research, a copy of an archived photograph. It was old and the colours had faded slightly the script on the reverse stated that it had been taken on the day that Eleanor Maurice had been promoted to the rank of Superintendent. She was the central figure dressed in a smart uniform that bore two medals, the purpose of which still had to be discovered. Standing face on she looked the very image of the person in a similar photograph that was on the memory block. To her left stood a young man and woman with a small baby, the annotations said he was her son Edward Clark and

Claris was his wife. Eleanor's right arm rested on the shoulder of a younger woman who was much smaller than she was; clutching a pink satchel she looked really happy as she gazed forward, seemingly right at the viewer. An annotation on the back gave her name as Oo-neh Maurice.

*The Ever-changing
and
Flexible Present.*

Eleanor Maurice plumped up the cushions, the late spring sunlight that cascaded through the western windows glowed orange as she readied herself to settle down with some mind numbing entertainment on the television. Oon-eh had left a quarter of an hour before to pursue her evening perambulations in the nearby countryside. What Oo-neh did exactly in the surrounding area that comprised mostly of heather covered moorland and fern lined defiles, Eleanor did not know. However Oo-neh was not expected back before Eleanor herself had gone to bed.

Earlier that day Edward had left, returning back to London to continue his studies in one of the colleges that proliferated in the capital. To his mother the fortnight he'd stayed had been to say the least, interesting. Eleanor's son had intended only to stay a couple of nights but he changed his mind for some unexplained reason, but then a lot seemed to have changed in her son since they'd last seen each other. On his arrival it had been tense, Oo-neh was there of course and Edward wasn't quite sure how to treat the strange girl he'd met in the capital in what seemed an age before.

Oo-neh had expressed some surprise that he'd come since it was her impression people were frightened of werewolves. He had replied, as though it was fact, that werewolves were big and hairy unlike her. What happened next both mother and son found hard to describe. No sooner had the words left Edward's lips than Oo-neh had traversed the distance between them, pirouetting behind him before bringing him down to his knees. Even as he knelt on the living room floor with shock setting in as his senses tried to re-orientate themselves to the rapidly changed circumstances. He was barely aware of Oo-neh standing behind him, feet now on his calf muscles. It was only when he felt the pain set in and her hot breath on his neck, the tip of her tongue barely touching the skin over the carotid artery, did he start to register what had happened. Then he heard her whisper into his ear, "Then I'll be a little vampire if that'th what you want."

Eleanor was less shocked as she had seen Oo-neh act similarly before but what fascinated her was the numbing shock response the event had had on Edward. It had certainly shaken him up a bit.

Over a cup of tea and biscuits Edward had remained quiet, his mind going over events to try and piece them together but the more he thought about it the less clear things became. It was as though he was trying to put a jigsaw together when half the pieces were turned over. Had she been that fast he wondered, that his brain had had little time to keep up with the changing scenario? That she had previously got him away from that weird guy Oo-neh called Oh-Four was known history, but he had never really considered how she had done it. Now he had more than a vague idea and she's only been playing with him. With that knowledge came respect for the person he had only really considered to be no more than a small interloper without merit.

When she had gone on to mention that Claris, his girlfriend, had seen him off at the station and that she still used 'Avail'. This mid-range value scent Oo-neh had pointed out to him had cost Claris more than she could really afford - and it really didn't suit her or him for that matter. The woman, on the other hand that he'd sat next to on the train, and to jog his memory Oo-neh went on to tell Edward that she had worn a pale blue woollen sweater, had used something far more fitting. She had used a dab or two of 'Composure' with its much more delicate odour and lower cost. After that Edward had to rethink his opinion of his mother's diminutive guest.

Eleanor had simply smiled at her son's discomfort but she wasn't going to tell him about Oo-neh's acute senses. To Oo-neh, Eleanor thought, Edward probably smelt to high heaven due to the various odours on his clothing. It was a short time later that Eleanor made a sudden realisation, as answers to questions she'd asked previously suddenly popped into her mind. She had often wondered how Oo-neh had known about the drug deal in the Brightly's café. The participants hadn't displayed their goods in plain sight. So it seemed reasonable enough, with the knowledge she now had, that Oo-neh had sensed, smelt or tasted particles of the drugs from her seat nearby. Somewhere, since her arrival in the U.K. Oo-neh must have had access to the various drugs in circulation for her to gain the knowledge of their different odours. Was that where her interest in drug dealers started she wondered. Eleanor had no real answer because it wasn't just drug sites; dealers or suppliers that Oo-neh had discovered; it was addresses; telephone numbers, and meetings. Things you couldn't smell or taste but then her hearing and eyesight were far better than the average person so maybe her other senses were too.

After that initial interaction the relationship between the younger people started to take on a different level of engagement. Part of this was due to Oo-neh inviting Edward to try out her games, which at first, as before, Edward felt might be a little beneath his abilities. An hour is a long time to learn you are wrong in every way. He was humbled. He had asked how he could get one of the units, to which Oo-neh had truthfully said, 'Live a very long time'. Edward had after that, presumably to try to gain the dominant position, started to pick friendly fights with his new found friend and Eleanor had called out for them to be careful, she didn't want anybody getting hurt. Edward had replied 'I'll be careful', only to be put down by Oo-neh saying, 'She wasn't talking to you'.

Two weeks later Edward had finally and regrettably returned to London after hugging Oo-neh with great brotherly affection.

So it had been an altogether interesting time, Eleanor was glad they had sorted out their differences but Oo-neh still didn't appear fully relaxed with him. Eleanor's own relationship with the little stranger was more relaxed. Truth to tell, even though they had now lived together for a few months, Eleanor still had a lot of questions she as yet didn't know the answers to. Questions relating to dead drug dealers, the detective in her couldn't rule out the possibility that Oo-neh was in some way linked to them. It seemed extremely unlikely that similar events a couple of hundred miles apart were unconnected. Both were places where Oo-neh had collated an immense amount of data, data she must have guessed was important to the authorities. How or why she had drawn that conclusion Eleanor had no idea. Maybe even in her time there had been a drug related problem or was it just that she was being useful to the security forces as her mother had told her to be. Even so she would still have to have known the problem she and her police colleagues were interested in. Probably just read the papers. She finally gave up wondering at that point.

The doorbell chimed causing Eleanor to look up from the remote control unit she held in her hand. Visitors were not usual, especially in the evening, even work matters started with a telephone call. Sighing she stood up and walked the short distance to the door, she opened it and paused as she appraised the people standing there, before saying, "Can I help you?"

Two females stood in front of the door, the older one about her own age and a much younger female who was possibly late teens or early twenties she thought. A man, judging from his size and shape stood further back in the shadow cast by the building.

"Is Oo-neh available please?" the younger speaker seemed barely to contain her enthusiasm, practically bouncing up and down. Her voice had a soft melodic accent; perhaps, Eleanor considered not dissimilar to Welsh or even some of the dialects from the Indian sub-continent.

"Patience sweetheart, where are your manners," said the older woman to the younger before turning her head back to face Eleanor. "Forgive my daughter she's waited a few years for this moment."

"And you are?" asked Eleanor.

"You do not know me but my name is Marine Maurice, this is

my daughter Silva and our companion is…"

Eleanor cut her off, her senses, as soon as she heard her own surname, became alert to possibilities; she scanned the two faces for similarities before examining the separate figure in the half light. "Forgive me, but I've met his like before, I know what he is."

"Ah, you must be referring to the agents Oo-neh mentioned. No, Captain Siven is a serving soldier; my husband insisted he accompany us to make sure of our safety."

Eleanor looked at Siven unconvinced. "Are you armed?" she finally asked.

"No Ma'am," replied the Captain in his monotone accent. "I have strict instructions to preserve the lives of Doctor Maurice and Silvana using non-lethal or life changing force."

"How do you know Oo-neh?" Eleanor addressed the older woman and wondering how the girl had waited a number of years.

"She sent us a message, quite a detailed one in fact and the consequences of that message certainly shook some people. That is why we are here. Professionally I want to see her because the images she sent, although of good quality, can never replace seeing the original."

"And your profession is what precisely?" Eleanor could feel herself tense up as she had a premonition of where this might be leading. Her eyes flickered back to the stationary soldier, his eyes told their own story. In her career she had seen some pretty cold, ruthless, emotionless men but none gave her the feeling this one did, he wasn't natural. So if he wasn't natural somebody made him that way, but whom? Was it this woman called Marine Maurice or somebody else? Whoever it was, it wasn't today or anytime soon. Eleanor drew her eyes back to the two in front of her, noting the unfamiliar hairstyle and the similarly unfamiliar style of clothing. Even allowing for some of the weird designs she had seen on catwalks, these clothes were work ware but stylish with it. She even asked herself why the younger of the two reminded her of Oo-neh with her darkened glasses, odd when worn in the late evening. "What year are you from?" she finally asked throwing caution to the wind and forgetting her previous question.

Then it was time for Mari Maurice to pause and take a quick breath, she hadn't expected such a direct question, especially not that one. She smiled, "Well that makes things easier; when we left it was twenty-three-oh-eight. May I ask what led you to that conclusion?"

"Your bodyguard, my senses tell me he isn't human in the way we are. Our technology isn't capable of creating anything like him so he must be from a time when it is possible. If that is true of him then it is also true about you."

"The technology isn't that old even from our perspective, it is still experimental. To answer your previous question I'm a genetic engineer specialising in evolutionary development."

"Then you may know Oo-neh's father, he worked in that field."

Mari Maurice paused noticeably, "No I don't know him but it is something we need to talk to Oo-neh about."

Finally relenting, Eleanor feeling no immediate risk to her or more importantly to Oo-neh opened the door wider to allow them in. On closing the door she found the mother and daughter looking at the picture of the bridge which hung on the lounge wall.

"Oo-neh bought that for my son, he's in college in London at present."

"The colours are a lot brighter than I imagined, in our time it is not so crisp, sadly the years or its owners have not been kind to it." Mari ran a finger over the textured surface of the painting as if to sense something that wasn't apparent.

"It's a bridge in Northern Ireland, near where Oo-neh was brought up." Eleanor said.

"It's not far from our home too, just over an hour's walk, on the western side of the solar arrays."

"Why don't we go and see it when we get home? That would be fantastic" Silva said.

"We could, couldn't we? You probably don't remember but we went ages ago, you were only two then. It was before the fencing and security measures were installed. You hung over the edge of the stone parapet, constantly dropping blades of grass into the stream then rushing across to see them come out the other side. It drove your father crazy."

"Was that the time he slipped and got his foot wet?" Silva responded nearly laughing.

"Yes, yes it was now you mention it, and you, you little monster were singing all the way home, 'squelch, squelch, squelch' every time your poor father put his foot on the ground. The things you forget. Sorry Eleanor. May I call you that? It is a bit awkward otherwise since we're both Maurice's."

"Of course; when Oo-neh gave the picture to Edward she wanted it to be an heirloom so that one day when the time was right and its price had gone up, it could be sold to fund someone's dream."

"It's strange you should say that, the picture, until a year ago was owned by my husband's cousin. He and his family were emigrating to the Australis Republic and he needed the money to help him get established there. Ewen, that's my husband was quite generous in my opinion but in view of recent events it seems as though it was meant to be. What I mean to say is, if Alwyn had taken the picture, he probably would never have found the diamond cell or if he had, its significance wouldn't have been recognised."

"Diamond cell, I'm not sure I follow you. Anyway do sit down," said Eleanor. "I don't think Oo-neh will be long she's probably already aware you are here."

Once they were settled Mari Maurice made a request, "Because of the importance of our being here we'd like to record the conversations, unless you have any objections. All it would mean is positioning four scanning units around the room, they would scan continually and when we collate the data it would create a record of things as though the viewer was actually in the room."

"Personally I have no objections but you'll have to check with Oo-neh. She's very private in some ways."

"Silva's the same; sometimes finding things out from her is more than an effort."

"Me, I'm an open book, it's not my fault you can't read what's in it," chirped up Silva as she grabbed a reason to feel included.

"I wish you were young lady and so does your grandma. Captain if you wouldn't mind putting out the sensors."

"Yes Ma'am."

"Well I'll just go and make a drink while you do that, tea alright?" Eleanor slipped out of the room giving her time to think.

Beneath a tree in the shadows outside Captain Noona kept watch for any possible intrusions. She sensed nothing amiss in the land around her. A slight rustling in the branches above gave no cause for alarm that is until a pair of small hands slipped in front of her eyes. For the first time in her life Noona was caught off guard. It being a new and novel experience she uttered a rare expletive.

"Gueth who?" a voice softly said by her ear.

Inside the cottage Captain Siven sensed Noona's reaction causing him to pause and look up.

"Something wrong Captain?" Mari Maurice enquired.

"No Ma'am I thought I sensed something, everything is fine."

Silva was talking to her mother and Captain Siven was co-ordinating the data feeds from the recorders when Eleanor returned to the room. She was not alone. The talk ended abruptly as Silva suddenly stood up, her mother Mari turned slightly to see what had suddenly excited her offspring.

"It's her, Oooo!" Silva was bouncing up and down with excitement, as she moved closer to Oo-neh. "Can I hug you?"

The reply she got perhaps wasn't as she had expected, "Why?" Oo-neh said without enthusiasm.

Silva undaunted moved a lot closer and lifted up her glasses so that they rested upon her head, "That's why" she simply said, no further comment was necessary.

Eleanor from her position beside Oo-neh saw the sparkling dark brown eyes. They were indeed distinctive, perhaps a little larger than normal as they were a reflection of the radiant smiling face. Eleanor tried to ascertain what her exact feelings were as her mind tried to cope with the horizontal lenticular pupils. She kept her surprise as masked as possible. Her mind raced to fit what she saw into some kind of perspective. Eleanor had never seen a human being with such pupils as those now before her. Because the iris was of a dark shade of brown, the blackness of the pupil itself didn't stand out as much as it might have done with blue eyes. Perhaps, Eleanor thought, in subdued light she could pass through a crowd almost unnoticed.

Oo-neh slid her glasses down slightly as she peered over the top of them to see the face of the young woman more clearly; this had the effect of exposing her own eyes to the strangers.

"Wow," said Silva in surprise, "they look better in real-life. Look Mama her eyes are really green. I wish I had eyes like yours."

"You don't, believe me," replied Oo-neh pushing her glasses back up along her nose. Curiosity however got the better of her as she reached out to feel the texture of Silva's hair. "Ith it real?"

"Real?" Silva frowned, "Yes of course, shouldn't it be?"

"No it ith good, nithely cut," then Oo-neh stepped forward and embraced Silva just as long as the custom of her time dictated, before standing back again.

"Silva remember your manners, you haven't even introduced yourself," reprimanded Mari.

"I'm sorry Oo-neh, ever since I saw you on the recording I have wanted to meet you." At the speed she spoke the words were nearly a song because of her accent. "My name is Silvana Maurice, I prefer Silva if that's alright. This is my mother, Doctor Marine Maurice and our companion is Captain Siven, he's on protection duty."

"Hello Oo-neh," Mari started to say, "I expected you to be taller from the images you sent."

"No, thith ith me, it'th all you get for your money." Oo-neh's hands swept theatrically down from chest height. Then her eyes flickered over the soldier, her tongue slid partially out, "You were here thix weekth ago."

"You didn't say," said Eleanor.

"I didn't know who they were at the time, all I knew wath that they didn't fit in. He wandered about a bit checking the village out and another one like him reconnoitred the area in the other direction."

"Captain?" Mari asked for some response.

The Captain leaned forward, "That would have been the last visit to check the area for possible threats, Captain Forten was with me." Although his voice remained flat his eyes showed an interest in the small figure in front of him. He had one thought and that was why neither he nor Forten had sensed her presence on that visit. He had yet to hear of Noona's full experience.

"Interesting," said Mari, then, "We had to perform several test runs with equipment to see what we were getting into and whether it was safe or not. I think they sent four black rabbits with sensors initially, to map out the terrain."

"Three," said Oo-neh, "the thecond one wath brown with a white front."

Mari just stared for a moment, "Then you knew we were coming?"

"It might have jutht been bonnieth, but I exthpected you would follow eventually, once the one with the camera arrived."

"Ah, now that caused a flutter back home, you nearly gave Doctor Dios a heart attack. The fact you were aware of our contact and responded spurred the program forward and that is why the three of us are here." Mari Maurice peeled back her sleeve to look at something affixed to her arm before continuing. "We have slightly more than an hour before the recall sequence triggers so we must press on. Oo-neh please sit down there are some things I need to tell you."

Oo-neh turned her head slightly to look at Eleanor, who smiled back encouragingly. "It's alright I'll be right here," Eleanor said out loud, inside her mind yelled out, 'Do you really think I am going to miss this?'

Oo-neh sat down.

"To begin," began Mari Maurice, "your message triggered a series of events, the first of which was the President authorising the building of a pilot project, the P.I.P Field Generator. After four years of work it was ready for systematic testing and it's what brought us here. Although the President was himself initially reluctant to commit public funds, you probably know the usual excuses, money, public danger, etc. but pressure from the scientific community on hearing of your existence swayed him. However he only authorised a limited program, after we return and report on events there will only a short period of time before the thing is shut down. It has been decided, if the linear theory of time holds true, that the risks of making devastating changes to our history are too great.

Now Oo-neh the President himself has become very interested in your position after finding out about Silva's uniqueness. She is like you Oo-neh, that is, we had to alter her genome to overcome abnormalities that prevented her coming to full term in the womb. Had the authorities known at the time, the pregnancy would have had to have been terminated by law. It was our secret and the open secret of the security forces that surround our home until four years ago when she won the World Aquatic Championship. That made Silva a national heroine, the consequences of that forced the President to make Silva a full citizen of the Republic of the United Islands. So when he heard about you I believe he was genuinely moved by your situation, so much so that he has empowered me to give you this on his behalf."

Mari withdrew a blue box from her pocket and flexed the lid open, inside lay a rectangular crystalline block.

"It is what we use to demonstrate our identity should we be asked." She removed a rectangular pad from an inside pocket of her jacket, it was smaller than the one Oo-neh owned but had many similarities. "I imagine this is like the one you have, except of course this is a civilian version without encryption facilities. The technology has only just become available to the public at home." She slipped the crystal into the side and displayed the contents in the air alongside the chair. "These details and the picture we took from your message cell. This isn't just a token; the President has bestowed upon you the full rights of a free citizen of the Republic. He also invites you to return to our time as he feels it will suit you more than," she paused slightly, "than this historical setting. Not his exact words, but I'm sure you get the idea. You don't have to make up your mind now. I am to leave this unit with you; on it we have collated images and data about our time, the world, the people and the technology so you have enough information to make a decision. There is a personal message from the President himself and my husband Ewen Maurice. Any questions Oo-neh before I continue?"

"You're not going to try and take me by forthe?" Oo-neh asked in a subdued tone after a pause.

"Absolutely not, it has to be your choice. Should you decide to follow us you will have a home at the Centre as part of our family until you get acclimatised. After that you are free to come and go as you wish."

Oo-neh sat thinking a moment, the tip of her tongue projected into the air beyond her lips.

"What we'll do is send a rabbit with a locator cell on it; all you'll have to do is fasten it to your skin and await the recall signal. We'll do that once a month for three months; if you decide to stay here then you take no action. There is plenty of time. It has been tested on a couple of live trials, Captain Siven sent back a local cat and dog when he was last here, that was part of his brief."

When no further comment appeared forthcoming Mari continued after flicking through the data files and projecting the image of a family tree. "There is something though that you will need to know, this is the family tree you sent us and this one is the family tree we have assembled about Ewen's family history. Edward Clark is here and you Eleanor are here. Edward marries a girl called Claris Woods and has three children not the two in your chart. One of his sons Philip Edward has two children one of which is the William in your chart, same date of birth after that it changes substantially. Ewen has the same day and month of birth as your father but it is one year later; I believe there was a miscarriage in the earlier year." She stopped talking allowing Oo-neh to look at the details then after a minute. "I am sorry Oo-neh but there never has been an Ioan Maurice in my husband's family. The only Margaret McLeod we found with any details similar to those you supplied works for a conservation group that ensures genetic diversity in some of our threatened species. As far as I am aware she is not known to the family. We believe the consequences of the change you made to Edward Clark's genome caused the family history to progressively move along a different track. I'm sorry Oo-neh, I really am."

"But.." Oo-neh started to say, and then she remained silent as she sucked in her bottom lip. Finally she stood up without saying a word and left the room leaving behind a heavy atmosphere.

Eleanor looked helplessly on then shifted her gaze to Mari as if to say, 'well done I hope you're proud of yourself'. Turning, she followed Oo-neh out of the room and found her sitting in a dark corner of the conservatory seemingly talking to herself. She didn't understand the words as they were spoken in Oo-neh's native tongue but from the tone it sounded like an intonation or mantra.

"I am Oo-neh Maurithe the lawful daughter of Margaret McLeod and Ioan Maurithe. I mutht have a good appearanthe, be polite and well mannered. Telling the truth at all timeth even though it may offend thome, I shall be rethpected. I mutht help the thecurity forthe at all timeth tho they will be aware I am a good and utheful perthon ath I blend in. Daily I mutht write my journal to have good hand-eye co-ordination, noting everything I have done and learnt. Each day I mutht extherthithe my mind and body in order to be good at all thingth. I shall do what I can and do what I mutht to thurvive." A single tear slipped beneath her shimmering glasses, "I mith you my mother, I mith you my father with all my heart, I have my grandmother who will love me, now she knows me, just like you said she would."

Eleanor didn't disturb Oo-neh until she stopped, then, crouching down, she wrapped an arm around her waist. "It's alright sweetheart you are not on your own. I don't pretend to know a lot about science or time travel, you're the expert here but maybe things are not as they seem. Maybe when you came here by, what was it, Project RoTos, you didn't travel backwards along the time line but side stepped into another one. If that's true then where you came from is still there, as is your father."

"Then he won't be cured because I gave the serum to the wrong Edward Clark," Oo-neh replied unhappily. "They told me not to change anything, now I know why. But why am I still here Mathair ? If my parentth never lived, why do I?"

"I don't know sweetheart, I wish I did, maybe it's because I need you, or maybe it is God's will. Whatever the reason you are here, you do exist and now a person you do not know has given you the gift of identity. He recognises your right to life. Now cheer up and wipe your eyes, I think our visitors may have more to say and little time to say it."

A few minutes later Oo-neh and Eleanor returned to the room, the trio watched their advance. After asking if Oo-neh was alright Mari continued on.

"Just to clarify the changes my husband Ewen occupies the position in the family tree your father held that makes Silva your alternative self. What might have been, had your father's line not had that genetic flaw. When we checked some of Eleanor's descendants, at least those we had viable DNA from, we discovered something odd. On the gene site you described as creating the illness that passed from father to son we found a gene combination that was way out of the ordinary. At least not something we had come across before. What we asked ourselves was why your father hadn't just edited out the problem and inserted a normal human counterpart. We think it was because he couldn't.

Genes never act in isolation there are all manner of switches and interactions. In the modelling we have done, it suggests that if he had done as we would have expected, then the outcome would have been fatal. Your father may have been ill but he wasn't suicidal; he was also a genius. How he did it I have no idea, it might have been calculated or just one of those serendipitous events that occurs too infrequently. Whichever it was we shall never know but what he created was an organism so complex that in its development the right genes came together. Genes that would provide a lasting cure and more importantly they were sighted in the right place. We believe he took that corrective combination, intending perhaps initially to give it to himself, but as things came about you gave it to Edward Clark instead and it has passed down through the male line ever since. So far as we know there is no aberrant behaviour or defective outcomes in the family line that suggests anything abnormal about the donor organism. Oo-neh," Mari Maurice paused briefly, weighing her words carefully, "you have that gene complex."

The room went silent as each individual considered what had been just been said.

"And that means what exactly?" Eleanor eventually asked.

"It means that the cure was found from a source on the female line, someone closely related to Oo-neh: or as I personally believe Ioan Maurice manipulated Oo-neh's genome intentionally to create this complex. What he did was far beyond what he needed to do to create a viable birth. You can see that with Silva, we manipulated only the genes we felt were creating the rejection problem. That is why I had to meet Oo-neh, I had to see what differences existed between the two."

"I wanted to enter an athletic competition ath a girl but my father told me it wathn't thafe, had the authoritieth found out what he had done, it would have been the freezer for me," said Ooneh in response.

"The freezer, what do you mean by that?" asked Mari.

Before Oo-neh could reply Eleanor interrupted, "That's how they executed people they didn't want in her world and they didn't want mutations or any other genetic disabilities they could easily get rid of."

Mari looked at Eleanor and Oo-neh in disbelief, she could tell from their expressions it wasn't a joke.

Eleanor continued, "I imagine what you had hanging over your heads was nothing compared to her everyday fear of discovery."

Oo-neh sat thinking about what had been said and about these people who appeared to offer so much to an orphan in time. She knew that some of the conclusions they'd come to were wrong, she also knew something they hadn't seemingly thought about. Finally she decided on a course of action. "I'm a meth really, thith ith all show," she waved a hand down her clothing, "to cover my inner anxthieties. I don't have any body hair; I'm ath bald ath an egg tho I have to wear a wig. I have an implant in each ear to help me with my hearing and I have to wear gloveth to hide an unthightly skin condition. Well, you've seen my eyeth but they are thensitive to light giving me another reathon to cover them up." She sighed perhaps a little too dramatically while looking at the floor. "Ath you notithed I'm thmall and I can't really run very fatht on my legth they are not long enough to win a rathe, but I like thwimming. I'm too thmall and inthignificant for anyone to take theriously."

"Then you have no skills or acute senses beyond the normal?" asked Mari.

Oo-neh only shrugged.

Eleanor having heard Oo-neh's description of herself before was nearly convinced but she knew it did not fit the actions she had witnessed. "Despite my little girl," she stopped dead realising what she had said, up to that point she hadn't realised how she really felt about Oo-neh. The few previous times she'd called her as such had been only to give Oo-neh some protection. "Despite Oo-neh's problems she is very intelligent, very hard working and she is also excessively well mannered. I have yet to meet anyone with a bad word to say about her. All in all I would be a very proud mother if she was my daughter; I would never have to worry whether she would ever disgrace me. When you consider she came from a very different society and technology to this one and has a very noticeable speech defect she has fitted in as to be almost unnoticeable."

"The perfect child then?" Mari said perhaps with a hint of rancour.

"Near enough, the only flaw that I have seen is that she can be slightly obsessive, but who wouldn't be if they'd been brought up with the constant threat of being frozen to death. You see, although Oo-neh has only lived with me for a few months, I have always, even at the beginning, found her very candid and open. Because of that I think I have got to know her pretty well." Eleanor replied with a straight face.

"Well as a mother I can tell you that all children keep secrets." Mari said defensively.

"Perhaps but then who doesn't? I know there may be many things I don't get told but if it ever became important I am certain Oo-neh would tell me. I trust her and I hope she trusts me."

Mari Maurice consulted her wrist again. "Time moves on, Silva would you take Oo-neh through there and show her the pad and where the files are, the interface may be different to the one she is used to?"

The younger Maurice smiled and jumped up grasping the opportunity to get away from the serious talk and spend some time with her opposite number on the family shrub which in truth was all she cared about. Behind her glasses Oo-neh's eyes drifted skyward, she couldn't help thinking that Silva was a bit immature and that was in a moment of generosity.

When the girls had drifted out of sight into the darker conservatory Mari asked Eleanor. "You've never seen her without her glasses have you?"

"No never, I once tried but she got very upset. I've never asked again," Eleanor said with a hint of sadness.

"I can understand why but her eyes are really quite beautiful. Does Oo-neh seem predictable in your experience?"

"An odd question," replied Eleanor, "but yes she is very predictable. She has her routines she always tells me when and where she is going and a précised update of what she's been up to when she returns. On her birthday she will present me with her handwritten journal for that year."

"Handwritten," Mari said with some surprise. "In our time that is almost an obsolete skill, Silva keeps a journal but it is a book file that her grandmother gets. My daughter sadly, whom I love dearly, can have bouts of unpredictable behaviour. If you surprise her you may well get a kick in the face if you aren't prepared for it. Her reflexes can be very fast, engaging before she consciously thinks things through. That is one reason the Captain is here, to protect us yes, but also to help control her if need be. She's never really ventured far from the known; she's always had a slow acceptance of places and people before she becomes comfortable. Since she won the championship her life has moved from the known, to a more varied and ever changing less predictable one. When one of the instructors saw her diving he offered to train her for the championships. We encouraged her to do it because we knew she was capable if she focused on it, and we hoped if she won it would boost her confidence. None of us expected the adulation that came after. The only reason she can bring herself to travel about the country is because Captain Siven and Team Phantom go with her."

As they continued to talk Captain Siven slipped into the conservatory where the two younger women sat chatting.

"Captain Thiven would you mind making a record of uth together?" Oo-neh asked doing her best to smile as she held out the tablet she had so recently been given.

The captain obliged, repeating the operation for Silva with her own piece of Diamond Lattice technology. Handing it back he checked the timer on his arm, "Silva we have but minutes, embrace your sister and join your mother and please gather up the recorders."

Silva and Oo-neh hugged each other tightly, then after parting Silva did as she had been bidden. Captain Siven remained, "Oo-neh may I also embrace you as a brother?"

Oo-neh nodded, he knelt and wrapped his arms around her and said, "You haven't told Eleanor Maurice what you are have you?"

Oo-neh just looked at him as he stepped away before shaking her head slowly from side to side.

"You must little sister; I believe she cares deeply about you. Don't let her find out from someone else. Be safe sister; be happy whatever you choose to do. They created us for their reasons not ours but you have your life now to do with as you please, you at least are free. Even so I wish you were part of my team. Captain Noona thanks you for meeting her; I believe it is the first time she has been taken by surprise." He winked at her as he turned to leave.

"Captain, Thilva cannot make it alone, she doeth'nt have the confidence." Ooneh said directly. "She needth your guidancthe."

"I know," Siven flatly replied.

"But you care about her, I jutht wonder why."

"Because little sister she is like me, although I have freedom I am not free. With our looks we never can be truly free and acceptable. As for Silva all she has to do is fulfil her dreams, something she never speaks of not even to her parents. She wants to attempt the annual challenge to recover the medal from the security tower. She can do it, of that I have no doubt, and when she does I believe it will give her the confidence to believe in herself, as you do. Especially with your so limited abilities," a rare smile creased the side of his mouth.

"Have you a location tracker fitted?" Oo-neh said after a little thought.

"Yes, I'd have to cut my leg off to be free of it."

"Mine wath dithrupted when I came here, the magnetic field corrupted thomething and it began thycling through the frequenthieth. It made it hard for them to track me for any length of time." She tilted her head sideways, suggesting it was something he might consider.

"A tragedy for sure," he said half smiling; another rare enough event. "Now I must leave you, try to be happy but I fear people like us can only ever be content. I'm glad I met you even though I shall not remember it. Do what you must."

Oo-neh stepped over to the doorway, watched Mari and Eleanor separate from an embrace before the former stood aside with her daughter and bodyguard.

"Five, four, three, two.." Mari counted, and then she and the others disappeared from sight, leaving no trace that they had ever been there.

"I don't think I shall ever get used to people disappearing like that," Eleanor said to nobody in particular.

A bright light drew her into the conservatory; Oo-neh was displaying the lifelike image that had recently been taken of her and Silva in the air by the corner. An almost silent click, imitating a camera shutter emitted from the less advanced piece of tablet technology she held in her hand. Satisfied with the result Eleanor's proxy daughter transferred the image file to a printer via the Wi-Fi connection.

Before Eleanor could ask what Oo-neh was up to, the girl in question walked purposefully past her and removed the oil painting of the bridge from the wall and started removing the screws from the backing board. A minute later she took out the diamond lattice memory cell that was held in place by a low tack clear adhesive. Then like a girl on a mission she took the printed photograph from the printer tray and wrote something on the back. Finally Oo-neh wafted the paper around her head to make sure it was dry before inserting it into a clear laminate sleeve. A few minutes later she retrieved it from the laminator; she then let it cool before inserting it into a brown envelope. This she sealed and fastened in place on the wooden board with a single staple and then, replacing the backing board she screwed it once more into place.

"I imagine there is a reason for this rush of activity," said Eleanor as Oo-neh replaced the painting onto the wall."

"Abtholutely," replied Oo-neh straightening the frame until she was satisfied.

"I think I shall make a drink," a bemused Eleanor said turning towards the kitchen.

It was only when they both sat side by side holding their hot drinks did Oo-neh finally relax once more.

"I put the memory thell into the frame a month ago." Oo-neh said, starting to explain the sequence of events that had led to the, 'interesting times' as Eleanor later described the events that had so recently occurred. "It wath intended to give a warning to my father not to make me the way he did but I forgot to take into account any changeth that might occur ath a rethult of changing Edward'th genome. I never exthpected for one moment that he might never be born. Well, I have taken out the memory thell, it ith to be hoped we have no further unexthpected people turning up."

"Why did you give up the chance to get back to your own time? Even if it isn't exactly the same, it must be technologically closer to home than this time," Eleanor asked.

"They were very kind to offer me a home and an identity but I think Captain Thiven wath warning me when he thaid I wath free. Perhapth I might not be there. Thiven ith better than the defectth Project leader Tyler made, I imagine they will theek to improve the project. Silva wath nithe enough even if she lacked confidenthe, I do not think she had the love and guidance from her parentth that I had from mine. I wath lucky I think to have such a mother that made me work at being normal." Oo-neh stopped talking and began looking at the floor seemingly in a reflective state of mind. "Well at leatht we know that time commentheth to rewrite the moment an alteration happenth. Perhapth I am here now becauthe I came before the alteration, making me fixthed in hithtory. I think, if I go to them, I might theathe to be on the way. Not to mention the pothibility that if I leave thith time hithtory will change, ath I may do things here that maketh their time come about."

"I wonder why they never considered that possibility?"

"Perhapth their ideath of time are different from mine. There ith thomething elthe they didn't conthider, the real effect of the gene change in Edward."

"How do you mean?" Eleanor sat up to pay closer attention.

"Two generationth from now, thomewhere about the turn of the twenty-thecond millennium it theemth the family tree ith cut back. From what I thaw on their version, only the male line from Edward continueth, no children from any female. I am guething but it may be that they died off, perhapth from an illneth or epidemic and only the male line continued becauthe of the altered gene, creating better immune protection. I never get ill; if the gene originated from me then they wouldn't either. After the change I made to Edward, in Thilva'th family tree they theem to have become more inventive, more creative when compared to my family tree. They appeared to have made a lot of money which allowed her father to develop hith rethearch laboratory whereath mine had to rely on selling an old picture to pay for it. If that ith true then the gene ith likely to change Edward'th mental ability, I think, make him more focuthed."

"Well that might not be a bad thing; he can be a bit scatty. Any improvement would be welcome." Eleanor considered other possibilities, then smiled to herself because if the same 'genius' gene had come from Oo-neh then she hoped it came with a 'modesty' gene as well, otherwise her son would be insufferable.

"Grandma?" Oo-neh said quietly.

Eleanor felt a cold chill; it wasn't so much the word as the tone that concerned her. She knew from past experience whenever she used that word in that way something was bothering her younger companion. It was the first time since moving into her home that Oo-neh had used the word. Directing her full attention on her 'daughter' she said finally, "What's wrong Oo-neh is something bothering you?"

Oo-neh stared at the floor. Eventually she said unexpectedly, "Thith ith a nithe house."

Eleanor was surprised, Oo-neh in her opinion was usually more direct but she only used this kind of distraction when she wanted to avoid something, so she said nothing.

"I like living here, it'th good," Oo-neh continued.

"Well I like having you here." Eleanor shifted her seating, moving onto a pouffe in front of Oo-neh. "What's wrong sweetheart, this isn't like you?"

"Captain Thiven thaid I should tell you what I am," Oo-neh's eyes never shifted from gazing at the floor.

"Well I know what you are silly. This is your home now for as long as you want to stay, there's no reason for you to think otherwise." Eleanor tilted her head sideways to see if her words had had any effect.

"Grandma do you love me?" To Eleanor the words sounded like a desperate plea. "Did you mean it when you thaid I wath your little girl?" Unusually Oo-neh started to sound very emotional not unlike that time on the last festival of the darkest day.

"Oo-neh, listen to me. I don't know what has caused this but there is no reason to tell me anything you haven't already said. It's not worth you getting so upset, it really isn't."

"Grandma, do you love me?" Oo-neh repeated but with more force, looking up to watch Eleanor's face. Her own face was a picture of total misery and fear.

Eleanor's heart went out to her young companion, "Of course I love you." She reached out and took Oo-neh's small hands into her own. "Once upon a time I wished I'd had a daughter after Edward was born, but I guess time and work just got in the way and it never happened. Then, unexpectedly, you came into my life and filled a space that I hadn't really known was there. Yes, you are my little girl, I hadn't realised it until I said it today; a Freudian slip I guess. That's something we subconsciously feel and can blurt out when we aren't thinking. I need you perhaps more than you need me."

"Grandma, please try to keep loving me, even if it's only just a little." Then freeing her hands Oo-neh reached up and pulled her glasses away from her eyes.

"Oh Shit," Eleanor couldn't remember later if she'd said it out loud or whether it was just part of her internal conversations. Either way she was unprepared.

The eyes that looked back at Eleanor from the tear-streaked face of Oo-neh Maurice were, it had to be said slightly larger than normal but that was of little significance when compared to the green irises. Each one was encompassed by a pale almost glowing yellow ring. The pupils, normally circular were convex in shape and set vertically. Periodically an opaque membrane slid across each eye.

Oo-neh watched Eleanor's reaction before pulling off her wig and removing her white gloves. To Eleanor, Oo-neh's skin looked pale but that wasn't unusual as many people had paler skin especially those with red hair. The now exposed hands did not appear to show any signs of a disfiguring skin problem. That progressively changed as she continued to watch.

Slowly the exposed skin colour started to change as Oo-neh sat back in her chair; initially it was mottled then gradually became more defined as it reflected the colours and pattern of the material the skin was in contact with. Oo-neh started to blend in with her background. Eleanor was appalled, all she could think of was Oo-neh's father and what a despicable piece of shit he was for doing that to his own daughter. It did however answer the question as to why her grandmother had left never wanting further contact. For if Oo-neh had been laid in her cot surrounded by white sheets all her grandmother would have seen were two glowing eyes looking back; unsettling to say the least.

Slowly Oo-neh replaced her glasses and wig before slipping on her white gloves, her intense emotions having evaporated she was back in control as she said, "I'm thorry that I'm a dithappointment to you Grandma," she stood up; "I shall go and pack my thingth. If it is no trouble, can I leave in the morning?"

Eleanor was still in slight shock, as she stood up she could feel the tears brimming in her eyes. Then cradling Oo-neh's face in her hands she bent slightly to kiss the upturned forehead. "Oo-neh you will never, ever be a disappointment, any disappointment I feel is directed at your father. I will always love you more than a little." Wrapping her arms around Oo-neh's slim frame she pulled her close, "Oo-neh," she said through the emotion, "this is your home and it always will be for as long as you want. I'm not your grandmother sweetheart but I will be more than that. You are so special Oo-neh and if people don't like it, well it is their loss." She felt the arms around her stiffen as Oo-neh hugged her close in reply.

Minutes passed before they parted and sat down again. Eleanor swept a finger across Oo-neh's forehead to move an errant hair back into place as she really considered how difficult this delicate looking young woman must have found life.

"My father," Oo-neh started to tell the rest of her story, parts she'd previously missed out, "my father had been approached by the military before I wath born becauthe of hith work on camouflaging a rodent. They asked if it could be done to a man, their aim wath to know if it were pothible to create an enhanthed soldier for infiltration work. Becauthe thecurity thystemth were getting tho advanced they wanted a tholdier capable of bypathing whatever thecurity measureth there were. They needed a perthon that could hunt and remove a thpecific target and gather information before returning; all without being dithcovered. A tender wath put out to theveral engineerth, Doctor Tyler came in firtht with a viable propothal, and his work produced the Oh-therieth of agentth. My father monitored the project initially and he wathn't happy with what he thaw after three yearth, hith final report wath very critical after that he detached himself from it all. The Tyler that created Captain Thiven did a much better job but it thtill wathn't right.
In between time my father did a lot of experimental work trying to thee if it wath practical, that work finally became Project 01x."

"But why did he use you, his own child to see if it worked, that I can't understand. The result could have been catastrophic," Eleanor said.

"I think it wath becauthe he had to change the DNA of a potential foetuth anyway to get a viable child that gave him the opportunity. If it resulted in something none viable, or a monster wath produthed then it could be dithpothed of. He could have used hith own ignoranthe or lack of thkill ath an excuthe. Later he could try to create a child again but without the project exthtension."

"Your mother must have been livid when she found out."

"I don't think she knew at the beginning, she wath happy to have a baby, even if did look like me, but then she mutht have thought thingth through. After that my father's life would have been awful, I believe she made him be a father to me even though he looked at me ath an exthperiment to begin with. My mother loved me I know that had she not I would have been tho different I think."

"How do you mean?" asked Eleanor.

"The military wanted a predator, that ith what my father designed, I think my mother taught me to be more human than I might have been. Captain Thiven thaw what I wath, becauthe he ith the thame, I do not believe however he had a mother like mine. That'th why the military thent the agentth after me, they finally realised what they had let thlip away, I wath better than anything they had. However, had they thought thingth through after I had delivered the viruth they'd have realised I wathn't the average theventeen year old. Fortunately they were more contherned about my mode of conthception and the thpread of the infection in the NAF. I don't think they even conthidered the pothibility that my father had achieved what they had athked for."

"Well you are unique that's for sure. Thanks Oo-neh, thank you for telling me that, it explains so much I didn't previously understand. It probably explains why you are such a good researcher." Eleanor didn't broach the issue of dead drug dealers because she knew, Oo-neh, if asked would admit her part in their demise and that would make her own position as a police officer difficult. "Better not mention anything to Edward, not just yet anyway, maybe never might be better. He has grown to like you and that's what matters. I think tomorrow we should talk about your future."

"What ith there to talk about?" Oo-neh asked. She had defaulted back to the tone she usually used, questioning but not threatening, calmly without emotion.

"Well you can hardly spend the rest of your life cleaning and polishing this place every day while I'm out. I certainly don't expect you to cook for me all the time."

"Don't you like my cooking?"

"Yes I do, you're better at it than Edward that's for sure and I thought he was good. Oo-neh for all your little quirks you are truly gifted, you have so much potential, so much talent that it would be truly wrong to let it go to waste. Do you remember that research you left me in the suitcase when I was looking for you? Everybody I know that saw it was highly impressed with the detail and the way the information had been collated. Literally they had seen nothing quite like it. You could make a name for yourself in that field; in fact you could become exactly what you first introduced yourself as, a researcher." She paused to let the suggestion sink in. "Anyway that's for tomorrow; do you remember the sergeant you first met when you came looking for me at headquarters?"

Oo-neh nodded.

"Well she's going to see her grandmother in Ireland in a couple of weeks or so, anyway she called me earlier today to ask me, to ask you, if you wanted to go with her. She reckons you would go down well, being a speaker of the old language. Not to mention that it would keep you in practice, be a shame to lose your mother tongue. You don't have to decide now; I think we've both had a bit of a challenging day, so sleep on it."

"Will your mother thtill come to thee us in three dayth time? You might not want her too."

"My mother has been eager to meet you since I told her you were living here. She'll love you Oo-neh of that I have no doubt."

"She might run away if you tell her what I am."

"I've already told her what you are, a lovely, clever, and funny young woman. The rest can wait, let her get to know you then, maybe we might tell her the rest later. Are you going out again?"

"No I think I shall give the foxeth a retht." Oo-neh said. "I've got a lot to write in my journal."

"The foxes, what on earth do you do to them?" Eleanor wondered out loud, but that was a story she'd hear another time.

2304 A.D.

Version three overwrite.

The celebration marking Silva's recognition as a full citizen of the Republic went on until just after mid afternoon but the Maurice family left well before that. Back at the Centre after brief congratulatory messages from the staff and students they returned to their private residence on the upper floor. Barely had they had time to change clothes before the intercom alarm sounded.

"Yes," said Ewen curtly.

The voice on the speaker was unabashed by the response, "Curator August Stener is here to see you, he says it's urgent."

"Alright send him up will you?"

The intercom went silent.

Moments later the Curator's head appeared above the floor as the moving staircase carried him up from the floor below.

"Good afternoon Curator, what brings you here so soon? Don't tell me you have found my picture is an over paint on a long lost master," Ewen began as he held his hand out.

The Curator shook it briefly, "Alas no, at least not yet but I have discovered something equally interesting."

"Oh, you intrigue me. Come this way, we might as well be comfortable. Can I offer you some refreshment?"

"No thank you, but you might need it afterwards."

After greeting the rest of the family whom he met in the lounge the curator removed a tablet from his bag and activated the in air display. The image of the picture currently in his care for cleaning appeared in sharp focus. The picture lay on a table covered in fabric.

"As you know for legal purposes we have to record all our actions when we are restoring paintings to avoid claims of negligent behaviour. Now just watch, I'll talk you through what is happening. This is your painting, in, as far as we can tell its original frame. As we turn it over it has on the back board some aged labels which look the part. They describe the painting; identify the painter as well as the dealer's marks and catalogue number. My research assistant has checked those details against our database and found that the numbers are in accord with the historical records. We noted that an alteration had been made as there were two catalogue labels with differing numbers, probably a clerical error. So to all intents this is an original work and your family appears to have been the only owner. It was originally purchased by a Miss Oonex Maurice in the year twenty-sixteen the year after it was painted.

This detailed image shows the screws, there are six of them; they appear to be made of steel, a commonly available product at the time. Note that they are rusted and show no scratch marks that would indicate previous or more specifically more recent attempts to remove them. Note also that there are no signs surrounding the backing board, which is made from pine wood that suggests a light line which would be there if the board had been removed and not replaced accurately. What I am saying, is that in my opinion this painting is in the original condition to that in which it was bought and has never had any work done on it. Now this is where it gets interesting, the board is removed to expose the back of the picture."

"What's that?" Marine said, not without a little excitement.

"Exactly my feelings when I first saw it," said Stener. "It is in fact a paper enclosure, a common item used three centuries ago. It is somewhat fragile as would be expected for something that old; this piece of bent metal, probably of steel holds it in place. But watch as I brush the dust away."

All eyes watched the floating image as the ephemeral hand of the curator used a broad soft brush to remove the accumulated dirt. In dark letters, that were slightly faded they could read the letters SILVA.

"You are joking surely," said Ewen.

"I am not, that is, as you have seen with your own eyes the exact same thing I saw. That is the reason for my urgent visit. What a coincidence you may think, after all, it is your daughter's name is it not? As far as I can ascertain, Silvana is a name that has never been that common, even more so the abbreviated form. The glue that once stuck the enclosure together has long since dried out and degraded so the flap sealing it is now easily opened." The Curator shut down the file replay and reached for his case, a small, rigid grey affair he used to carry documents and occasionally paintings, in a secure manner.

"Did you open it?" asked Silva with barely suppressed excitement.

"Patience young lady, you wouldn't want to deprive me of building the drama, would you?" He removed a clear lockable folder and placed it onto the table top in front of him. "Like I said the actual enclosure is quite fragile so I have kept it at the workshop for preservation, I can return it to you afterwards if you so wish."

"What was in it? Silva said trying to see through the lockable folder's translucent lid.

"Why do you think there was anything in it?" Stener teased.

"Because nobody would bother putting an empty enclosure in the back of a picture, what would be the point?" Silva's patience was beginning to wear thin.

"Quite right, inside I discovered a picture. A picture encased in a film of some type of synthetic material, which is quite brittle so I ask

you not to handle it until we have had the opportunity to stabilise it."
He slowly snapped the locks back on the folder case, as dramatically
as he could manage. Lifting the folder case up he turned it around for
all to see. "Now how do you explain that young lady?"

The picture they could all see clearly was a little faded due to
pigmentation degradation but it was still, due to being stored in a light
free environment, full of clear detail. The picture showed two girls,
both wearing tinted glasses, smiling and waving at the camera, one of
those girls looked unmistakably like Silva.

"It's impossible," commented Ewen.

"That was my thought exactly, but I stand by my earlier
comments, in fact I'd stake my reputation on it. This picture has not
been opened for centuries; it most certainly hasn't been opened or the
contents put together in the last twenty years."

Silva peered at the print, "The glasses are the same as mine."

"Any idea who the girl is?" enquired Stener.

"No idea at all," answered Marine, "do you know her Silva?"

"No, I don't think I'd forget her if I did, I don't know that many
girls."

"May I?" asked Mari. Taking a careful hold of the case she
peered at the image, "Dear God, Ewen look at this, in the window
behind the girls."

Ewen Maurice moved closer to look at the area his wife
indicated, his pupils opened perceptibly, "That looks like Captain
Siven. This is more than impossible, for this to be genuine it would
have had to have been placed inside the frame fairly recently, less than
six months. Silva didn't have those glasses before then."

"Then you'll be even more surprised when you read the
inscription," said the Curator.

"What inscription?" Mari said not without surprise.

The curator turned the box over allowing the contents to drop
gently onto the table top, the hand written text was plain to see.

"Hand writing like this is very uncommon these days, in fact
only artists of one type or other tend to be the only practitioners. It
hasn't been in common use since the third quarter of the twenty-first
century, adding other proof that this document is not of recent origin. I
shall have it properly dated in due course."

Silva read the text slowly as the letter formation wasn't exactly
like the styles she was familiar with.

'Silva, you must listen to your heart and act accordingly. Go to
the tower and take what is there. You know that you can and must do it
if you want to discover who and what you are. Only by doing what

you feel is right will you learn to be free, free to be yourself. I know Siven will help you. Love 0|x'

The trio seemed to hold their collective breaths, finally Mari said, "Well Silva she appears to know you and Captain Siven. I think we should ask him who she is."

"But I have never met her; I don't know who she is. I'd remember those glasses they look great, better than mine and her clothes are a bit out of date. Who wears green these days?" Silva protested all the while wishing she did know her, she'd never had a friend that signed off 'love' before.

"Then Curator Stener we have a puzzle, draped in a conundrum and boxed with a riddle and encased in an enigma. By all means preserve this and the other item and should you have any thoughts on the answer to all this please let us know."

"Well the only safe answer at present, the answer that makes sense is that at sometime in the past your family had a young woman in the family that looked like your daughter, even with the same name."

"Which doesn't make sense if you read the letter, was there also a Captain Siven then? After all his name is derived from the sequence coding of his conception." Silva commented.

The fact that Silva's genes had been manipulated, ruled out the likelihood of any ancestor looking like her because of heredity thought Ewen. What to him was more disturbing was that the tone of the letter suggested they had at least met, something his daughter denied, and there was no reason to deny it. She was far too intelligent to think this joke would pass inspection, so joke it was not. All anyone had to do was explain how the photo image had come about and that would need a lot of research. What an interesting diversion, he at last said to himself.

"Perhaps you might research the image paper and mode of reproduction Curator. That may give some light as to its possible origins."

"Indeed so, a brief micro-scan suggests it is a powder based pigment pressed into the paper, an old technology. I shall examine it further," Stener replied as informatively as ever.

Soon after Captain Siven, on being questioned said he had no knowledge of the other girl either and there the matter rested.

Silva was taken away shortly afterwards from all that she was familiar with, to meet her admiring public; it would be weeks before she could settle once more into the comfort of her home. An exact three dimensional copy of the artefact was given to her to hang on her bedroom wall and periodically she re-read the reverse and it finally prompted her to action. To achieve her heart's desire of bypassing the security systems and taking the winner's medal from the tower, she would have to train and develop skills, skills she had denied and allowed to remain dormant. In due course she attended regular runs around the perimeter of the base and the Solar Array with Team Phantom. On the runs the team members would point out where the sensors and cameras were positioned, what type and with what effectiveness. Finally as the year turned, Team Phantom applied to be in the annual competition which caused a stir in the security teams that protected the sites. As would transpire, while all the attention was focused on Team Phantom a small figure would pass unnoticed into and through the sensor fields. Bypassing active and passive scanners she would slip unheeded through the solar arrays finally accessing the anti-climb coated tower's structure. Designed and constructed externally to resist any attempt to scale it, internally several securely locked explosive resistant doors barred the stairwell to invaders. The tower had been built to prevent access to any human being that tried but the hand that lifted the medal was something of a different order.

It would be a few weeks after her victory trip around the Republic that Silva would once more turn her attention to the family research she had sporadically paid attention to. Her mind on other pursuits she idly watched a series of images she had stored flash into the air in front of her. The pictures weren't in any particular order as she had yet to collate them with the personal data on file. An image flashed on and then as it was replaced Silva sat up straight. Suddenly reaching for the floating virtual controls, she marched the images backwards until what had drawn her attention hung in the air before her. Something totally unbelievable had occurred forcing her to look again at the three dimensional image she had of two laughing girls on the wall. Hanging suspended in the air was a reproduction of an old photograph, on the left of which was a girl with a happy half smiling face wearing a pair of the most adorable glasses, She was called O-one-x, it was she who originally bought the picture and had signed off the message 'Love 0|x'.

Finis

Thank you for purchasing and reading this book.

If you enjoyed this book let me know at kadeyckaries@yahoo.co.uk.

Why not leave a review where you purchased this book?

Other books by Alan Grieveson.

Fiction.

Kadeyckaries:

It was today that Henry Drake would realize his water supply was running dry. A few months before, his wife had been told she had a few months to live. It was the darkest time of his life – he needed a miracle.

It was today that the military forces of Texas would start their daily routines, as would the civilians of a small township in the foothills of Western Texas. Nobody foresaw the events that would change not just their world but everybody's.

As she rose from the rails, the crew of the Tharion Class Kadeyckaries saw today as the start of another mission, by the end of the day it would be anything but normal.

For everybody - today everything would change forever.

Shadows of Kadeyckaries;

The story continues.

Rook:

The war with France and Napoleon is over.

Alistair Ponsonby has returned home to his native country, a land he'd left ten years before. A self confessed horse dealer to the army, although he never specified which army, he'd spent his time in the Peninsular and France.

Unexpectedly he received a message, summoning him back to France as quickly as possible. The message bore the seal of the Bishop of Toulouse. Without delay he made preparations to travel back into France, a country still in chaos.

Joshua Marshall was a convicted thief who was sentenced to transportation seven years before. He had escaped his fate and in the belief he would go unnoticed amongst all the returning soldiers and sailors, he slipped back into England. His past however cast a long shadow and soon the officers of Bow Street were on the lookout for him.

Events would draw these two socially different men together as with a single purpose they left their homeland once again.

Soon they would find a common cause in which they could either stand or fall against the detritus of war. All they needed to succeed was trust, a rare commodity in both their lives.

Non-fiction.

The Complete Realistic Numerology.

After three decades of research and 'number crunching' the author offers an in-depth look at the real history of Numerology, not the unsubstantiated claims made in many commonplace books.

The second part of the book shows the real distribution of numbers through various careers. The author performed over three hundred thousand calculations to extract the number data from names and dates of birth using two different systems, so the results are actual and not fanciful.

The third part offers to the reader a new way of looking at the numbers and their interpretation based on the principle that you should never reduce the numbers to a single digit.

Made in the USA
Columbia, SC
16 May 2017